TOBIN IN PARADISE

STANLEY MORGAN

Copyright © Stanley Morgan 1974

Originally published by Mayflower Books Ltd
Frogmore, St Albans, Herts AL2 2NF Reprinted 1976

All rights reserved. No part of this work may be
reproduced or stored on an information retrieval
system (other than for purposes of review) without the
prior permission of the copyright holder

This is a work of fiction. Names. Characters and
incidents are the product of the author's
imagination or are used fictitiously, and any
resemblance to actual persons, living or dead is
entirely coincidental

This edition published in 2023 by White Marvel
Books

All rights reserved.

ISBN: 9798864653234

FOREWORD

This book was written in 1973 and, as such, contains depictions of society, particularly around gender roles and sexual orientation, that may seem at odds with the modern values of 2023.

Therefore it feels necessary to acknowledge this, and duly warn the reader that occasional stereotypes and offensive language of the times lie ahead.

Rather than edit the manuscript to remove these elements, it was decided to leave the original content unexpurgated as it provides a fascinating insight into British life and attitudes at the very start of the 1970s.

Aside from all that, the action takes place almost entirely on Paradise Island in The Bahamas, with Stan's usual flair for capturing a time and place. The islands will be much changed from the playboy decadence of the 1970s. For example, the Cafe Martinique, where Russ & Stud eat, was used as a location in the James Bond film "Thunderball" and while it still exists today, it has since been fully subsumed into the Atlantis resort (or as it was back then the Britannia Beach Hotel).

We hope that you enjoy spending some time with him once again

.

CHAPTER ONE

Well, now, I promised I'd drop you a line and let you know what happened if I ever got to the Bahamas, didn't I? Well, I did, so I am, so here goes.

Unbelievable.

That's the only word to describe what happened down there. And it all started three hours before I even *got* to Nassau - in the transit lounge of the John F. Kennedy airport in New York, for that was when and where one Stud Ryder stumbled into my life - and I choose the verb advisedly.

Ah, these tiny accidents of fate that can so drastically change the course of our lives. What sort of a holiday it would have been if I hadn't run into ... if Stud hadn't run into me is anybody's guess, but I rather imagine it would have been a simple fortnight of sun, sand and sea; a little gentle exercise by day, a quiet solo dinner in the evening, then early to solo bed. And if you believe that you'll believe anything.

However, all this was not to be. Our paths crossed, the fuse of instant friendship was ignited, and any chance of a quiet, celibate vacation was blown to bits by the ensuing explosion. Thank heaven.

CRAASSHH!

I was standing just inside the door of the crowded lounge, looking around for an empty seat, when something like a twelve-stone body smote me in the small of the back and sent me teetering arse-over-armpit over my hand-luggage to land in a lump five yards away.

Dazed, I turned and saw him, He was lying prone among

a pile of hand-luggage and parcels, squinting disbelievingly at a spreading pool of ... sniff... sniff ... whiskey, oozing from one of the packages.

'Hot damn! ' he muttered, then looked up at me and blinked. 'Heck, I'm sorry - the swing door ... are you all right?'

'Sure. I was going to sit on the floor anyway, there aren't any seats.'

He gave me a relieved grin, blinding me with a sparkling set of choppers. 'Well, that's nice of you.'

He was an extremely handsome lad about my own age, twenty-six, with dark curly hair worn long at the collar and humorous blue eyes, a touch like a young Tony Curtis. He peered woefully at the spreading whiskey and gave a sigh. 'If I'd known that was gonna happen I'd have smashed it in Boston - would a saved me carrying it.'

I got to my feet, dusted off my dark blue suit and went over to him 'Can I help?'

'Sure,' he grinned. 'Get that scotch back into the bottle.'

'I could get two straws from the bar and cut your losses.'

'Ah, a thinking drinking man. Glad to know you.'

He got to his feet and bent down, picked up one of the parcels then picked up another but dropped the first back into the whiskey, picked that up again but dropped the second.

'Hot damn,' he cursed.

'Here,' I laughed, 'give them to me. You get the luggage.'

Gingerly he picked up the dripping cases and tip-toed out of the puddle, wrinkling his nose. 'Phew. I'll have to get a waiter to clean this up.' He began moving away towards the bar, saying to me, 'Would you mind just hanging on to the par ...'

Crraasshh!

He ran smack into one of the low coffee tables, cracking his shin a beaut. Dropping the cases he clutched his leg and hopped around like a flamingo with its foot on fire. 'Oooohhh ... ooowwww!'

I couldn't help laughing. 'Here,' I said, 'let me have the cases, too '

'Oh, *baby,* that hurt.' On one foot he picked up the cases and hopped back to me, shaking his head. 'Man, I'll tell you, if you've got any sense you'll get out of range - fast. I've got this habit of killing folks who get in range. I've slaughtered four already this year an' it's only April.'

'There's a seat over there,' I laughed. 'You can forget the waiter - he's coming over now with a mop and bucket.'

'Oh?' He turned. 'Oh, yeh - he keeps it handy in case *I* fly in. Last trip I cleaned six beers off somebody's table - shattered every glass, neat as pie.'

'You really make an impression on a room, don't you?'

He shook his head. 'Accident prone - the whole family. They've banned us from the local supermarket up in Boston, we do so much damage. Only last week my ma demolished a display of ten million tins of Goodboy dog food with one swing of her trolley. They got her for dangerous driving. She claimed a blow-out but no dice, she did the same thing last year.'

He sat down on the empty seat, still rubbing his leg, then held out his hand with a grin. 'Stud Ryder - and thanks.'

'Russ Tobin and think nothing of it. It passes the time.'

'You should try Russian roulette - it's safer. What time's your flight?'

'Two-thirty'. I'm going to Nassau.'

He gave a groan. 'Oh. my God ..

"You, too?'

'Me, too. Look, Russ ... do yourself a big favour, hm - go book a later flight and live. With me on board the wings'll drop off.'

'I'll risk it, I can't get there fast enough. I hear it's a fantastic place. Have you been before?'

'About eight hundred times - I work there. Are you on vacation?'

'Yes, a couple of weeks. You work there?'

He nodded. 'In the casino on Paradise Island. I'm a dealer - a croupier '

'Really? Ah, then you can tell me something. I met an American chap in a bar in Nairobi a couple of months ago and he painted such an exotic picture of the Bahamas I just had to come and check for myself. He was a copywriter in advertising so I couldn't tell whether he was telling the truth or if he'd succumbed to his own brochure blurb. He was also extremely shickered at the time which also might have coloured his prose.'

He laughed. 'What did he say about them?'

'I will quote. "Tobin . .." he said, in a voice quite tremulous with passion, "... until you have strolled those sun-kissed sands, swum in that azure sea, you have not lived. The Bahamas are the islands of languid do-as-you-please, where time is unknown and sensual pleasures are a full-time preoccupation ..." '

'Yeh?'

'"Go!" he commanded, "fill your days with wish and whim ... fish, water-ski and swim ... or simply sit on your fanny and watch the babes ..." and at this point he became quite overcome. "Man, oh, man ..." he said, shaking his head in disbelief, . those incredible babes." End of quote. Now - was he telling the truth or was it hogwash?'

Now *he* was shaking his head. 'Russ, there's no doubt about it...' 'Hogwash, eh?' I said miserably.

His eyes grew big. 'Heck no! He was telling the truth ! '

'He ... was?'

'Man, if anything he was understating the situation. Even for an advertising copywriter it is not easy to do the scene justice ...'

'Really?'

'Truly! Listen ...' he moved closer, warming to the subject, sensing himself in the presence of an appreciative bird-fancier. 'The situation is unbelievable. There is so much talent on New Providence alone you'll go blind in the first hour ...'

'Get away,' I gasped

'Believe me. It *pours* into Nassau by the boat-load - every single day. As Nassau is only a hundred and fifty miles from Florida, swarms of American birds can afford the trip even for a week-end Russ ... *three* boat-loads come in from Florida alone every week.'

'Good God ..

'Then there are the *foreign* cruise boats - from Britain, Europe - especially Scandinavia. At least *six* of them hit Nassau every week ..

'My sainted aunt..

'And then there're the pigeons who come in by plane - mostly from the States. Hundreds of them!' He shook his head. 'Yes, sir, that advertising guy was definitely understating the case. There is a positive cornucopia talent out there - to say nothing of a glut. And never enough time to more than skim the surface.'

'Sounds like you need some help.'

'We do, we do ...' he sighed. 'The situation in the casino gets quite embarrassing at times - them climbing over the tables to get at us and us beating them back with our sticks Quite embarrassing ..

The elderly, crumple faced waiter drew up, made a wry grimace at Stud and nodded at the bucket. 'So what was that - the whiskey chaser to the beer yuh shattered last time?'

Stud grinned contritely. 'Sorry to give you so much trouble.'

The waiter shrugged fatalistically. 'You guys wanna drink while I'm here?'

Stud looked at me. 'Beer?'

'Great.'

'Two Buds,' he told the waiter.

'Sure. You gonna knock 'em over here or you want I should throw 'em on the floor by the bar?'

He departed, chuckling to himself.

'So ...' I said, still stunned by what Stud had told me. 'It congregates in the casino, hm?'

'Listen - may it wither and drop off if I'm telling a lie - but that place *bulges* with it. There are eighty-seven of us dealers there and even on bad nights there's six birds for every one of us ..

'My aching back ...' I breathed.

'Well, there's a reason for it. The casino is Fantasyland for them. It's glamour ... excitement - even if they don't gamble. Any little secretary bird from any old hick town can walk around there and pretend she's a princess - and there isn't even a cover-charge. For the price of a Coke she can sit up in the gallery bar, rub shoulders with millionaires and make believe she's the female lead in a James Bond movie.'

'Yes, I can see it.'

'Ah, something happens to them in there, Russ. They get carried away by the glamorous atmosphere - like they do in the pits at the race track. But in there it's the croupiers they go for in place of the drivers.'

'Yes?'

He grinned diabolically. 'Hot damn, they do. Things happen in there you wouldn't believe.'

'What sort of things?'

'Well ... take last month. I was working roulette one night when this great-looking blonde came in, swathed in mink, with a guy old enough to be her great-grandaddy. Within a few minutes she's giving me the eyes something awful and leaning across the table, showing me everything. I was getting so worked up I couldn't think straight. And then my twenty-minute break came up - we get one every hour to relax from the tension. I handed over the wheel to my relief and went into the bar for a Coke and suddenly she was at my elbow, telling me she'd excused herself to powder her nose and how did I fancy a quick drink up in their hotel room - they were staying in the complex. Five minutes later we were in bed and she was tearing holes in my back. Incredible! And before my twenty minutes was up she was back at the table, nibbling sugar-daddy's ear and squeezing him for another grand.'

'Good God,' I gasped.

'Swear it's the truth. Funny thing is they don't seem to stop and think we're just working fellas, not glamorous big-time gamblers. We're not even *allowed* to gamble. But it doesn't make any difference. It's the image that hits 'em - the evening dress, the fast action, the slick way we deal. Boy, those guys in there are exhausted all of the time. Some nights they even creep out the back exit just to get a few hours' sleep. It's one hell of a life, I'll tell you.'

'Terrible. Er, Stud ... how do I go about getting a job as a croupier?'

He laughed out loud. 'You serious?'

'Desperately.'

He paused for thought then went on more seriously. 'Had any experience?'

'No, none.'

'Oh. Well ... it's not easy. There's a lot to it, Russ, and this casino only hires experienced men. Even so, it would be quite a while before you could start. They'd have to get security clearance for you from England ... then you'd have to apply for a Bahamian work permit - that could take anything up to three months alone ...'

'Oh.'

'Anyway - what do you need to work there for, all you've got to do is walk into the place. You'll get more than you can handle, I promise you.'

'You reckon?'

'Hell, I know it. But in the unlikely event that you *should* need help - well, just holler.'

'Thanks, Stud.'

'Listen, it's my pleasure. Come to think of it, I'd get a big kick out of showing you around.'

'Well, thanks again, I'd appreciate that.'

'Where will you be staying?'

I shrugged. 'Don't know, I haven't booked in anywhere. I thought I'd take a look round first.'

'O.K., we'll fix that. I reckon Paradise is the place for you.'

'By the sound of things the whole island is Paradise. But what is this place ...?'

Just then the waiter hobbled up with the beers. 'Here yuh go - two Buds.'

'How much?' I asked him, reaching for my pocket.

'That'll be eighty.'

'Cents?'

He shot me a curious glance. 'What else d'yuh have in mind?' Stud cut in, 'I'll get these, Russ,' and handed the waiter two dollars. 'That's for all the trouble I've caused you.'

The waiter raised an approving brow. 'No trouble at all,

mister. At a buck twenty a time yuh can wreck the joint.'

He moved off, walking on eggs, his feet killing him.

Stud raised his glass. 'Well ... here's to Paradise.'

'And pulchritude, old buddy.'

'May you never know what hit you.'

We drank some beer and lit cigarettes, then I said, 'You were about to tell me about Paradise.'

'Oh, yeh. Well, Paradise Island is just off-shore from the town of Nassau - they're linked by a toll-bridge ... look, do you know the lay-out of New Providence Island ...?'

'Stud, I don't know anything. The brochure I picked up in Nairobi showed a cluster of islands due east of Florida and there was an arrow pointing at all of them that said Nassau ...'

'O.K., well, let's do the thing right, hm?' He took a ballpoint pen from his pocket, turned over the beer-mat and drew an almond shape. 'New Providence Island ... sixteen miles long and eight miles wide ..

'It's that small?'

'Minute. Right ... Nassau, its only town, is on the north coast, about ... here. The airport is left of centre ... here. When we land - just to give you an idea of direction - we take a short drive north to the coast road, then turn right and drive straight along the coast into Nassau. That's along Bay Street which runs almost the whole length of the island. O.K.?'

'Fine.'

'Right ... then we drive on through the town, get to the toll-bridge and cross over it on to Paradise Island - it's about three hundred yards off-shore.'

'And Paradise is a much smaller island,' I presumed, because he'd just drawn a much smaller island.

'Minuscule - four miles long and only a mile wide, but, baby, that's where *all* the action is - the casino complex ... big hotels ... beautiful beaches ...'

'What d'you mean by "complex", Stud?'

'Well, it's more than just the casino. It's a whole bunch of buildings all joined together. There's a hotel, a theatre supper club, four restaurants, two bars ... it's really quite something. Then, of course, there's the "piece de resistance" - the glamorous Cafe Martinique which is only a couple of yards from the complex. That, buddy, will blow your mind. It overlooks a magnificent lake which at night is all lit up by flickering gas lamps on the far bank. It's an elegant place and the food is superb. I tell you, take a pigeon out there for dinner, get a table on the terrace near the water's edge, order lobster and cold white wine under a skyful of tropical stars - and if you don't make homebase after that, pack your bags and take the first jet home, you're a born loser.'

'Stud, I can't wait.'

'You don't have to, our flight's on the monitor. Come on, let's get aboard.'

With a surge of excitement I finished my beer and gathered up my hand-luggage, impatient, now, to get there. The Bahamas. Only a couple of hours away; so close I could hear the surf, feel the hot tropical sun on my back.

'Ready?' asked Stud.

'Ready,' I nodded.

'O.K., let's go and kill 'em.'

Out of the door we went and along the labyrinthine corridors to the waiting jet, escorted all the way by a sense of bubbling well-being. This, I knew, was going to be one heck of a holiday.

And, hot damn, it certainly was.

CHAPTER TWO

Slowly, we moved with the crowd of passengers along the narrow boarding jetty and as the forward door of the jet came into sight Stud went up on his toes, craning to look inside the plane. Then he came down, all of a doo-da.

'Russ, we're in luck! We've got a couple of air stews I know very well - a real couple of go-gos.'

'Yes?'

'Take a look.'

Up I went. Sanding in the doorway, greeting the passengers, were two blondes, both lovely-looking lollipops, especially the one on the left. She was a gorgeous, sultry creature with a soft, sexy mouth, naughty eyes and a belting figure. I fell in love with her on sight.

I dropped back down to Stud. 'Wow!'

"Not bad, eh?'

'Not bad? They're terrific.'

'Lucinda Lee and Bunny Doyle. They come into the casino a lot and I've flown with them a few times. I took Lucinda to the Martinique a couple of months ago ..he grinned satanically, 'boy, she really flies - no pun intended.'

'And . ... which one is Lucinda?' I asked, knowing he was going to say the lovely bird standing on the left.

'The one on the right.'

'Oh? Really ...?'

Up I went on my toes for another look. Bunny Doyle. I was more in love with her than ever, now.

'You know,' I said, dropping down again, 'I never thought it was possible to date an airstew unless you had four rings on your sleeve. They always look so aloof.'

10

He grinned. 'Aw, it's all a big game. They're only human under the uniform. Sure, they do mostly date aircrew because they're with them all the time, but if anything else comes along .. .'

'Stud, you don't suppose ...'

'Russell, I am way ahead of you and working on the possibility right now. Wait till we get inside.'

We shuffled on, reached the platform that led into the jet and finally came into the airstews' view. Lucinda's big blue eyes, warmly smiling her professional greeting, widened with delight as she recognized Stud. 'Well, hey ... look who's here !'

The sultry Bunny also registered delight but immediately gave a groan of pretended dismay. 'Oh, my God, disaster ...'

'Hi, girls, how've you been?' beamed Stud.

'Very happy,' sighed Bunnie. 'Until just now.'

'Not a serious accident since you were last on board,' Lucinda added. 'Though we *are* still paying for the crockery.'

Stud wrinkled his nose. 'Nah, don't be like that. Girls ... say hello to my English pal, Russ Tobin - you'll love him.'

'Hello,' they chorused dutifully.

'Didn't I tell you,' he said, nudging me. 'A couple of great girls.' He turned back to Lucinda. 'I was telling Russ ...'

'Ryder,' drawled Bunny, 'you do realize you're holding up the entire line ...'

'Mm? Oh ... well, see you later, then.'

Laconically, Lucinda held out her hand to him. 'Stud, if it's not too much trouble, may we see your boarding card?'

'Mm? Ah! Oh ... yes, now just a minute ...'

Juggling with his parcels and hand-luggage, he managed to get a hand to his inside pocket and poked around with growing dismay. 'Now, that's funny ... ah! I know ...' Everything was transferred to the opposite side then he explored that pocket, his expression unchanged. 'You know, I could've sworn ...'

The girls sighed and exchanged weary glances.

'He's back,' groaned Bunny.

Lucinda said to him, 'Look, Stud, would you mind standing to one side so the other passengers ...'

'Ah! No - I know where it is! It's in the case ... Russ, could you just... whoa ...!'

The parcels hit the deck. Stud went down after them. 'Sorry about that ...' As he stood up, one of the cases burst open and out shot a ton-and-a-half of assorted rubbish - shaving gear, books, underwear, a gross of french letters. The girls gasped, then exploded with laughter and Stud turned bright puce with embarrassment.

'All prepared for the season, I see,' muttered Bunny.

'Hot ... damn ...' muttered Stud, diving for the condoms and hustling them under cover.

'Look, what's the hold up in front?' demanded an irate female voice from the rear. 'Come on, now, I've got two tired kids here who wanna sit down!'

I glanced round to see who it was and met the fiery eyes of a graduate-hippy mother in a big floppy hat and a crumpled brown dress she'd lived in all year. At her side stood a little girl of about three and a boy of seven, a real long-haired weirdo dressed in jodhpurs, cow-boy vest and a sou'wester. 'No goddam consideration for kids,' mother told the crowd, evil-eyeing me. 'Move it along there, f'Crissake.'

Flinching from her glare, I turned back to Stud then stooped to help him get the things back in the case. Then, to hurry things up, the two girls went into a crouch to help and I got a glorious eyeful of Bunnie's knickers.

'Ryder,' groaned Lucinda, 'why can't you ever come on board normally like everyone else - or maybe fly Army transport or something?'

'Here's the boarding card,' I said, fishing it out of the mess.

As she stood up, Bunnie took it from me and checked the seat number. 'About half-way down on the starboard side. D'you think you can make it or would you like an escort?'

Stud grinned sheepishly. 'I sure would appreciate an escort.'

She transferred her half-smile to me. 'And where's *your* boarding card? Down in the luggage bay, I suppose?'

'Nope - right here.'

I gave it to her.

'You're three rows in front of Stud but sit with him - if you're crazy enough to want to - we're flying light.'

'Thank you.'

'Don't thank me - just keep this guy pinned to the window seat.'

'Come *arn*, what's the hold-up! ? ' rapped the hippy. 'What's so damn difficult about gettin' on a plane?'.

'Here,' said Lucinda, taking Stud's parcels from him. 'Now, come on before we have a riot on our hands.'

As we followed her swinging bottom down the aisle, Stud turned to me and winked. 'Cute, hm?'

'Terrific.'

'You dig Bunnie?'

'I'd love to.'

He chuckled. 'Wait till we're in the air and I'll see what can be arranged.'

'For *tonight?'*

'Why not? They'll be stopping over in Nassau ... oops!'

Lucinda had stopped and he ran into her.

'Sorry, angel, I was walking backwards ...' he stammered.

She gave a wry sigh. 'Would it make any difference? Go on, get in before you wreck the ship.'

She threw his parcels on to the aisle seat, then, squeezing past me to return to the forward door, she murmured, 'Take care of him, he's kinda nice.'

'Sure.'

We stowed our hand-luggage under the seats and finally got settled down. 'Phew! ' I said, 'I reckon I'm going to need a holiday by the time we get to Nassau.'

'Aren't they something, though?' he said excitedly.

'They're wonderful. What d'you reckon the chances are of taking them out tonight?'

'Well, all depends on whether they've already got something lined up, of course.'

'Mm. Boy, that would be a terrific start to the hoi...' I broke off because Bunnie was coming towards us, leading the hippy mother and the two kids. She came right up to us and shepherded the hips into the three seats opposite, then, with her flock seated, she leaned over the kids to fasten their straps and presented me with a heart-stopping close-up of her wonderful legs.

'Wow!' I whispered to Stud.

'Yeh!' he breathed, eyes popping.

Having strapped the kids in she stood up and turned to us. 'Well, well, we finally got you two bedded down, hm?' Oh, the thought of it! 'Fasten your seat belts, there's good children.'

'We, er, don't know how,' Stud said plaintively. 'Do we, Russell?'

'No,' I said, shaking my head at her. 'We don't know how.

This is my first flight.'

'Ha!' she went and strode back up the aisle.

'By the ... *heck*, Stud, you've got to do it, man ... you've *got* to.'

'Leave it to Uncle Stud, Russell. If it's at all possible it will be ...'

BAAANG!

I leapt out of the seat at the terrific explosion on my left. It was the hippy boy in the aisle seat. He'd blown up his sick-bag and burst it.

Momma tutted disapprovingly. 'Paul, darling, you shouldn't have done that - you may need it. Now what are you going to do if you get sick?'

'I'll do it on the floor - there,' the kid said, pointing at my feet and mean-mouthing me at the same time.

'No. Paul, I don't think that would be a very good idea.'

'Marmy ... that man's lookin' at me.'

Mother's eyes swept over to me defiantly. I looked away murmuring to Stud, 'Trouble.'

'Yeh, two thousand seats on the plane and we had to get them.'

Through the corner of my eye I saw mother open a book and she began to read aloud. 'And who's been sleeping in *my* bed ...'

'Not me for a start, love,' I murmured to Stud and he burst out laughing.

'Marmy ... those two men are laughing at you,' snitched

the kid.

Quivering silence. I could feel mother's searing gaze on us. 'What we do is no concern of anyone else, Paul. Perhaps the gentlemen would like to amuse you for two hours instead of me ... Elizabeth, don't do that, darling, you'll make holes in your knickers ... and who's been sleeping in *my* bed,' she continued, 'and broken it aaaallll up ...'

'Oh, man ...' I groaned. 'Two hours of flaming Goldilocks coming up.'

'Dirty little sod,' commented Stud, staring past me at the kid.

'What's he doing now?'

'Picking his nose and flicking it at you.'

'Eh...?'

I whirled, catching Paulie in mid-flick. 'Hey, you stop that ...'

Like lightning, his hands were down on his lap. Momma looked up, glared across at me. 'Are you talking to my son?'

'Yes, I was, madam ... he was picking his nose and flicking it at me.'

She gasped. 'Paul ... were you doing that?'

'No, marmy - he's lyin'. He just made that up. He's pickin' on me -.

Mother's eyes narrowed. 'Why are you picking on my boy?'

'I ... I ...' I choked.

'Never mind him, Paul, turn this way - don't look at them. We all know there're some mean people in this world and we just have to ignore them. Now, let's get on with the story ...'

She continued reading but it was obvious Paul, darling, wasn't listening. His expression was furtive, cunningly thoughtful, and I just knew he was plotting something quite diabolical. Between the two of us, war had undoubtedly been declared.

'Been meaning to ask you,' Stud said then, taking my mind off Paul, 'what were you doing in Nairobi?'

'Ah, I was working out there - as a courier for a photographic safari firm - you know, escorting people into the bush to photograph animals.'

'No kidding! Hey, now, that sounds like fun, tell me about it.'

Well, I began telling him about Africa, then got on to my season as courier in Majorca with Ardmont Travel, making him chuckle at the things that had happened to me out there with my mad pal Patrick Holmes. Then, prompted by his questions, I went further back still to my days as a sewing machine salesman and debt collector in Liverpool and, later on, to the TV presenting I'd done in London. I must have talked for a good half hour, I suppose; something I hadn't done in a long time, but he was an easy man to talk to and I enjoyed it. Funny how you can meet a complete stranger like that and get on so well with him right from the start. I felt I'd known him for years.

'You've certainly had some fun,' he grinned. 'Wish I'd been along.'

'So do I. Still, I've got a sneaky feeling the next two weeks are not going to be exactly *dull.*'

'Not if I've got anything to do with it. You know, it's going to be a real pleasure showing you around. We'll get you fixed up in a hotel on Paradise and then start planning a good time.'

'By the way, where do *you* live?'

'On Paradise. I've got a small pad in an apartment block near the Holiday Inn Hotel. It's just a one-bedroom place but it suits. I don't dig hotels - not enough privacy.'

'Sure,' I laughed.

His eyes shifted up the aisle. 'Ah ha, here come Bedworthy Bunnie and the Lush Lucinda now.'

The girls were moving towards us, quickly dispensing trays of food to the widely dispersed passengers. When they finally reached us it was Bunnie who leaned in with our trays and leaned too close for comfort, bending my mind with her perfume.

'You're doing a grand job,' I murmured to her, my voice wobbly with excitement.

She looked at me, now very close, shockingly intimate, and smiled ruefully. 'So are you - just keep him here out of mischief.'

She stood up and passed on, then it was Lucinda's turn to pop in.

'What would you like to drink?' she asked us.

Stud took advantage of the moment masterfully. 'Well, now ... how about a couple of martinis first ... then a bottle of ice-cold Niersteiner with the lobster?'

'Mm?' she went. 'Lobster ...?'

'Sure - the one you're having with me tonight at the Martinique.'

'Huh!'

'Bunnie's already said yes to Russ.'

That got her. 'She ... has?' she frowned.

'Sure - just now.'

She glanced along the aisle but Bunnie was far down it. She came back to us, eyes narrowed suspiciously. 'You're lying, Ryder ...'

'Cross my *heart*,' he protested. *'And* scout's honour.' He held up two fingers.

'I'll check it out, of course,' she said lightly, opening two cans of beer.

'Lucinda ...' he pouted, 'would I lie to you?'

'Only through your teeth,' she said sweetly, plonking down the beers and moving on.

'Very smooth,' I said, 'but what happens now - when she checks with Bunnie?'

'Have no fear - that was only Phase One of the diabolical plan.'

'I see. And what is Phase Two, pray?'

'Aha - wait and see,' he said cunningly.

Within a few minutes the girls had finished serving and were coming back up the aisle to the forward galley. Watching from the corner of his eye, Stud allowed Lucinda to pass, then, as Bunnie reached us, he called to her. Again she came in close.

'Yes?'

'Bunnie ... Lucinda, Russ and I are having dinner at the Martinique tonight and we wondered whether you'd like to join us.'

'Uh?' she went, regarding him suspiciously. 'You and

Lucinda and *Russ* are having dinner ...?'

'Yes. You see, Russ hasn't been to Nassau before and I've promised to show him round. And Lucinda, bless her, said she'd like to help. So, naturally, we thought you'd like to make it a foursome ..

Her frown of suspicion deepened. 'Lucinda said *that?*'

'Sure - just now. She's ordered lobster - crazy about lobster.
How about you?'

'I... I love lobster .. .'

'Fine - lobster all round. What time do we pick you up?'

'Hey, now ... didn't Lucinda tell you?'

'No - she said she'd leave it to you. How about eight o'clock - that early enough?'

'Well... yes ...'

'Good - eight o'clock, then. Oh, just one more thing - Russ hasn't booked into a hotel yet and he wondered what yours is like.'

'The Sonesta? It's fine ..

'Great. He can have a look at it when we pick you up. See you at eight, then - at the Sonesta.'

'Hm,' she said, distrustfully, then went off hot-foot for the galley.

Chuckling, Stud attacked his rubber chicken in the tin-foil tray. 'Theeere yuh go, buddy - one romantic dinner coming up.'

'Fantastic,' I laughed. 'My God, Stud, I've seen some smooth operations in my time but that one takes the Oscar.'

He shrugged modestly. 'Nuthin' to it, really.'

'But ... won't they be conferring, right now? Won't they rumble what you've done?'

'Not at all.' He tapped his head with his plastic fork. 'It's all psychology, you see. Bunnie will go in there and say, "I told them to pick us up at eight, honey - was that O.K. with you?" Lucinda will say "Fine" and that'll be that.'

'By golly, I have got to hand it to you ...' '

'Well, thanks, but it was really nothing. A little applied psychology, a little devious thinking ... it's got to work every time ..

'Er, Stud ... don't look now but I've got the sneakiest of feelings that...'

Lucinda was bearing down on us, firm-mouthed and fiery-eyed. In she swept, driving me back into my seat, and with venomous whisper attacked Stud. 'Ryder, your sneaky game is exposed. You lied to me! You asked Bunnie *after* you asked me and told her I'd already accepted, *didn't* you?'

'I... I... well, you see ..'

'*Didn't* you?'

'Lucinda .. baby .. .' he gulped.

'And if you think for one *minute* that we'd go out with a coupla bums who'd try to pull a fast one like that on two sweet, innocent, unsuspecting airstews . '

'Lucinda ...' he groaned.

'... you're dead right. But pick us up at eight-thirty, we need long, hot baths. O.K.?'

Then she was gone, striding back up the aisle.

Stud gaped at me. 'Hot... *damn,* would you believe that?'

'No,' I grinned.

'Well, now ...' he sighed. 'You know, Russell, I do believe it's gonna be *quite* a night.'

'*I'll* drink to that, old buddy.'

'Hot... damn,' he gasped, raising his glass.

The little hippy monster began his attack the moment momma got up to go to the loo. Splat! A spoonful of raspberry jelly shot across my bows and got Stud smack in the ear.

'HEY ...!'

I gasped and turned. Splat! I caught another spoonful plumb between the eyes. 'You little ... BUGGER ...! '

'Don't you touch me! ' he yelled. 'I'll tell my marmie ... ! ' In panic he scooped up a third spoonful and lined it up on my nose. Flicking jelly off my brow I lunged. Ping! He fired. I ducked. Stud got the lot in his hair.

'Aw, you little bastard ...! '

I was out of the seat, grabbing for him. Biff! I got half a bread roll in the teeth. Then, behind me - CRAAASSHH! I whirled. Stud's tray was in his lap - upside down. 'AAAA-AHHH! ' he cried. Hot gravy was coursing down his trouser leg and the can of beer was lying sideways in his lap, emptying fast glug .,. glug ... glug.

'YYAAA!' he yelled and jumped up, throwing the tray on to the floor. There was chicken and jelly and peas and gravy all over the place.

'Now look what you've done! ' I stormed at the kid, who by now was brandishing a knife above his head and about to stab me through the hand.

'You hit me an' I'll kill yuh! '

Then: 'What the hell's goin' on here! ' It was momma, back from the loo. 'What are you doing to my child! '

I stood up and faced her. 'What am I doing to *him I*' I pointed at my face, then at Stud. 'He flicked his jelly all over us ...'

She wagged her finger under my nose. 'Now, you listen here, mister, you keep away from him or I'll report you to the goddam captain, you ... you *child* molester ...! '

By now, Bunnie and Lucinda were racing down the aisle.

'What's happening here?' Lucinda came to an abrupt halt and gaped at Stud, hair covered in jelly, trousers soaked with beer and gravy like he'd wet himself. 'Oh, my ... God,' she groaned miserably.

'I want to report these two men to the captain,' bellowed momma. 'They've been molesting my child ...'

'Don't be bloody ridiculous,' I said, getting me paddy up now. 'He started it. He flicked jelly at us with his spoon.'

'I did *not*! ' the brat shouted. 'He *hit* me - soon as you'd gone, marmie.'

'There! ' thundered momma at Lucinda. 'Get me the captain! '

'Now, madam ...' Lucinda said gently, 'I don't think that's at all necessary ..

'Well, I do! And if you won't get him I will - these two maniacs need locking up! '

'Madam,' Bunnie cut in firmly, 'we happen to know these two gentlemen personally and ..

'I ... just ... *bet* you do,' snapped momma. 'Now, let me

through, I want the captain.'

'Ah, siddown!'

Momma whirled to face the man who'd spoken, a tough looking cookie with a face and voice like Bogart. 'You keep outta this!'

'The guy's tellin' the trute, lady. The kid started it. I saw him flick the jello. He needs a damn good pastin'. You oughta learn him some manners ..

'You mind your own goddam business, mister ... I'll raise my kid *my* way! '

'There's only one way ta raise him, sister - that's two feet off de ground wid a right hook ! '

'Ohh!' she gasped. I thought for a second she was going to bash him one but Lucinda quickly took over, grabbed my arm with one hand, Stud's with the other. 'Would you two gentlemen please come to the galley and we'll clean you up. Right, now, would everybody please sit down, it's all over.'

Stud and I were hustled along the aisle by Bunnie who had taken over from Lucinda. 'In the galley you two ... mush! '

The three of us crushed into the tiny kitchen and no sooner had Bunnie drawn the curtain than it flew open again and Lucinda squeezed in. 'Oh, boy, oh, boy ... it just *had* to be you, Ryder, didn't it?'

'It wasn't *my* fault,' he grinned. 'It was ...'

'Oh, sure. Just look at you ... jelly in your hair ... and what in *hell* have you been doing down there, for God sake.'

'It's beer,' he said meekly.

'Huh! Gravy all down your trousers ...' She transferred her glare to me. 'And you're no better - brawling with seven-year- old kids. You were supposed to be looking after this guy.' She squeezed past us to get to the tiny sink and held a cloth under the tap. 'Come here, let's get the gravy off.'

As she worked on his leg he looked across at me and slipped me a wink, thoroughly enjoying it.

'I just knew it ...' Lucinda was going on. 'Soon as I saw you, Ryder - disaster.'

'Well, what did *I* say?' said Bunnie. 'Next time, Ryder,

you stay in the toilet the whole flight - though no doubt you'd find a way of creating some kind of mayhem in *there*! Probably flush yourself out of the pla ... hey, now, there's a thought ! '

'There,' said Lucinda, 'that'll have to do for now.'

Stud looked down at his flies. 'Er, what about the ... beer? Couldn't you just...?'

She slammed the wet cloth into his hand. 'No, I couldn't just.'

He burst out laughing and began dabbing at the beer stain. 'Kinda ... cosy in here, Russ, wouldn't you say?'

'Listen,' said Lucinda, wagging her finger at him, 'you leave this poor guy alone - and hurry up and get out of here, we've got work to do.' She turned to me. 'And if you've got any sense at all, you'll fly back with us tomorrow morning and get to know some nice quiet harmless people in New York - like the Mafia, for instance. But then again - the way Ryder's shaping up you won't *see* tomorrow morning, so take a flight out tonight.'

'Aw, come on, I'm not that bad, am I?' grinned Stud.

Lucinda cocked a wry eye at Bunnie. 'Bunnie ... is he that bad?'

'Worse - and this one's no better.' She ripped off a piece of paper towel and turned me towards her. 'Come here, you've got jelly in your eye ... close it.'

Very gently she wiped it away. She smelled so good I ached to get hold of her. Well, maybe I would, later that night, if we went dancing. The prospect was unbearably delicious.

'Thank you,' I said.

'Hmm,' she went, looking me over with a hint of a smile.

'Come on, you two, outta here,' said Lucinda. 'There are a couple of empty seats right outside, sit there. I'll get your things.'

'You are quite adorable,' sighed Stud. 'What would we do without you?'

'My God, I shudder to think. Move it.'

For the rest of the flight we had a marvellous time, sitting there right outside the galley, making cracks at the girls, having a lot of fun, and when the girls finally went to strap themselves in their seats for the landing, I said to Stud, 'It looks very good, buddy, and I think we're in for a lovely evening.'

'Russell,' he grinned, 'it is going to be a *lulu,* hot damn, if it ain't.' He gave a chuckle and rubbed his hands together exuberantly. 'A *lulu!*'

CHAPTER THREE

In boisterous spirits we said a temporary goodbye to the girls at the door of the plane, ran down the steps and made our way across the tarmac towards the terminal, and now, for the first time, I was able to think about Nassau.

It was five o'clock and the heat had gone from the day. The cloudless sky had begun to take on its first hint of evening mauve, the air was sensuously warm and the gentle breeze brought with it the salt of the sea and the heady fragrance of tropical blossoms.

I took a deep breath and went a bit funny in the head. 'Just sniff that air, Stud, me boy. Ah, I reckon this is the place for me. I was born to live in the sun, you know.'

'Yes, me, too. Can't stand the cold. If I can help it I'll never spend another winter in Boston.'

'Ditto London for me. From November to May I used to walk round like a zombie - all stiff and 'orrible. Nah, this is the stuff for me ... yeeer ... hooo !'

We entered the terminal and had to pass through a small cubicle in which stood a young giant, a six foot four Bahamian immigration official immaculate in starched khaki uniform. Sternly, he checked my passport, then Stud's, then unexpectedly his severe countenance softened with a beaming smile.

'Welcome to the Bahamas, sir,' he said to me. 'Have a good holiday. Hope you enjoy our island.'

'Thank you.'

We passed through into the Customs hall and minutes later our luggage was arriving from the plane. A young Bahamian porter humped our cases on to an inspection bench and then an official arrived, dressed for the heat in white shirt-sleeves, grinning good-humouredly at Stud.

'Hi, man, good trip?'

'Too much, Charlie, but glad to be back as always.'

'Sure, why not,' laughed Charlie, slapping colourful clearance stickers on the cases with practised speed. 'Take it easy now — leave some fo' tomorrow.'

And that was the formalities completed.

The porter wheeled our luggage out to the entrance to where a line of saloon-car taxis was waiting, and as we came through the doors a big American Ford left the line and hurtled towards us, stopping with a skid in the flurry of dust.

Out climbed *another* Bahamian giant, bigger even than the bloke in Immigration, six feet six and shoulders like a sofa.

'Yo' wanna taxi, sayah?' he drawled sleepily, grinning familiarly at Stud.

'No, we're waitin' for a train,' answered Stud, then laughed. 'Hi, Johnnie, how're things?'

'Oh, up an' down, man, up an' down,' grinned Johnnie, picking up all four cases as though they were empty and taking them to the boot.

'Know any other way?' asked Stud.

'No ... but Ah'm workin' on it !'

As Stud and I climbed into the back seat, I said to him, 'Do you know everybody on the island?'

'Most of the residents, I guess - because of the casino - by sight if not by name.'

Big Johnnie swung into the driving seat. 'Paradise?'

'Where else?' said Stud. 'Johnnie - meet Russ Tobin from London. This is his first visit.'

Johnnie nodded to me in the rear-view mirror. 'Hi - welcome to the Bahamas.'

'Thank you.'

'This is Jonathan McArthur,' Stud explained to me. 'If you ever want a taxi in a tearin' hurry, get this one - it's the only speed it does.'

'Yeh ... man!' laughed Johnnie, gunning the Ford away from the terminal.

'Well, how's life bin treating you?' Stud asked him.

Johnnie's shoulders slumped dramatically. 'Ah'll tell yuh de truth, massah, bad times is surely hittin' de poor folk. Us poor chillun done work from sun-up ta sun-down fo' hardly next ta no pay t'all.'

Stud tutted sympathetically. 'I know, I know ... I can see you're havin' a real tough time, Johnnie - by the new gold watch you're wearing.'

Johnnie cackled a laugh and shook the watch at us. 'Ain't that somethin', though?'

'Something,' agreed Stud. 'And I hear you put in a take-over bid for the casino while I was away.'

Grinning, Johnnie shook his head. 'Couldn't quite make it, man - I wus a million short. I didn' do no over-time that week!'

While all this nonsense was going on, we were cruising along a wide, beautiful modern avenue lined with slender palm trees and masses of multi-coloured flowering shrubs. Everywhere I looked the vegetation was lush and exotic, as though it had just been brought freshly alive by recent rain.

'Johnnie's giving you the scenic tour,' explained Stud, perhaps reading my mind. 'There is another road to Nassau that cuts across the centre of the island, but this is the impressive one.'

'Sure, why not,' shrugged Johnnie. 'We want Mr. Tobin to be impressed with New Providence.'

'John, you're all heart,' Stud said solemnly.

As Stud had described on the plane, within a few minutes we reached the ocean, then we turned right on to Bay Street and followed the shallow white beach very closely towards Nassau, passing, on our right, countless beautiful villas set back from the road beyond lush, colourful gardens.

'Mostly British,' offered Stud. 'Mostly retired folks escaping from the taxman.'

'What do they do out here to amuse themselves - apart from gamble?' ,

'Oh - swim, fish, sail, play tennis, golf, go to the races, drink, fornicate ... all the usual stuff.'

'Rough,' I tutted.

'Rugged,' he grinned.

Now the coast road would occasionally meander a short way from the sea, allowing villas on that side as well as on the right, and as we turned a corner we came upon a huge, ultra-modern hotel to our left.

'The Sonesta Beach,' announced Stud. 'This is where the girls are staying.'

"Wow - looks beautiful.'

'Well, it's certainly got everything - four restaurants, six lounges, bars, pubs, clubs, golf course, a big pool and its own private beach.'

'And some mighty good-looking airstews,' added Johnnie.

'Oh, really,' said Stud aloofly. 'I didn't know that.'

'Oh, didn't you know that, sir?'

'No, I didn't know that.'

Immediately beyond the hotel a cluster of villas hid the ocean from our view, but as we passed them we once again came upon the open sea, and there, surprisingly close to the shore, plodded an enormous, glittering white cruise ship, heading for Nassau.

'Aha! ' laughed Stud. 'There you are - just what I was telling you about. That's one from Europe coming in for a one-night stop-over. By golly, the casino will be jumpin' tonight.'

We quickly overtook the lovely ship and very soon were entering the outskirts of the town, but at this point we had to leave Bay Street and cross Nassau by a series of back-streets which took us away from the harbour in an encircling one-way system.

'We can't go through town along Bay Street,' Stud pointed out. 'It's one-way, east-to-west, but we'll see it tonight when we pick up the girls.'

'Government House,' announced Johnnie, pointing to the right, and through a high, wrought-iron gate I caught a glimpse of a stately colonial house set in glorious gardens.

Here in the back-streets the town disappointed me. The buildings were a cluttered mixture of decaying wooden colonial and ultra-modern, strung together with little sense of planning or devotion to history', and I found myself hoping that Bay Street had more to offer.

On we went, crossing the town in no time at all, to rejoin Bay Street at the eastern end of the harbour, and now, quite close, I could see the slender white Paradise Island bridge reaching out to touch Paradise some three hundred yards offshore.

Johnnie swung the car on to the bridge and climbed its steep arch quickly, slowing at the top to give me a view of the harbour.

Down to our right lay the yacht harbour, a forest of masts and gleaming white hulls tucked up for the night along the jetties. To our left lay Nassau, and in its harbour two immense cruise ships dominating the little town. Everything was much smaller than I'd imagined it would be.

On we went, over the apex of the bridge, then descended to a toll booth. Here Stud took a couple of dollar bills from his pocket and handed them to Johnnie, saying to me, 'It's a pretty stiff toll - two bucks a time,'

'Two dollars - every time you come over! ' I winced.

'Well, not me personally. Residents get a pass.'

Johnnie collected the receipt and drove on. Paradise, I could see immediately, was very different from Nassau. It was spotlessly clean, quite luxurious, a beautifully landscaped parkland of flowering shrubs and tall, feather-leaved casuarina trees. I felt I'd just entered a wealthy, private residential estate.

Within a short distance the road divided, leading right, so a sign indicated, to 'The Ocean Club and Gardens, the Flagler Inn, and Paradise Island Golf Course'.

'You can just see the casino roof from here,' said Stud, pointing through the trees, 'but we turn left here. We'll take a look later.'

The road we took led, so another sign said, to 'Paradise Island Stables, the Beach Inn, the Holiday Inn and to Paradise Beach'.

Johnnie now drove with uncharacteristic sedateness through an extensive grove of the towering, graceful casuarinas, passing the Beach Inn Hotel and drawing up finally in the forecourt of the Holiday Inn Hotel, a brand-new, multi-storeyed place overlooking Paradise Beach.

'End of the line,' Johnnie announced. 'There's nowhere to go from here except back the way you came.'

'How much is it, Johnnie?' I asked him.

'Heck, no, I'll get it,' Stud offered.

'No, you got the toll.'

'Normally,' said Johnnie, 'that would be one hundred and thirty-eight dollars ... but seein' it's your first visit I'll make it six dollars fifty.'

I gave him eight which seemed to please him, then we got out and he lugged the cases from the boot.

'Have a good visit, now,' he bade me. 'An' don't forget - any time yuh need a cab in a hurry ... adios, Stud, keep it clean, man.'

The cab departed in a squeal of tortured rubber and in the ensuing silence I stood for a moment, listening to the woosh erf the distant sea and the rustle of the casuarina fronds.

'Quite a place,' I sighed.

'Yes, it's beautiful all right. I try to get down to the beach every day - to compensate for the casino. I do a bit of sailing, snorkling ... come on, the pad's just behind the hotel.'

'What sort of hours do you work, Stud?' I asked as we moved off.

'Heck, all sorts. Sometimes noon till midnight, other times late afternoon until dawn ..

'The casino's open until *dawn*'

'In principle you can play the slot-machines twenty-four hours a day ...! But the other games don't start till after noon - blackjack, craps, roulette, baccarat ...'

'I'm dying to see it.'

'Russ, it'll knock your eye out - always does first time. It's quite a place.'

The apartment block was as I'd expected, modem, unpretentious, and his flat on the third floor likewise. It was cool, clean and comfortable, nice, under furnished, but including all the essentials for a randy young bachelor - a well-stocked liquor cabinet, a stereo cassette system and a well-sprung double bed.

'Veeery nice,' I commented, looking around.
"Dump the cases there and take a look at the view while I get us a drink.'

I opened the balcony door and walked out, feeling the warmth of the breeze after the coolness of the air-conditioning. It was quite a view - the deserted beach below, ringed by palms and casuarinas, the vastness of the ocean, and to the left a glimpse of twinkling Nassau and the harboured cruise boats. Now the stars were out in the darkening sky and way down on the far horizon a big, fat yellow moon was waiting for its cue. All was peace.

'What would you like?' Stud called.

'Got any vodka?'

'Vodka, gin, rum, whiskey ..

'Vodka's fine,' I laughed. 'Got any tonic?'

'Tonic, soda, tomato juice, lime, orange ...'

'Show off. Tonic would be terrific.'

He came out a minute later with a glass six feet high, chinking with ice. 'Heere yuh go. Well... here's to everything.'

'The works.'

We took long swallows, leaned on the rail and lit cigarettes.

'Well,' he asked, 'what d'you think?'

'It's great, Stud. Man, I'll bet the little pigeons go weak at the knees up here - under those stars ... with a moon like that coming up.'

He grinned evilly. 'Well, now, I will admit there have been one or two occasions.. .'

'I'll bet. Stud ... what's that hotel like?'

'The Holiday Inn? Great. Why, were you thinking ...?'

J shrugged. 'Why not?'

'Sure ... why not? Hold on..

He disappeared into the lounge and a moment later he was saying into the phone, 'Hi, honey, Stud Ryder ... give me Joe, will you ...' A pause. 'Joe ...? Stud ... how you been?' Another pause followed by a lecherous laugh. 'Yeh, me, too ... I've got two weeks catching up to do. And speaking of that, I've got a kindred spirit with me, met him on the plane. He wants a good room for a couple of weeks - can do?' Pause. 'Wonderful. His name's Tobin. We'll be over in half an hour. See you.'

He put down the phone and came out to me. 'You're in.'

'Stud - is there anything you can't fix?'

'Yes ...' he said thoughtfully, 'the telephonist I spoke to first. Try as I will.. .'

'Anyway, thanks very much.'

'Nah, my pleasure. I told you - I'm looking forward to this two weeks as much as you. Hey, did you ever do any snorkling...?'

'Yes, in Majorca.'

'Good. Maybe we'll go out tomorrow.'

'Fine ... but, er, about *tonight*..

'Yeh?'

'What d'you reckon will happen?'

'Happen? Well, now, we'll pick the girls up, bring them to Paradise, ply them with an exotic dinner at the Martinique, dance a little, have a stroll round the casino, and then ...'

'Yes?'

'Well, as a gambling man, I'd lay ready money that you and Bunnie...'

And what's more, he'd have won.

Hot damn, he would.

CHAPTER FOUR

At eight o'clock, showered, shaved, shampoo-ed and feeling terrific, we drove back across the bridge in Stud's yellow Mustang, smelling like two extras from an after-shave commercial.

Stud was looking quite resplendent in a midnight-blue velvet suit and I was doing my best in a black-jersey job I'd just bought in London. Altogether, and in all modesty, a couple of very sexy-looking fellas.

'Cal ... a ... forn ... ya ... here we come,' he was singing, driving with light-hearted abandon and slightly faster than Johnnie McArthur. Up and over the bridge we went, round the roundabout, then straight down Bay Street, holding the waters of the harbour channel closely on our right, into town.

'Nassau!' he announced. 'Jewel of the Caribbean!'

'Caribbean? I thought we were in the South Atlantic.'

'So we are, but it sounds so damned unglamorous. On your right - Rawson Square - daytime home of the famed Straw Market. If you should ever feel in need of a straw handbag, this is the place for you.'

'As a matter of fact,' I lisped, 'I do need a new one. Me old one's in tatters from bearin' off the fellas.'

The shops along Bay Street were, again, a mixed lot - dowdy, down-at-heel lock-ups cheek-by-jowl with modem glass-and-chrome boutiques, giving the impression that Nassau could not make up its mind whether to languish in the nineteenth century or take a decisive step into the twentieth.

As we drove through the town, Stud kept up a running

commentary, pointing out bars, restaurants, telling me where I could buy this, that and the other, then, suddenly, we were through, having reached the rambling, pink-painted British Sheraton Hotel which marked the western end of town.

'Is that it?' I asked, surprised.

'That's it, baby - the works.'

'Funny, I always imagined it to be ... I don't know - a glittering, swinging place..

'Oh, it swings all right - in its own quiet - to say nothing of parochial - way. Now, maybe, you can see why Paradise is so popular. The planners were very smart - they figured that if they supplied everything there, folks wouldn't want to leave and spend their money in Nassau. So they did supply everything.
Sometimes I don't cross the bridge for a couple of weeks.'

'Damned clever these Yanks.'

'We have a saying back home ...' he droned, all folksie, '"if'n you're goin' at all - go big".'

I looked at him. 'Do you really?'

'Something like that.'

We were now on the stretch of Bay Street we'd travelled along coming in from the airport and here, on the straight, Stud applied a little accelerator, bringing us to the Sonesta in rather a hurry. Into the driveway we swirled, braking hard under the cantilevered entrance, bringing a uniformed Bahamian doorman down the steps with a grin and a flamboyant salute.

'Good evenin', gentlemen.'

'All right if we leave it here for a couple of minutes?' Stud asked him.

'Sure thing - right over there.'

We ditched the car and went up the steps into the luxurious foyer, fragrant as a garden, then used the house phones to call the girls.

Bunnie's voice gave me a little shiver of anticipation.

'Bunnie - it's me, Tobin.'

'Who else with that accent. Hey, you're early.'

'Couldn't wait any longer.'

'How nice. You'll have to give me five minutes - I'm replacing my eyes, they fell off in the shower.'

'Take ten - I don't care anymore.'

'Did you get settled into a hotel yet?'

'Yes, the Holiday Inn - on Paradise. Thought I'd better stick close to Stud, keep an eye on him.'

'He's still alive! How incredible.'

'Alive and kicking - rarin' to go.'

'And you?'

'I've been rarin' to go since I left the plane.'

She gave a low chuckle. 'Down, boy. O.K., we'll put you out of your misery soon as we can. See you in the lounge?'

'Fine. 'Bye.'

I put down the phone with thumping heart. Stud was still at it, chuckling down the phone. 'You did ...? You naughty girl. O.K., see you in ...' he turned to me, 'Bunnie ready?'

'Ten minutes.'

'Bunnie's ready now,' he lied into the phone, winking at me.

'O.K., doll, see you.'

He put down the phone and did a little jig. 'Hoop-de-doo- de-diddle-um..

"What's got you?'

He made a grab for me, got me in a dance hold, made three wild pirouettes before crashing into the porter's desk and knocking all his pens and four hundred pamphlets on to the floor.

'Oh, hell, sorry ... here, let me ...'

We scrambled around, picking the stuff up while the porter looked on with considerable disdain.

'Sorry ...' said Stud, dumping the stuff back on the desk, then, catching me by the arm, led me into the open lounge, quite beside himself with glee. 'Oh, *boy,* oh, boy - what a night this is goin' to be..

What's happened?'

'Nothing ...! Except she's feeling *very* loving and is all set for a super, knockout evening..

Wonderful.'

'And what is more - Bunnie is feeling the same.'

'She is?'

'Huh huh. Apparently they have just spent a pretty arduous couple of months up aloft, changing flight schedules willy-nilly, and this is the first bit of fun they've had in weeks, *Hoooop-de-* doo-de-hot-damn, I feel good. So, Russell, old son, we two have just got to *see* they have a super, knockout evening - hm?'

'Stud, you are not wrong. So ...' I said thoughtfully, 'Bunnie is also feeling very loving, is she ...?'

'Bunnie is feeling rather well disposed towards you in every direction - according to Lucinda.'

'She is?'

'Hm-mm. You are apparently the first Englishman she's ever dated and the uniqueness of the experience intrigues her no end. There are, I hear, one or two things she's got to find out for herself about you Limeys and the prospect of the investigation quite appeals to her.'

'Oh? What sort of things?'

His grin was something really quite obscene. Well, for one - there's this rumour going around that all Englishmen are cold- hearted, cold-blooded, overtly shy, stiff-necked boobs - in short - lousy lovers. Russell ... you do realize what this means, don't you?'

'Er ... no. What?'

'Well, it means, old chap, that this very night the reputation of an entire *nation* could well be resting on your shoulders, Think about it.'

'My God ... you really think so?'

'An entire nation!' He shook his head. 'Terrible responsibility ... awful! '

'Enormous,' I agreed. 'Well ... one can only do one's best,
' Stud.'

'Stout fellow. I know you can be relied upon to give your all.'

'Oh, boy...'

'And heeeere they come ... man, oh, man don't they look something...'

I spun round, catching my breath they looked so

beautiful. Lucinda in an ankle-length black-and-silver gown that clung delightfully to her legs, and Bunnie also in a long creation of brown-and-white silk, cut tight on the thighs and low at the bosom to show off her wonderful breasts. Bearing in mind what Stud had just told me I went weak at the knees and lost control of my voice.

'Hi!' they greeted us, looking us over.

'Hello,' I croaked, disintegrating under Bunnie's smile.

'My,' cooed Lucinda, 'but don't we look elegant.' She stroked Stud's velvet lapel and kissed him on the cheek. 'Real cool and *very* handsome.'

'You, too, doll - but beautiful.'

She gave a sigh. 'Then our labours have not been in vain.
Come on, we're both starving.'

Slipping her arm round his waist, she led him off, Bunnie and I following, for the moment walking apart.

'He's in high spirits,' she laughed. 'A nice guy. How long have you two known each other?'

'About... seven hours.'

'You're kidding! I thought you were life-long friends, the way you behave.'

'Nope. He ran into me in the Transit Lounge in New York - knocked me flat... about three minutes past one.'

She laughed. 'He did *what?*'

'Came hurtling through the door and knocked me over.'

'That's our Stud,' she sighed. 'I *do* hope he stays out of the lake tonight - just this once.'

When we were settled in the Mustang, Lucinda turned to Bunnie with a wink. 'How're you doing, babe?'

'Me ... ? I'm doing great ...' Unexpectedly she slipped her hand into mine and gave it a squeeze. 'I've got me a date with a lovely-smellin' fella. How are *you* doing?'

'Likewise,' said Lucinda, leaning over to Stud and blowing a kiss down his ear.

'Hot ... damn!' he gasped and hit the accelerator.

We were on Paradise in seven minutes.

Stud abandoned the car right outside the casino and as we went up the steps a uniformed doorman, recognizing

Stud, pulled open one of the big glass doors and ushered us in with a salute.

'Good evenin', sir,' he said to Stud, grinning at him. 'Ah do hope you have both a pleasant and profitable visit.'

Stud made a remark I didn't catch and the doorman exploded with laughter.

'I hope so, too, sir - I surely do.'

As she passed through the door, Lucinda hissed, 'And what filth was that, Ryder?'

'Filth? Me?'

'You.'

The girls entered ahead of us, giving Stud time for an aside to me. 'Everything all right?'

'Fan-tastic.'

'Well, whatever happens, keep your pecker up. England depends on you, you know.'

We joined the girls inside and there, on a dais overlooking the room, we stopped to survey the scene.

The casino was everything Stud had said and more - vast, breathtaking, a cathedral f elegance bathed in a rosy glow, its tables dramatically lit by spotlights hidden in the ceiling, forming pools of intrigue in a sea of subdued excitement.

To our left and right stood banks of slot-machines, literally hundreds of them, garishly coloured, parading like flamboyant soldiers in squads of twenty, ten back-to-back with ten.

Down the long, long length of the room ran the gaming tables - first, from left to right, the dice tables, then blackjack, then roulette, the furthest ones almost disappearing from our view in the gloom.

In the far left-hand corner of the room and open to it in a slightly elevated position stood the Gallery Bar with people seated at tables at its rail, watching the action below. Next to it - Birdcage Walk, an elegant arcade of shops leading, so a sign above it said, to the Bahamian Club, the Brauhaus Grill, the Coyaba Room, the Villa d'Este Italian Restaurant, the Marine Room Restaurant, the Brig Bar, and the Britannia Beach Hotel.

To the right of this arcade was the entrance to the theatre

supper club, Le Cabaret Theatre. Further right still - yet another bar, the Casino Show Bar. Then another arcade, leading, according to its sign, to the Paradise Island Hotel and Villas and to the Tradewinds Bar.

It was all unbelievable - a multi-million-dollar complex of stupendous proportions; an extravagantly conceived and executed dreamworld providing every conceivable service for folks just dying to spend their money. And I could understand now why Stud rarely left Paradise. There was no need.

He moved to my side, grinning. 'Well...?'

'Fabulous.'

'Come on - let's have a drink at the Gallery.'

As we crossed the sumptuously carpeted floor I nodded at a table set apart from the room on a raised plinth behind a rope guard-rail and asked Stud what was played on it.

'Baccarat. The big-money boys like a bit of privacy.'

'How big, Stud?'

He shrugged. 'Oh ... a thirty- or forty-thousand-dollar win or loss isn't unusual.'

I winced. 'Wow. Me - I'm a gambling coward. If I lost a hundred I'd be sick for a week.'

'You and me both,' added Bunnie. 'Though I'm going to have a go on the slot-machines later. Those I adore.'

'O.K., you're on,' I said. 'I can never resist a few bob on them myself.'

We sat at a table near the rail and ordered drinks, then gazed around the room, watching the people. It was easy now to understand the casino's attraction. As Stud had said, for the price of a drink this was rubbing shoulders with bigtime glamour, and I had to admit just sitting there made me feel very James Bond-ish - a beautiful girl at my side, the trickle of the roulette wheels, the calls of the croupiers. No wonder the girls made a bee-line for Paradise.

'Just supposing,' I said to Stud, 'I wanted to train as a croupier - what is involved? How long would it take me?'

'Well, it varies, of course. The odds are the most difficult thing to learn. Take craps, for instance ..he nodded towards the dice tables. 'A customer can play either Pass Line or

Don't Pass - one being the reverse game of the other. And at any time during the game, players can also bet the Boxes. Now - a seven rolled in Pass Line pays 5:1; Craps 3 pays 16:1; Eleven pays 16:1; Craps 12 pays 31:1. On Field - an even money bet on one roll - you win with a throw of 2, 3, 5, 9, 10, 11 or 12 and lose on any other number. Any Craps is a one- roll bet which wins 8:1 on a throw of 2, 3, or 12 and loses on all the other numbers. Craps 2 wins ...'

'Woooaaahhh!' I cried. 'Holy Mother, you lost me after Pass Line and Don't Pass.. .'

'You have to remember all those odds!' gasped Bunnie.

He grinned. 'Not only remember them but calculate all the players' winnings on each throw and pay out - and rake in - in seconds.'

'Oh, brother,' I groaned. 'Well, how about roulette is that any easier?'

'Not much. The table is divided into three rows of twelve numbers - plus 0 and 00 - I'll show you later. That's thirty-eight numbers in all, but in addition you've got bets on Black or Red and Odd and Even. A punter can bet on a single number or a series of numbers - like Five-line which is 1, 2, 3, 0 and 00. That pays 6:1. A single number - called Straight Up, pays 35:1. Six-line pays 5:1; a Row or Street pays 11:1; Corners 8:1; Dozens 2:1; Columns 2:1...'

'Stud...?'

He laughed. 'Yes, Russell?'

'Let's talk about the one-arm bandits, they're much more my style - dead simple.'

The drinks came then and for the next half hour Stud kept us entertained with stories about the casino, the big gamblers, the eccentrics; then we had another drink and this time the girls took over, making us chortle at their experiences in the air. Finally Stud looked at his watch and said, 'Shall we make a move - I booked the table for nine thirty.'

We sauntered along Birdcage Walk, looking at the shops which sold everything from expensive jewellery to beach balls and water wings, finally entering the foyer of the Britannia Beach Hotel. Then, leaving the hotel, we walked a few yards down a landscaped drive and into the fabulous Cafe Martinique.

We were met at the doorway of the main dining room by a small, dark maître d' who looked Italian. He grinned at Stud, ogled the girls, nodded to me and led us off at a fast clip through the dining room and out on to a tree-shaded patio where a group of three Bahamians was making some very nice music. Across the patio we went and down some stone steps to a lower-level patio where a dozen or so tables were set beneath colourful umbrellas, secluded, intimate, and over-looking Paradise Lake.

With speed and Latin flair we were seated, drinks ordered, menus distributed, and then we were left to gaze at the lake. It really was a sight, its rippling water reflecting not only the leaping gas-flames on the far bank but also the radiant light of the high, full moon.

Very romantic.

'Isn't this heavenly?' Bunnie said to me. 'It's our favourite place.'

'Didn't I tell you?' Stud muttered, behind his menu.

'Didn't you tell him what?' demanded Lucinda, eyes narrowed suspiciously.

'Oh ... just that ...'

'Just that this is *the* place to seduce a bird,' she answered for him.

'No, not at all...'

'Well, it is,' she snapped. 'And I *love* being seduced here - and if you don't - goodbye, Ryder. And what am I doin' holding this thing ...' she threw down the menu, 'I know what I want - so does Bunnie. Come on, let's dance.'

As they got up, both the drinks and the head waiter arrived simultaneously. 'Lobster for four, Tony,' said Stud. 'And three bottles of Niersteiner ..

Three?' frowned Lucinda. 'Listen, if I'm gonna be seduced I want to be alive to see it.'

'You'll see it,' Stud insisted, taking her arm and leading her off up the steps.

'How about you?' I said to Bunnie. 'Would you like to dance?'

'I thought you'd never ask,' she smiled.

As we reached the small, crowded dance-floor she turned and came into me, very close, the soft warmth of her startling my heart. For the whole number we didn't speak, just clung together, her hair soft scented against my cheek, the press of her breasts immensely disturbing. As the number ended she broke away and smiled up at me, telling me everything was just fine, then, as the next tune began, she came in again, closer still, slipping her arms around me intimately, showing me what she wanted. A very passionate girl, not overburdened with need for protracted preliminaries.

The number ended and this time I broke away and wiped my forehead. 'Phew! '

'Warm?' she smiled, her eyes misty, playing with me.

'It's ... you.'

'Oh?'

'You're doing awful things to me.'

'I am?'

'You know darned well.'

She chuckled devilishly. 'What ... sort of things?'

'Well ... for one thing you're ruining my appetite ... at least for food.'

'That's nice.'

'But who needs food?'

'Yes ... who?'

We came together again and by the end of that number I was in such a state I could hardly stand up straight. She made a move to leave the floor but I pulled her back. 'Hey ... stay here.'

She widened innocent eyes. 'Why, Russ ...?

'You know damn well.'

She laughed and came in close again, pressing against me. 'Having ... trouble, are we?'

'You'll have to stay here, I can't walk off like this.'

'We could dance off - do an Astaire and Rogers down the steps.'

'Very funny.'

'Come on,' she chuckled, 'I'll walk in front of you.'

'You're taking a terrible chance.'

'Now, *there's* a thought.'

We finally got back to the table, with me bent over as though inspecting my shoes, very glad to sit down. Bunnie was in pleats. Then the other two arrived and it was patently obvious Stud was in the same predicament.

'Damn it,' he was saying, glancing at his shoes, 'that woman really caught me one ...' Walking like Groucho Marx he came round the table, held Lucinda's chair, then sank into his own with a grunt of relief. 'Cooorrr,' he gasped and all four of us hooted with laughter.

'It's all right for you women,' he complained, 'nothing shows.'

'Serves you right, you randy devil,' said Lucinda, then, to Bunnie, with a glance at me, 'And I noticed yours is no better.'

'*He's* disgusting,' grinned Bunnie, slipping her hand into mine and squeezing it. 'Quite disgusting.'

The dinner, I vaguely recall, was wonderful, then it was more dancing and a lot more agony until we'd all had enough and Stud suggested the casino, more, I'm sure, as a means of getting Lucinda closer to the front door than from any desire to gamble.

As we walked back along Birdcage Walk, Stud and Lucinda a little in front of us, I asked Bunnie, 'Well, how d'you feel now?'

'All nice 'n floaty,' she laughed. 'It was a gorgeous dinner.'

'Do you really want to gamble?'

She shook her head. 'Nope.'

'Me, neither. What would you like to do instead?"

A small, smiling pause, then, 'You.'

I gulped. 'Oh.'

'You ... never did tell me what it was like, you know.'

'Mm ... what *what* was like?'

'Your hotel room.'

'Oh. Well, it's sort of difficult to describe, really ...'

'Easier if I saw it for myself, you mean?' -

'Infinitely.'

'Hmm.' She sighed. 'Well, I'd better see it, then ...'

'You mean ... now?'

'Now.'

'What about the other two?'

She smiled. 'I ... somehow think they wouldn't object too strongly. There isn't much time - Lucinda and I fly off at eight.'

'At eight! Does Stud know?'

'Unless I'm very much mistaken ... she's telling him right now.'

The other two had stopped in the arcade. Stud was frowning, and, as we approached, he turned to us, grinning sheepishly, pulling his lip. 'Er ... folks ...'

Bunnie squeezed my arm and murmured, 'Make him suffer for a bit.'

'Yes, Stud?' I said innocently.

'Er ... Lucinda and I were just wondering ... if you'd kinda like to skip the casino ... you know, sort of call it a night and..

Bunnie groaned petulantly. 'Oh, *Stud* ... oh, I'd be so disappointed. We were so looking forward to you showing us around...'

He frowned at her, open-mouthed. "You ... were?'

'Well, of course! We want you to take us round *all* those tables and explain those *fa*scinating odds to us. We want to watch craps and blackjack ... and roulette ...'

'And baccarat,' I added, making him wince.

'... *and* baccarat,' Bunnie went on, 'and then we'll have a fling on the one-arm bandits. I want to have *fun* ... stay up till dawn.. .'

Lucinda sidled up to me, murmured, 'Is she for *real?*'

'Pulling his leg,' I muttered.

She grinned, then joined in. 'Sure - why not! We've never gambled the night away, Stud. Let's watch the dawn come up and toast it with champagne ...! '

'Lu... *cinda*! ' he groaned.

'Well ... we'll be down here again in a couple of months, lover, maybe next time ...'

'O.K.! ' he agreed desperately. 'A quick five bucks on the

slot machines and then...'

'Oh, no,' Bunnie said adamantly, 'we want the works - I feel lucky.'

'Tobbbiinn ...!' he wailed. 'Do something!'

'Well,' I said hesitantly, 'I must say, Stud, I'm inclined to agree ... I really would like to see all those fascinating odds in action - all those columns and craps and five-lines and...'

'Are you *crazy!*'

'No more argument!' insisted Lucinda, grabbing his arm. Bunnie took the other and they turned and marched him off, down the steps and right across the casino floor, as though heading for the one-arm bandits. But they didn't stop. Out through the front door they went, down the steps to the car.

'Come on, come on,' Lucinda urged him, 'get the damn thing started. You're wasting precious time, Ryder, we've only got seven hours.'

'Yes ... ma'am,' he grinned, fumbling for his keys.

Three minutes later we were at the Holiday Inn.

'G'bye, Stud,' said Bunnie, kissing his cheek. 'And *try* to stay alive - and keep this guy out of trouble, will you?'

' 'Bye, baby - sure, I'll keep an eye on him.'

'Huh!' went Lucinda.

I said goodbye to her, then winked at Stud. 'See you tomorrow some time?'

'Sure - Paradise Beach ... ten o'clock?'

'I'll be there.'

We watched them drive out of sight then entered the hotel, alone for the first time.

There was no need for lights in the room; it was bathed in moonlight. Bunnie kicked off her shoes and went out on to the balcony, calling to me, 'Come here and look at this.'

We stood in the moonlight, arms around each other, relishing the warm, scented breeze and the sound of the sea far below.

'A heavenly night,' she sighed.

'Yes ... it was.'

She gave a quiet laugh and turned into me. 'It was beautiful, Russ.'

'And not over yet.'

I drew her close. Her arms went around nay neck and I kissed her. Her mouth was warm, tremulous, suddenly hungry. We broke away, gasping, looking at each other, then in a breathless whisper she murmured, 'Let's go inside.'

Standing by the bed she came into me again, slipped her hands inside my jacket and eased it from my shoulders, saying with a sexy, quizzical smile, 'Ever had a woman undress you?'

'No,' I croaked.

'You have now.'

Slowly she undid the buttons on my shirt then slipped her arms inside, rubbed her check against my body, murmuring, 'That's wonderful ...' My belt parted suddenly. The zip went down ... then slowly she sank to her knees, taking my trousers with her, and with a stifled gasp swallowed me.

She drove me wild, using her tongue and hot, moist mouth, tickling and caressing, uttering soft moans of pleasure. Then quickly she was on her feet, reaching for her zip, dropping the dress and shedding her underclothes, standing before me breathtakingly naked.

'My God,' she gasped, her eyes twinkling with excitement, 'just *look* at him'

My voice was croaked, my whole body aquiver. 'What d'you expect - doing things like that?'

'I love doing it.' She came into me, pressing her body hard against me, whispering urgently, 'I *want* you! ' then moved to the bed, taking me with her, pulling me over her.

'Oho, no you don't ...' I said sternly, moving away. 'Why should you have all the fun?'

'What d'you mean?'

'Lie still.'

'Russ ... please! '

'No. Lie still and do as you're told.'

'What ... are you going to do?'

'You - extremely slowly. It may take days.'

She gave a low chuckle. 'So this is what they mean by "an

Englishman needs time".'

'This one does...'

'Well ... just as long as I'm on that plane by eight ... oh! My God, that's crazy ... Russ ... what are you *doing* to me! Oh, baby, that's fabulous . . .fabulous! ' It was only moments later that she gasped, 'Ye Gods ...! Russ, I'm coming ...! Russ ... I'm COMING! OHHHHH!! Oh my... GOD!'

Fingers and teeth clenched, she arched her wondrous body in repeated paroxysms of piercing ecstasy then collapsed and lay gasping, shuddering, staring in wonderment. 'Dear *God,* what hit me? That was fan ... tastic! Ohh, baby ... baby ...'

Chuckling at her delight I caressed her gently for a while, then suddenly, she came to, sat up quickly, eyes narrowed fiendishly. 'All right, Tobin, if that's the way you want it ... Now, *you* lie down - and I'll show you how a Yank makes love ...'

I stretched out on my back and she knelt at my side, gazing down at me with wide, hungry eyes, then she began. I shuddered at the first touch of her hot mouth.

'Oohh ... Bunnie ..

'Mmm?'

I jumped as her tongue pierced me, gasped at her vibrating caress, then suddenly she broke away. 'Oh, my God ... this is ridiculous...! '

'What's the matter!?'

'I'm *coming* again! '

'But... I'm not touching you! '

'I know ... I know it's ohhhhh! OHHHH !! '

She curled into a tight ball, shuddering, pressing her body against me, murmuring plaintively until her climax was done, then, quite mystified, she raised her head and whispered, 'It's never happened before! What are you *doing* to me?'

'Well,' I chuckled, 'certainly no more than you're doing to me.'

She came forward quickly, rolled on top of me. 'Oh, you are something else again, Tobin. If I were you I wouldn't plan on getting too much sleep tonight.'

'No?'

She shook her head. 'No way. This is once in a lifetime. I'm going to remember this when I'm ninety.' She kissed me tenderly, then began to descend very slowly, kissing my body until she was back where she'd begun, and then began all over again.

She was right. It was a night *I'll* remember if I live to be three thousand.

I awoke with a start, knowing time had flown, and looked at my watch on the bedside table. It was almost six.

I turned to her, asleep in my arm, one leg thrown across me and her hair spilled across my chest.

I kissed her on the nose. 'Bunnie ...'

'Mmm?' She wriggled closer, hugging me tightly.

'Honey, it's six o'clock.'

For all the effect it had, I could have said 'Happy Christmas'.

'Baby ...' I shook her. 'It's six o'clock!'

She gave a start, lay still, staring at my stomach.

'Hate to wake you, but it's almost six.'

'Six!' she gasped. 'I must go!'

I tightened my hold on her, brought her close. 'I don't want you to go. I want to lie on the beach all day with you ... then come back here and do it all again.'

'*All* of it?' she grinned. 'Did anybody ever tell you you were a sex maniac?'

'Huh, you can talk. I reckon you broke a record or two last night.'

'Well, it was all... his fault.'

'Bunnie, don't do that...'

She smiled and rolled into me, kissing my cheek. 'You're a hell of a lover, Tobin ..

I shook my head. 'It takes two, Bunnie.'

'... a rare and beautiful thing, hm?'

'Yes, it is. When will you be coming to Nassau again?'

She sighed. "Not for a while. We switch to the Miami run when we get back.'

'Miami? Well, now, maybe I'll see you over there.'

'You're going to *Miami?*'

'It's possible. I want to see something of the States while I'm so close and Miami is the logical place to start.'

'Oh, do come, Russ ... I want to see you again.'

'And I you. Where can I reach you?'

'We stay at the Eden Roc - it's on the beach.'

'Eden Roc. It's a date.'

She kissed me on the nose. 'I must go, babe,' then skipped out of bed and made for the bathroom, tall, lithe, gloriously naked. At the door she turned with a puzzled frown. 'Well ... are you comin' or not?'

'Mm?'

'For a shower. I *need* you.'

She made the plane with about three minutes to spare, totally exhausted but very, very clean.

And I returned to Paradise.

CHAPTER FIVE

Suddenly the sun went in. I opened my eyes and found Stud standing over me, weaving with exhaustion but managing a grin.

'Hi, down there.'

'Hello up there. Jeez, you look terrible. You'd better sit down.'

He dropped like a stone, face-down on the sand, and uttered a tortured groan.

I laughed weakly. 'You, too?'

He nodded ponderously. 'How ... about you?'

'Me, too, son ... knackered.'

'You reckon ... you saved ... rep'tation of the English ... male, then...?'

'I believe her opinion ... was adequately re-orientated, yes.'

'Good man ... I'm.,. proud .

He was asleep.

We woke two hours later. The sun was high and hot, the beach busy. We sat up, squinting at the dazzling ocean.

'Come on,' he said, getting to his feet. 'Last one in's a fairy.'

I staggered down the loose sand after him on legs of jelly and hit the cool revitalizing water, surfacing a new man.

'Wow!'

'Oh, man ...' he laughed, 'that's better.'

We swam out at a fast crawl, then turned on our backs and floated face-up to the hot blue sky.

'Boy, oh boy ...' he laughed, shaking his head. 'What a

night! That baby can really fly!'

I laughed at his exuberance. 'Bunnie damn-near missed the plane. We were still at it at seven - in the shower.'

'Hot *damn,* but that Lucinda's' got an imagination.'

'I've arranged to meet up with Bunnie again in Miami. She reckons there were one or two things we left out, though I'm darned if I know what they could be. I thought we'd just about covered everything.'

He gave a laugh and rolled over, disappeared beneath the surface for an alarmingly long time, then shot up like a cavorting porpoise.

'Hey, how about some snorkling?'

'Sure, but what do we do for gear?'

'Hire it - on the beach over there - *and* one of those sailboats.'

'I don't know how to sail.'

'I can handle it - come on!'

We raced each other into the beach and hired a flimsy, flat- bottomed sailboat and some flippers and masks. The boat looked wildly unstable from the start - little more than a fibre-glass raft with a sail stuck on it, but Stud sounded very confident.

'Nothing to it,' he said, as we pushed the thing out into the shallows against a lively breeze. 'I'll have us skimming over the briney before you can say ... look out!'

A brisk gust caught the sail and spun the thing round like a top, the bow catching Stud a good thump on the arse. 'Ow!' he yelled. 'Russ ...! Catch that line ... no, man, the other one on the ...' Whhoosshh! Another gust ripped into the sail and the mast came down like a felled pine, right on top of Stud. With a yell he disappeared under the spread of sail and for a minute or two the canvas jumped and bucked with pummelling fists, then he dived, emerging like a drowned Old English sheepdog, hair plastered down his face, coughing and spluttering.

'Hot... *damn!*'

'Hey, I thought you could handle this thing!' I hooted.

'So I can, so I can. It's just gettin' the bloody thing started...'

We got the floating tea-tray upright again and managed to climb on board.

'O.K., O.K. ... here we go!' he cried, yanking on the sail rope. He swung the tiller, brought us around to face the open lagoon, then the wind hit us again and over we went.

'AAAAAAHHHH!!'

We both shot into the sea.

'Aw, hell, S ... Stud!' I spluttered, breaking surface.

'P ... Patience, Russell ...' he gasped, grabbing the boat again.

'Where did you learn *your* seamanship - the S ... Swiss navy?'

'Veeery funny ... O.K., up we go!'

This time he got it going, missed colliding with another boat by an inch, almost decapitated a bald-headed swimmer, and then we were streaking out to sea.

'Ho ho ...!' he laughed, 'now this is the life! The salt breeze in your hair, the tang of the sea...'

'Tight gallons of water in your lungs ... the bruises coming out nicely...'

'Oohhh ... a life on the ocean waaave ... and there isn't a girl in siiight...'

'If I don't get off this flamin' shiiip ... you're gonna get yours toniiight...' I lisped.

About a mile off-shore he slackened off the sail and brought the thing to a halt. 'Right - over you go, Russell.'

'Aren't you coming, too?'

'I'd better look after this thing - we'll take turns.'

'As you say, skipper.'

I donned flippers and snorkel mask and slipped over the side.

'Head out in that direction,' he said. 'The coral is fantastic.'

'Aye, aye, sir.'

Down I went to about ten feet.

My first sight of the coral was so breathtaking I almost took <u>in</u> water. The colours, the shapes were really spectacular. And the fish! Hundreds of them! All colours of the paintbox - blue, green, yellow, red, spotted, striped and wavy.

I swam slowly over a huge bed of waving eel-grass that was infested with tiny, multi-hued tiddlers that darted away in a perfectly precise cloud as I approached. I was really enjoying myself. Maybe, I thought, I'd do this every day, trying a different part of the lagoon, coming out by myself if Stud was working.

I crossed a deep ridge of magnificent pink coral and stopped to watch its waving fans and the multitude of weird and wonderful fish swimming around and through it, then I went on. diving, a moment later, for a big pink shell but discovered it was an eel's house and abandoned it.

Surfacing briefly for air I dived again, continuing in the direction of the open sea and encountering another fascinating ridge of coral with a deep, mysterious-looking trench beyond. I slowed, swam for a while up and down the ridge, then turned and crossed it, entering the plummeting valley ... and there, in the misty murk of the deeper water, came suddenly face-to- face with holy terror.

He was monstrous - at least five feet long and solid as a shark. And his mouth! A gaping *cavern* of cruel, terrifying teeth, two ... three inches long, pointed like knives! He was staring straight at me with huge, fierce eyes, poised for attack. I froze with terror, heart hammering. This was it! I was going to be eaten alive!

Then in he came.

Rigid with fright I backed away, hypnotized by the evil glassiness of his eyes, then, propelled by a surge of panic, I turned and streaked for the surface, flippers kicking wildly, arms beating at the water.

I broke through, desperately searching for Stud.

'Stud! ' I yelled. 'Stud ...! Help...! '

I could sense the devil right behind me, its cavernous mouth stretched wide for the snap and swallow. My skin crawled, nerves screamed. I'd seen the film 'Blue Water - White Death' and the appalling mess the White Shark had made of the skindiver was, I knew, about to be made of me. I could feel the great razor-sharp teeth scything into my flesh, hear the crunch of bone as they severed a limb with one stupendous bite ...

'Stud ...! HELP!!'

He was racing towards me, crouched at the tiller, staring with apprehension. 'What is it?!' he shouted, now only twenty yards away.

"F ... fish! Enormous!'

"Where ... Where?'

Now he was half-standing, balancing precariously, peering down into the water, the emergency paddle in his hand, ready to strike.

"Right *behind* me!'

'I see him ... I see him! God, he's gigantic!'

'I bloody know!'

I lunged for the side of the boat, hauled myself up, fell on to the deck, unable to believe I'd still got both legs on. Then ... behind me ... a horrifying splash! Stud had gone overboard!

He'd fallen in! And it was my fault - I'd tipped the boat! I spun round. There he was ... down there with the monster! My God, how terrible ... he'd be eaten alive! I searched frantically for a weapon ... anything. There was nothing. It would have to be bare hands and a kick in the balls. I scrambled up, crouched for the dive, expecting as I took the plunge to see the water boil as the fish attacked, turn bright pink with Stud's gushing blood. I'd seen it happen in the film ... great chunks of whale flesh ripped away with a single bite ... the billowing clouds of gore...!

With toes curled over the edge of the deck I paused, summoning non-existent courage, saying goodbye to the world I loved ... and then I paused some more. Funny ... the sea wasn't boiling. And the monster wasn't attacking! It was down there all right but absolutely still - looking at Stud with really quite a benevolent air ... allowing him to approach ... to reach out ... to touch it! Dammit, he was *stroking* the bloody thing! Tickling its belly! For a good ten seconds he stroked the flaming thing's turn then swam to the surface and hauled himself on board, killing himself laughing.

'Grouper,' he panted. 'Always very friendly. Man ...' he

chuckled, 'you should've seen your face.'

'Oh, very, bloody funny . . .! The standard rookie joke around these parts, I presume?'

He nodded, 'Couldn't resist it. You had enough?'

'More than, thanks very much.'

'Seriously,' he grinned, 'what did you think of it down there?' 'Fantastic - until the grouper. Really beautiful.'

'Right - take over the Q.E. 2, I'll have a go.'

He pulled on flippers and stood up and was about to put on his mask when he did a double-take and gazed off across the lagoon, shading his eyes. 'Aye!'

'Now, what have you spotted - a bleeding whale?'

'No ... unless I'm very much mistaken - a couple of damsels in distress!'

'Where ... where?' I was on my feet in a trice.

'There,' he pointed, 'and having lots of lovely trouble ... woops! They're in!'

I was in time to see a sail topple and two bikini-ed figures leap into the water.

'Ta-ta ... ta-ta! "went Stud on his bugle. 'Navy to the rescue. Crack on all canvas, Mr. Christian ... bring the helm aport ... haul in the sea anchor ... tote dat barge ... lift dat bale ...' he broke into a dance, '... get a liddle drunk an' yo' land in jail ...'

In seconds we were approaching them.

'Have no fear - the navy's here!' Stud called to them.

Two tanned arms waved in response.

'Hee hee,' laughed Stud. 'Thiiis ... iiis our lucky daaayyy,' he began singing. He had a lousy voice.

As we drew closer our hopes were rewarded richly. A couple of nice little pigeons, one so tanned she could have been Mexican or something, her long dark hair floating around her like seaweed, and the other a pretty-faced thing with short blonde hair and a cute snub nose.

'Gee, thanks,' this one called to us. 'Could you please help us get this thing upright?'

'Sure!' grinned Stud. 'No problem - but let's get you out of the water first - the sharks, you know.'

'Sharks!' they gasped.

'And barracuda,' he added nonchalantly, 'And stingray ...'
'My Gard! ' gasped Button-nose.
'Here - give me your hand,' he said to her, reaching down.

I did the same to Consuela.

I gripped her mitt and gave a mighty pull. Out she came with a rush, the pressure of the water yanking down her bikini top almost to her waist and completely exposing her gorgeous breasts.

'Ohh! ' she yelled, horrified, and hung out from the side, struggling with one hand to pull the top back into place.

'Never mind that! ' I commanded. 'The sharks ... the sharks! '

'Eeek! Let me go ... no, pull me in! '

'Which do you want?'

'Pull me in ... pull me in! '

Delaying as long as I could I finally hauled her in. 'Sorry about that,' I grinned.

I heard Stud chuckle.

Flustered and blushing she wrestled her charlies back into harness and slumped down on the deck and wrung out her hair.

'By ... golly, you had a narrow escape there,' Stud said anxiously, shaking his head at Snub-nose. 'Oh, by the way ...' he snapped a salute, 'Captain Ryder - Stud Ryder - at your service. And this is my First Officer Russell Tobin.'

'Well, thanks a lot,' said Snub-nose. 'I'm Jeannie Gilmore ... and this is Marie Todd. We're sure grateful for the rescue ... but are there really sharks in this lagoon? I'd have thought they'd have warned us before renting us the boat.'

'Surely they can't get inside the reef,' added the lovely Marie, in a tone that was tinged with more than a hint of growing suspicion now that she'd had time to analyse the situation.

'Oh, good heavens! ' exclaimed Stud, peering around the lagoon. 'Are we inside the reef? Ah, well, no ... in that case there aren't any sharks ..

Snub-nose narrow-eyed him. 'Or barracuda ...?'

'Er, well ...'

'Or stingray ... ?'

'Erm..

'So it was all a trick to get us on board?'

Stud slumped and placed a contrite hand over his heart. 'Madam, I cannot tell a lie - it was all Tobin's idea. He spotted you in the water and quickly devised the whole dastardly plan. Captain, he said, how would it be if we went and rescued those two lovely creatures and invited them to spend the day with us - take them out to lunch ... laze away the afternoon on the beach ... then show them a real good time tonight. Tobin - didn't you say that?'

'Yes, I said that,' I nodded dumbly.

'So - how about it?'

They were both smiling and swapping glances.

'How can we refuse?' smiled Marie. 'But what about our boat?'

'Ha! Leave that minor matter to us,' Stud said gallantly.

'But you won't be able to sail it - the sail's torn.'

'A mere bagatelle. We'll tow it ashore with this. Tobin - overboard.'

In we dived and swam to the capsized hull, now thirty yards away, and there in its lee, we conferred.

'Hoo hoo,' laughed Stud, 'what luck! That Jeannie is a scrumptious little piece ..

'Man, oh, man, did you get an eyeful of Marie's buswarms! Right little handfuls ..

'Well, listen this is how we'll play it. I reckon we ought to take them to Kelly's for lunch - it's right on the beach so we won't have to change - then afterwards we ...'

'Well... g'byyyyyeeee, fellas! And thanks a lot! '

The shout came distantly from Jeannie. Stud gaped at me ... me at him. We hauled ourselves up, peered over the hull ... and there they went, flying before the breeze, heading for shore.

'Hey! ' gasped Stud. 'Our boat! '

'Oh, you can have ours! ' shouted Marie.

'But what about toniiiight?'

She gave a heartless laugh. 'I don't think our boyfriends would go for it! '

'Watch out for the sharks, now!' laughed Jeannie. 'And the wolves!'

'Oh ... bollocks,' groaned Stud, sliding down into the water.

'What a mean, low-down trick.'

'Yeh - almost as low-down as ours.'

He looked at me and burst out laughing. 'Yeh, how about that? Come on, let's get this thing upright. Ta heck with dames. Come to think of it, I don't want to see another one for a week. I need a rest.'

'Me, too.'

'Right - it's a pact. No women for a week.'

'Done!'

We didn't quite make it somehow. Later that night we were knee-deep in it again. We were in the casino. Stud was back on duty, on roulette, and I was standing there watching, feeling a mite jaded from the night before and from all the fresh air and sun of that day and contemplating, if any<u>thing</u> at all, an early night. And then it happened.

The Contessa came in.

Boy, oh, boy, what a night *that* turned out to be.

CHAPTER SIX

'Thirty -six ... red,' droned Stud, eyes drooping, looking really shagged.

Mechanically he raked in the losing bets, paid out the winners, picked out the ball, slowed the revolving wheel and sent the ball round the groove again.

Zzzz ... zzz ... zzz ... tinkle ... tinkle. Silence.

'Twenty-two... black.'

Everyone lost. No excitement at all. I stifled a yawn and as he picked the ball out again he turned and caught me at it, slipped me a wink and pulled a face, telling me he felt the same.

'Place your bets, please,' hf droned and the game continued.

Suddenly there was a commotion over by the main door. A party of people entered, about thirty of them, elegantly dressed, boisterous, noisy, in high spirits. For a moment they milled around on the raised dais, collecting themselves, laughing and joking, then, from their midst, emerged a woman, a flamboyant creature with flame-red hair running riot. Expensively gowned in glittering green silk and trailing a huge white fox fur, she descended the stairs, not too steadily, then swept across the floor, chin high, eyes twinkling, her voluptuous hips swinging and swaying sexily like an old-time movie-queen.

Now her entourage fell in behind her, though none closer than a tall, handsome, immensely tough-looking young Negro in immaculate evening dress, who clung to her heels like a limpet.

Half-way across the room her progress was momentarily

impeded by, I presumed, the management. Hands were shaken, heads bobbed, then on she came again - straight for us.

I looked at Stud and found he was watching her approach, the expression on his face one of anticipation, half delight yet partial dismay, obviously knowing who she was.

On she came, beginning now to smile in his direction, and then, at twenty paces, she let out a cackling laugh that completely shattered her regal image and bellowed, 'Stud ... ! Yuh good-lookin' son-of-a-bitch, how are yuh!'

Grinning bashfully, he gave himself helplessly to her big bosomy hug and a smacker on the cheek.

'I'm fine, Contessa. Nice to see you again.'

'Hell, man, how dare yuh go on vacation when I'm on the island! Two goddam weeks I've bin here - an' lost a motherlovin' fortune every night! Here, everybody - meet Stud Ryder, the handsomest dealer on Paradise and the only son-of-a-gun that lets me win!'

Her followers clustered around the table, jockeying for position, and what a puzzling assortment they were - young, old, slim, fat, some of them young swingers and others looking like respectable, middle-aged businessmen. But all, as I said, well- dressed. A very odd bunch.

'Now, Ryder,' laughed the Contessa, 'are yuh gonna let me win on my last night - or do I have ta sic Benjie on yuh!' She threw a nod to the Negro at her side who was watching the proceedings without a glimmer of amusement.

'Heck, Contessa,' grinned Stud, 'with your talent I don't have to.'

'An' ain't *you* the lover,' she laughed, pinching his cheek.

'O.K.., you crumbs, let me in there ... let the bitch see the rabbit. Hi, Barney ... hi, Joe,' she nodded to two punters on the next table as she slid her voluptuous ass on to a stool. 'There ya go! Now, let's get some action movin' here. Benjie - give Stud two grand for openers - an' gimme a light, baby.'

The Negro took a thick wad of bills from his inside pocket, peeled off two and threw them on the table for chips. The Contessa fitted a Lucky Strike into a long silver cigarette holder, then accepted a light from Benjie's gold lighter. And while all this was going on I was having a good look at the Contessa.

As a young woman she'd undoubtedly been a real beauty. It was still there in her fine green eyes and high cheek bones, despite the lines and pouches. But an awful lot of living had been done since those days and now she was falling to bits nicely.

But who gave a damn? *She* certainly didn't. With a king's ransom in diamonds and emeralds around her neck and another on her fingers she was not only worth a fortune but was obviously determined to spend it having a high old time.

But what, I wondered, was the 'Contessa' bit all about? A nickname? Must be. With that voice and vocabulary she was as much aristocrat as an alley-cat. But whatever her background was it was a dead cert to be colourful. And so it turned out when I got the story from Stud on his next break.

'O.K., roll, baby! ' she told Stud, slapping a blue chip on Red and another on Even. 'Five hundred on each an' don't let me down or by God ...' she leaned close to him and muttered something that made him laugh out loud. 'An' I ain't kidding!' she threatened.

'I'll do my best, Contessa.'

'Hell, it's good t'see yuh back. Yuh know I only come to this crummy joint to see you, don't yuh - otherwise I'd sail the goddam tub to Monaco! '

Stud grinned, looking overwhelmed and a bit sorry he was standing there. 'Right - no more bets, ladies and gentlemen. Here we go.'

He slowed the wheel and flicked the ball into the rim. The Contessa's eyes followed it avidly, afire with excitement. 'Come on, yuh S.O.B. - even an' red ... even an' red! '

At her elbow the Negro's eyes, heavy-lidded, panned slowly around the group and around the room, alert for any threat to the Contessa's person or diamond fortune. Unexpectedly they switched suddenly to me, perhaps feeling that I was watching him, and their flint-hard hostility shocked me. Quickly I lowered my eyes to the table but could feel his lethal gaze on me for some time after. A very nasty gentleman.

The dropping of the ball into a slot aroused excitement around the table and broke the tension between us.

'Eighteen . ... and RED! ' announced Stud, and the crowd erupted in a joyful cheer. The Contessa let out a whoop of delight and brandished her fists aloft, then came off her seat and threw her arms round Stud's neck.

'Baby, I *love* yuh! Didn't I tell yuh - you're my lucky piece!' Sitting down again, she slammed a pile of chips on to the table. 'Go on, sweetheart, do ya woist - see if yuh can take momma t'the goddam cleaners! '

'Place your bets, ladies an' gentlemen! '

In great excitement the Contessa ground out her barely-smoked cigarette, shakily stuck a fresh one into the holder and clicked her fingers. Benjie was there with a light instantly.

'Thanks, honey. 'Kay, Ryder, let 'em roll! '

The wheel was slowed once again. Zzziiipp went the little ball into the groove. A sea of faces stared in concentration.

'Come on, come *on* ...' the Contessa breathed fervently. 'Drop in that mother-lovin'..

It did drop ... ran across the slats ... tinkle ... tinkle ... tinkle.

Silence.

All I heard above the exploding cheer was Stud's 'Four .. but I knew it was also red.

'Jesus!' gasped the Contessa. 'We hit ... we hit! Both goddam barrels! '

The noise around this table was now so outrageous that I took a look around the room to see what effect it was having on the other gamblers and did an amazed double-take. There wasn't a soul in the room! We'd got the lot!

'O.K. - it's a sign! ' exclaimed the Contessa breathlessly. 'Tonight we bust the bastards! Get back some of the goddam fortune I've dropped in this joint. Come on, Stud, let her go, baby! I'm hot... I'm hot! '

As Stud once more gathered the ball, slowed the wheel

and flicked the ball in, the tension was electrifying and almost the only sound in the entire casino was the metallic zizz of the little pill - apart from the rhythmic click ... click ... click of chip against chip in the Contessa's nervous fingers.

The ball slowed ... dropped from the rim ... rippled across the slats ... stopped.

'Twenty-six ... red! '

The Contessa threw back her head and let go an ear-splitting 'YYYYY ... IIIPPPEEEE! ! ' and the cheer from the crowd was a roar.

In the next twenty minutes she won six more times and lost only three, leaving her a net gain of six thousand dollars and deliriously happy. But then ...

It was time for Stud's break. His relief arrived, upsetting the Contessa no end. She implored Stud to stay but the house rules won in the end. Finally she relented but with little grace.

'O.K., yuh bum - but twenty minutes on the nose - not a second longer, yuh hear!'

'Twenty minutes, I promise.'

She gave him a rueful grin. 'If yuh not back on the stroke - Benjie will come an' get yuh! '

'I'll be back,' he laughed, then pushed through the crowd, indicating the bar to me with a flick of his head.

I joined him.

'Jeezus! ' he gasped, wiping his forehead. 'Do I need a drink! '

'I'd say ... yes, you need a drink.'

'Man, oh, *man* ... what a woman! '

We climbed the steps of the Gallery Bar and he collapsed into a chair. Instantly there was a waitress there, no doubt anticipating his need.

'Vodka?' he asked me.

'Please.'

'One vodka tonic, honey - and my usual when under stress.'

'What's that?' I asked him, when she'd gone.

'A good slug of Bacardi lost in a coke. Officially we're not allowed to drink on duty but needs must when that particular devil calls.'

'She's a real character, isn't she,' I said, glancing across the casino as another cheer went up. 'Who is she, Stud? Not a real Contessa, surely?'

'Oh, yes ...'

'What! '

'A genuine Italian Contessa ...'

'Good God.'

'... by marriage - naturally.'

'Ah.'

'It's quite a story.'

'It's got to be.'

He paused as the waitress came up with the drinks, thanked her, then raised his glass and swallowed a third of it. 'Ah, that's better.'

I gave him a cigarette and a light and as he exhaled he said, with a wry grin, 'As you might suppose, she wasn't always a countess ...'

'Yeh, funny you should say that. What was she before - a longshoreman?'

'No - a stripper.'

'Of course ... what else with a figure like hers? I'll bet she was a real cracker in her time, Stud.'

He nodded. 'By all accounts a knockout.'

'And what happened?"'

'As I heard it from one of her crowd last time she was over, just after the Second World War, one of those dispossessed Italian counts arrived in New York without a bean. There must have been hundreds of them floating around in those days, having lost everything to the Germans or the Allies or somebody ...'

'Sure, ten a penny.'

'Anyway, this guy - whose name was Da Vichi - was apparently not averse to doing a day's work for his bread, borrowed a few bucks, opened a pizza parlour in Little Italy and started making a bit - his gimmick being his title - Count Da Vichi's Pizzas. I imagine the folks flocked in to see a real live count making his own pizzas, found they were good and went back for more. So he was on his way.'

'And the Contessa was one of his customers, I suppose?'

'Nope - he was one of hers. Being a normally randy sort of fellow he liked to pop into the strip joints in town and that's where he fell head-over-pizza in love with her - she then being a voluptuous red-haired lovely rejoicing in the improbable name of Blossom Kalewski ..

As though mention of her name had prompted it, a tremendous cheer went up from her table at that moment.

'Jesus, she's killing us,' laughed Stud.

'Go on, this is great stuff.'

'So - the count proposed. Blossom apparently took one look at this little squirt and was about to laugh her tassles off when she caught the title Count and the bit about three thriving pizza parlours and had a swift change of heart. And so, incredibly, she became the Contessa Gabriella Da Vichi.'

'Gabriella?'

'Well, under the circumstances she could hardly stay with Blossom, hey? Anyway, as soon as they were married the Count put his foot down - no more stripping - but in way of compensation he gave her half the business. And Blossom knuckled down, helping him manage the parlours and five years later they were doing very nicely.

'Then - disaster struck. The Count's lungs packed up and he was advised to move south to the Florida sun. So they sold up and moved down to Miami.' He paused to check his watch. 'Seven more minutes.' Hastily he swallowed some more Bacardi. 'And if I'm not back on the dot, she damn-well *will* send Benjie for me. Anyway, there they were in Miami with a lot of bread but the Count too sick to work ...' He paused, then began on a new tack. 'Russ, did I ever mention Fort Lauderdale to you?'

I frowned. 'No, but I've heard of it. It's near Miami isn't it?'

'Yes, it is - and it's one of the most luxurious residential areas in the States - a real millionaires' paradise, built right on the water like Venice. Some of the homes there are unbelievable - yet only a few years ago the entire area was nothing but dense mangrove swamp that you could buy for nothing an acre, though who'd want to?'

I grinned 'The Contessa?'

'Close. The Count. The old boy took one look at the Miami sun and figured that one day people would be flocking down south in their millions - especially during the northern winter - trying to get a piece of it. So he bought a thousand acres of swamp and everyone thought he was nuts. But during the next ten years the development he'd predicted began to happen. He sold off some of the land then for a monstrous profit but kept a couple of hundred acres in reserve. Then he died.' Again he looked at his watch, drained his glass and made to move. 'So the Contessa, old buddy, still owns a couple of hundred acres of Lauderdale.'

'At... how much an acre?'

He shrugged. 'Oh, about a million dollars. I must go.'

I followed him down the steps. 'She's worth ... two hundred million dollars!'

'Hell, no ...' he grinned, stretching the story. 'She's a shrewd cookie - so are the people with her. They're some of her advisers, by the way. She's into everything these days ...' he laughed, 'even pizza parlours. It's rumoured she's worth five hundred million and probably is.'

'Good ... God!'

'Twice a year she goes on the toot - loads her pals on to her yacht and heads out here. You should see the yacht! You'd mistake it for one of those cruise ships! But she doesn't stay on board - she's also got a villa here ...'

'Naturally,' I sighed.

'Just a small place - about forty rooms.'

'I understand.'

'Which - unless I'm mistaken - you'll be viewing before the night is through.'

'Uh?'

'This is her last night and she always throws a farewell wing- ding at the villa. I'm sure I'm going to get an invite - which means you will too if I ask her. How d'you feel?'

'Ha!'

'Thought you might.'

'Have you been to one before, Stud?'

'No. The last time she was here I was working till dawn and couldn't make it - but I've heard about her little parties. The whole island has. I hear they're really something.'

'Oh, boy ...'

'Stud, you bastard!'

Stud jumped. The Contessa was on her feet, tapping a diamond-studded watch. 'Twenty-one goddam minutes - you're late ! '

'Heck, I'm sorry, Contessa,' he grinned, nodding to the relief dealer and taking his place. 'How've you been making out?'

'Baby, I'm up ten grand - no thanks to you, yuh bum - an' I'm gonna make it twenty! So hit that wheel. I'm not leaving this goddam table until I get twenty back from those pikers - even if I have ta stay here for another mother-lovin' week! '

'O.K.,' laughed Stud, 'let's see what we can do for you. Place your bets, ladies and gentlemen ..

During the next hour her fortune soared to seventeen thousand, then, in a bad fifteen minutes, plummeted to six thousand, finally recovered to twelve thousand. Then, in an unbelievable run of eight straight red-and-even drops, rocketed to twenty thousand, the noise and excitement building with each win to a state of near-hysteria.

As the last point was made, the Contessa leapt up from the stool, threw her arms round Stud's neck and damn-near suffocated him. 'Yuh *did* it ... yuh *did* it! Yuh made it for momma! ' She fetched him a big wet one on the lips and turned to the crowd. 'O.K., everybody - the party's on me! Floyd, cash in the chips! Frank - get the cars! Here, Stud - that's f'the boys ... ! ' she tossed him two blue chips - a thousand dollars! 'Now - what time d'you finish tonight - an' don't tell me dawn like last time or I'll buy the goddam place an' fire yuh! '

'No - two o'clock, Contessa,' grinned Stud, quite abashed by his popularity.

'O.K. ...' she patted his cheek maternally, 'now, you get over to the villa soon as you finish. Momma's gonna see you get a beautiful time.'

'Thanks, Contessa. Er ... will it be all right if I bring a friend along ...?' He turned to me. 'This is Russ Tobin, he's on vacation here.'

Twin green fires devoured me, then, slowly, a sexy smile lifted the corner of her mouth. 'Sure, why not ... he's a nice-lookin' guy. Bring him along.'

'Thank you,' I said.

'O.K., see ya later.' She turned to the Negro. 'Benjie - my stole. Let's get going.'

Across the casino -she swept, hips swaying, the long white fox slung carelessly over one shoulder, sweeping the floor behind her. All that was missing was the razzy stripper music for her exit.

Then she was gone and the casino returned to sanity.

'Wow!' gasped Stud. 'Boy, when she hits a place it sure staggers.'

I laughed. "Yes - and if she behaves like that in *here* - what's the party going to be like?'

'Interesting,' he grinned and returned to the game.

I looked at my watch. It was nearly midnight - two hours to go. I was disinterested in the game now and impatient to get to the party, knowing in my bones it was going to be a right old pantomime.

It was.

But what I didn't know was that I'd already been chosen for principal boy !

CHAPTER SEVEN

Two thirty found us roaring in a southerly direction along Coral Harbour Road under a blazing moon, both of us in extremely high spirits and not entirely sober. We'd managed a couple of stiff quickies at the Gallery Bar before leaving because there's nothing worse than arriving at a full-blooded party clearheaded and sensible.

'Gimme the moonlight ... gimme the girl ... and leave the reeeessst tooo meee,' warbled Stud.

'So tell me what you heard about the Contessa's last party,' I asked him, more to stop him singing than anything else.'

He gave a chuckle. 'Well, now, I don't think I should - just in case this one doesn't come up to scratch. Maybe it's best we just take it as it comes.'

I shrugged. 'All right.'

'I mean - if I told you a pal of mine was kidnapped and raped by a couple of Chinese girls, you might be disappointed if it doesn't happen to you.'

'I'd be livid. Is that true - he was really raped?'

"Yup. They kept him locked up in a beach hut for twelve hours and raped him repeatedly the whole time.'

'But how ... I mean, how could they manage it?'

'With a lot of help from him,' he laughed.

'Is it likely to happen tonight?'

'With a bit of luck. Mind you, I'm not all that particular about them being *Chinese* - any nationality will do.'

'Oh, sure - one has to be reasonable. How far is it now?'

'About half a mile. Here's the sea coming up now.'

We had reached the ocean at the south coast. Turning

right we ran along the coast road for a while, then turned off on to a narrow private road and drove through a glade of casuarinas for some distance before finally arriving at a pair of tall iron gates in a ten-foot wall.

As we came to a halt, one of the gates opened and a uniformed Bahamian guard approached, flashing a torch on us.

'Hi,' said Stud. 'We're guests of the Contessa - Ryder and Tobin - from the casino.'

'Sure thing. I'll open the gate for you.'

He snapped an enthusiastic salute as we drove through.

The grounds were vast. At first we couldn't see the villa for shrubbery but eventually the gardens opened up and there it stood, massive and magnificent, a white Spanish palace, bathed in moonlight, built high above sweeping lawns to overlook the sea.

Stud slowed the car. 'Ain't that something? And all from one pizza parlour.'

'Stud,' I sighed, 'you ever get the feeling you've got a long way to go yet?'

He drove on.

Although almost every one of the eight thousand rooms in the house was lit, the activity was undoubtedly taking place around the pool situated to the right of the house behind an ornamental wall. We parked the car with a hundred others and wandered through an open gateway, then stood there for a moment taking in the scene.

The patio containing the pool was immense and landscaped with flower beds and many trees, including palms. The pool was enormous, big enough to take a thirty-foot board, and all around it were yellow sun-chairs and umbrella-ed tables.

The bar was over to the left, attended by a couple of Bahamians, and beyond it three barbecue stands were going full blast, lighting the people around them in a rosy glow.

On the right about fifty people, all in swimming togs, were dancing with abandon to a group of four exotically-dressed Bahamian fellas who were pouring their life-blood into a wild calypso.

It looked and sounded like a very good party.

'Hi, there ... come on in!'

We turned to the voice and found a gorgeous-looking redhead in a tiny white bikini weaving towards us, a huge drink in one hand and a hamburger in the other. On the way over she stopped to take a gulp and dribbled ice-cold whatever-it-was down her thrusting bust. 'Yow - that's cold I'

'Here, let me,' grinned Stud, pulling out his hanky.

'Sure,' she laughed, proffering her charlies.

Stud took the challenge, and while he was dabbing away she was cocking an interested and somewhat glazed eye at him. 'Would one of you fellas be Stud Ryder?'

Stud's brows shot up. 'Yes, main - *I* would.'

'Really I Hey, that's nice ... my name's Holly. The Contessa asked me to keep an eye open for you - see you had a good time.'

'Really?' He turned his head and slipped me a wink. 'Well, here I am, Holly - rarin' to go.'

'Well, come on ...'

'Er, where to exactly?'

She looked us both up and down. 'You guys brought swim trunks?'

'No,' Stud answered. 'We didn't realize it was going to be a swimming party.'

'Well, you gotta change - no clothes allowed. Never mind - I'll get you fixed up ... hey ...' she moved closer to him, peered at him, 'you're sober, too. No sobers allowed in here either. I guess I'll have to fix that, too. Come on ...'

'Er ... what about Russ?'

She looked at me and shrugged. 'The Contessa didn't say anything about him.'

'You go ahead,' I said to Stud, 'I'll look after myself.'

He frowned. 'You sure?'

'Sure I'm sure. Meet you some time by the diving board to compare notes. Go on - off you go. Never keep a lady waiting.'

'Lady?' he grinned.

'So - what do you want... elocution lessons?'

'O.K., see yuh. Keep out of trouble.'
'Huh!'
Off he went, catching up with the red-head and slipping his arm round her waist, taking a sip from her drink, heading for the bar.
Well now ...
I had a good look around the patio then made towards the dance floor with nothing more in mind than giving Stud time to collect a drink and disappear with Holly, but as I got nearer to the group the wild beat took charge of my feet and the sight of the bikini-ed girls began stirring the adrenalin. They were a wonderful sight, hair flying, breasts bouncing, bottoms wiggling, and before I knew it I was among them, dancing through them and out the other side, heading for the bar, noting that Stud was no longer there.
Panting, I reached the bar and was approached by one of the barmen, a good-looking fellow with a ready grin.
'Yeh, man, what'll it be?' he beamed, blinding me with a hundred and thirty-seven snow-white choppers.
'Got any vodka?'
'Sure we got vodka. You wanna glass or a bottle?'
I laughed. 'A glass'll be fine - with tonic if you've got it.'
'Man, we got ever'thin'.'
He yanked the cork out of a bottle with his teeth, slopped in nine inches of voddie and dripped in an afterthought of tonic.
'There yuh go - one Contessa Special. If yuh can drink four o' them you win the swimmin' pool - but as you can see, nobody's won it yet! '
He bellowed a laugh that rattled all the bottles on the counter and went to serve a weirdo dressed in Bermuda shorts, bowler hat and waistcoat.
I took a gulp and choked. No wonder the pool was still intact. It was a miracle that anyone was standing.
'Hi, there.'
She was sitting on a low wall, swinging her legs and nursing a glass, wearing a puce bikini and shouldn't have been, not with that figure. No one would have noticed if she'd been wearing the cups at the back. The glazed smile

told me she was on her third Contessa Special and about to fall backwards over the wall any minute.

'Hi,' I answered cautiously, veering away.

'I bin wash ... watchin' you.'

'Oh, really?'

'Yeh, really.' She took a swig from her almost empty glass, leaning so far back to drain it I thought she was going over. 'Why else you dressed like that?' she went on, recovering miraculously.

"Well, because ..

'And anuther thing ... I don't like your manners.'

I wasn't so bleeding mad about hers, either.

'Here we are ...' she continued, waving her glass around, 'bin talking for hours ... an' you haven't asked me to have anuther drinkie yet.'

'How very remiss of me - would you like another drink?' I said, intending to get the barman to bring her one.

Her eyes narrowed, her lip curled. 'Oh, no you don't ... I know your type, mister. You're just tryin' to get me drunk so's you can take advantage of me ...'

Th?'

'I know your type ...!' she said louder. 'You're a LOUNGE LIZARD ...! A seducer of eneb ... inebri ... women. You wanna get me in the bushes ... ! '

Everyone at the bar was laughing. 'Sssh, you mustn't say things like that.'

'Why not - it's true!'

'It is *not* true, madam.'

'Well, why the hell not! ? Don't yuh think I'm good enough ta screw, Mr. Fancy Pants ...! '

I was off. Geez, you meet some balmy buggers, don't you? There are times when I think the whole world is full of nutters.

I circled the pool again, keeping an eye open in case she'd taken it into her tiny mind to follow me, and then I was in among the dancers again, captivated by the stirring 'goombay' beat, getting the Contessa Special down nicely now I'd got the taste and having a lovely time dancing by meself.

But not for long. Suddenly she was there in front of me, head down, face hidden by a curtain of long, shiny black hair, a coffee-skinned angel in a gold bikini.

'Come on, now, shake it, man, let's see yuh go.'

'Hello,' I said.

'You sunburnt or somethin'?' she asked with a laugh. 'Why've you got all those clothes on?'

She looked up then, swept the hair from her face, and stopped my heart with its beauty. *What* a face. Long sweeping lashes framing oval eyes of lazy fire and a wide full mouth just begging to be kissed.

'I... I've just arrived,' I stammered, deep in shock.

'Oh, you're English,' she said, as though it explained why I had my clothes on. 'Ain't you gonna swim?'

'I haven't got any trunks.'

She laughed naughtily. 'I'll lend you mine if you like.'

My eyes dropped to her slender hips. 'That'd be fun.'

'If yuh want , I'll find you some.'

'You will? It mightn't be a bad idea, I'm beginning to feel a mite overdressed.'

'This the first party you've bin to here?'

'Yes, it is.'

'Hm mm. You, er, by yourself?'

'Well, sort of. I did come with a pal but he's preoccupied right now.'

She stopped dancing, looked me up and down, then with a smile held out her hand. 'Come on, let's get you fixed up.'

I paused to empty the glass, swallowed and coughed. 'Boy, oh, boy ...'

'What was that?' she laughed.

'Jet fuel. A Contessa Special. Y'know, I do believe I'm getting blitzed.'

'Good - you don't look in party spirit yet. What's your name, by the way?'

'Tobin - Russ Tobin.'

'Mine's Delphi - Delphinia Orme.'

'I'm absolutely knocked out to meet you. You're awfully nice.'

'Thank you,' she laughed.

'And extremely beautiful.'

'Thank you again.'

'Are, er, *you* here by yourself?'

'I... was,' she demurred.

'Meaning ... now you're with me?' I asked hopefully.

'See anyone else around?'

I looked. 'Nope.'

'Then I guess I'm with you. Come on.'

I didn't care where she was taking me, she was adorable. She led me into the villa by a rear door and eventually into a huge hallway crowded with people. I was busy gazing around when suddenly she jerked me to a halt and brought me face-to-face with none other than the Contessa herself, looking resplendent in a long flowing gown of mauve silk, holding in one hand a crystal goblet of champers, and in the other her long cigarette holder.

'Hi, babe,' she said to Delphi, then transferred to me with a puzzled frown. 'Now, I've seen you before somewhere, handsome ..

'Russ Tobin,' I smiled. 'Friend of Stud Ryder ...'

'Oh, sure! Hell, I shoulda remembered. And where is the bum ... did he get here?'

'Oh, yes, we came together. He was intercepted by a red-head at the pool gate and she took him off somewhere to find swimming trunks.'

'Red-head ...? In a white bikini?'

'That's the one.'

' 'Kay, I know where ta find him.' She turned back to Delphi with a naughty smile and began talking about me as though I wasn't standing there. 'He's kinda nice, huh, kid? Where you takin' him?'

'To find some swim trunks - get him loosened up a little.'

The Contessa nodded in approval. 'Do that, he looks like he needs it.' Then she said to me, 'Have a good time now, you hear? Let yourself go, we don't mind. If yuh feel like doin' it - dam well do it, you're only here once.'

'Thank you,' I grinned.

'See you later, baby,' she nodded to Delphi, then turned away and bellowed across the hall, 'Hey, Max ...! ' and floated away.

'Come on - upstairs,' said Delphi, and led me up a grand, sweeping staircase to a galleried landing, then along it, turning left into a corridor, right into another, then left again. There were rooms everywhere, people everywhere, a regular ants' nest. Suddenly she stopped at a cupboard door, opened it, searched inside and brought out a pair of white trunks, held them in front of me and said, 'There yuh go. Go in that bedroom and change - leave your clothes in there, they'll be safe. And don't be long, huh?'

'Two minutes.'

I opened the door and went in. It was a large room with a big double bed in it, piled with clothes. I took off my jacket and shirt and was standing on one foot to get my trousers off when I ran into trouble. The Contessa Special hit me. Suddenly the room was spinning. I lost balance, teetered backwards, tripped over a trouser leg and fell on my ass. It was awful. The room was whirling. I rolled over, got up on my knees, finally got to my feet and started all over again.

Sitting now on the edge of the bed I tried to get my socks off
- not an easy matter when your feet keep disappearing. Finally I was naked and started on the trunks — not a bad fit though a bit tight round the artichokes - and had no sooner accomplished that when nature - plus in all probability the Contessa Special
- necessitated a trip to the loo.

Then, conscious of rapidly passing time, I weaved to the door, pulled it open, and was gripped by dismay. The corridor was deserted.

'Delphi ...' I cleared my throat. Del... phi ...!'

My spirits plummeted. She'd gone - but who could blame her? I must have taken hours getting changed. Oh, buggerit.

Quite dejected I started off along the corridor, trying to keep the carpet in sight. At the end I turned left, went along, turned right ... and ended up in a bathroom. Rather bewildered now, I back-tracked, followed another corridor, turned left off it, then right ... and ended up in the same bathroom. The place was enormous! And I was lost.

Suddenly - voices! Around the comer came two fellas, swapping a bottle.

'Excuse me! ' I went towards them. 'Can you tell me the way to the main staircase?'

'Yeh, sure ...' said one, taking a swig and pointing, 'first left... second right... second left.'

'Thanks very much.'

'You're welcome, Have a slug.'

'I will.' I took one. Oh, boy ...

Now ... first left ... second right ... what did he say ... first left... left again ...

I found a staircase that was certainly not the main one but at least it led down. Down I went, emerging at the side of the house, near the pool.

A hand grabbed me. 'Here y'are - here's another one ! '

I was pushed, rushed and hustled, through the crowd and across the patio to the edge of the pool, completely flummoxed. Something big was happening - a game of some kind. The pool was full of men wearing snorkel masks, and the sides of the pool were lined with women, all holding sticks with strings and hooks dangling from them.

'Here - get. this on! ' A mask was crammed over my head and while I was adjusting it I felt someone encircle my waist with a belt of some kind.

'Right - in you go! '

I was given a push and in I went into the shallow end, up to my waist, and as I hit the water a Whistle blew. All around me men pulled down their masks and began to swim, going round the pool at a steady crawl, staying close to the sides.

'Hey, you - get going! '

A wet towel hit me in the back of the neck. I looked up - at the line of grinning birds.

'Get swimming, lover! ' one shouted, 'or I'll have you right now!'

She dropped the dangling hook in front of my face. I gaped at it ... at the shoal of swimming men - and then I saw them! The rings on the belts they were all wearing! We were going to ' be fished for!

I was off like a shot, making for the inside of the shoal, the underwater scene looking quite hellish, all arms and legs, thrashing and plunging. I came to the surface, heading for the deep end, then another whistle blew and a great cheer went up. SPLASH! A hundred hooks hit the water. Cold steel trickled down my back. Zonk! One hit me on top of the head. Biff! another one caught me in the ear. Then suddenly - jerk! The belt almost cut me in half. I was hurtling sideways, lifted almost clear of the water. A voice shouted, 'Orl right, you ken stop svimmink - you're lended! '

I lunged for the side and stood up, water in my mask and in my eyes.

'Here - put out your hend! '

A hand shot down in front of my face. I looked up. Jesus Christ - she was enormous! A great, strapping, broad-shouldered, huge-breasted Amazon in a bikini eight sizes too small. German by the sound of things.

'Give me your hend! '

Gingerly I proffered it. Whoosh! I was up with a rush, standing in front of her. She was bigger than me!

'Ha ha! ' she laughed. 'Ja, you will do fine,' looking me up and down. 'Vas is your name?'

'Er, Russ Tobin, actually.'

'Mein Gott - Eenglish?' Her smile had vanished.

I straightened my shoulders. 'Yes, English.'

'Just mein luck - O.K., let's go.'

She grabbed my wrist with talons of steel and began hauling me away from the pool. 'Go *where?*' I stammered, really very perplexed.

'Kom, I show you. I do not like the house.'

I went - towed by Tugboat Annie right across the patio, away from the house, and into a thicket of dense bushes. On and on she ploughed, bashing her way through, and then, after fifty yards or so, we broke through and there was the beach, bright with moonlight.

'This vay - I know a place, Ver' cosy.'

'C ... cosy ... what for?'

She glanced severely at me. 'Your leetle joke - no?'

'Er, no ...'

'You Eeenglish - alvays jokink.'

'Look, madam ..

'Ziss vay! '

Along the top edge of the beach we went, then suddenly she cut back into the bushes, turned this way, twisted that, finally emerged into a small sandy clearing.

Here,' she proclaimed proudly. 'Vat do you think?'

'It's ... very nice,' I said, massaging my wrist.

'O.K. - here ve do it.'

'Mm...?'

'Kom ... let me haf a look et you.' She advanced on me, arms outstretched. 'How about a leetle kees to varm up, huh? Kom - give Helga a kees.'

'Eh?' I backed away, appalled at the prospect.

She stopped dead, glared at me. 'Vas da madder - are you qveer or sumsink?'

'No, I am not! ' I said indignantly. 'Look, what's all this about anyway ...? What are we supposed to be playing?'

She gaped at me. 'You ... don't *know!*' She smote her forehead. 'Jesus Krist, vot haf I fished oud! Have you not been to ze Contessa's parties before?'

'No, I haven't.'

'Unt you've never played ze fishink game before?'

'No...'

'Ohh, Mein Gott - just mein demned luck.' Her voice softened. 'Veil, never mind - ve are here now. Kom. Let us sid down ...'

'Sit down?'

'Sure ... kom.'

She grabbed my wrist again and pulled me down on the sand, toppling me backwards into her lap and pinning me there. 'Ha, zat iss goot ... you haf a goot body ... firm and strong ..Her great mitts were all over me, massaging my chest, kneading my shoulders.

'Now, look .. .' I tried to get up, managed it.

'You like sex, hein? Veil, I give you a vonderful go. See ...' Her hands darted to the rear and in a flash her bra was off.

Huge, fleshy breasts exploded from captivity. Then she was on her back and wriggling out of her panties.

'Kom! ', she whispered hoarsely, beckoning me between her open thighs.

'Now, look ...' My heart was beating wildly.

'No need to be shy. Look, I help you ...! ' She was on me pulling at my trunks. 'Lie down! ' She knocked me backwards, slipped her hands into the top of my trunks.

'No ...! Stop ...! Look ... give me a few minutes.'

She stopped. 'A few minutes?'

'Yes, to ... get used to the idea. It's ... all a bit of a surprise ... and I really am shy.'

'Hmm.' Slowly her fingers came out of my trunks and she settled back on her heels. 'O.K. - a few minutes. Zen we do it?'

'Oh, sure - like the clappers.'

She laughed coarsely. 'Like ze clappers. O.K. - I go for a quick svim - two minutes. Don't go avay.'

'Not likely.'

She got to her feet, towering monstrously above me in the moonlight, all tits and tarbrush and quivering thighs, then she was off, lumbering down the beach. And I was up after her, watching her all the way, and as she hit the water with a splash they could hear in Texas I was off as fast as my trembling legs would go, back to the pool.

Breathless and weak I broke out on to the patio and headed straight for the bar, badly needing a drink. The same barman came up, still grinning.

'What'll it be this time?'

'Vodka tonic - if you please ... but make it a small one, hm?'

'*Small* one?' he frowned.

'Two fingers - not a fist like last time.'

'Small one,' he repeated. 'Don't get much call f'them - Ah may be a bit out of practice.'

'Try your best, there's a good chap.'

' 'Kay ..'He hefted the bottle and yanked the cork with his teeth. 'Shay when.'

'Woah! '

He held up the glass and frowned at the size of the shot, then shrugged, quite mystified. 'Well, ours is not to reason why, daddy, but that is the meanest-lookin' dribble Ah ever did. see.'

'It's called an English pub treble,' I explained.

'Oh, that's what's the matter with it.' He poured in some tonic and handed me the drink, quite hurt. 'Man, you're gonna be a long time hittin' the moon on that.'

'I've just been up there - on that Contessa Special you gave me. I prefer it down here. No offence, though.'

'And none taken. Each to his own - that way lies peace for all.'

'Cheers.'

I took a slug then automatically reached for my cigarettes, realizing as I did that I'd left my pockets in the bedroom. Now, that would never do, I just had to have one. So, taking the drink, I made my way into the house, keeping one eye open for Delphi and another for the dreaded Helga but seeing no sign of either one.

Up the main staircase I went and then it got complicated. Which way did Delphi bring me? I turned left ... then right. No, not along there. I turned back, took the first on the right ... aha! A cupboard door - with a bedroom next to it!

Confidently I pushed open the bedroom door, stepped inside - and froze.

'Oh!'

The exclamation of mild surprise came from the brunette lying on her back on the bed, one leg in the wall-cupboard and the other hanging out of the window. The big muscular guy sprawled between them stopping bouncing up and down and gasped, 'Wha's the matter - am I hurtin' yuh?'

She curled her lip at him. 'You kiddin'? No - we got company.'

The guy's head shot round, glared at me.

'I ... I'm ... terribly sorry,' I stammered, starting to pull the door shut.

'Hey!' he shouted.

'I'm sorry ... I was looking for my cigarettes!'

'Hey, don't go!'

The door was now almost closed.

'Come back here!'
And get thumped? Not likely,
'What is it?' I called, ready to sprint.
'You wanna watch?!'
'Eh ...? No! I mean ... I was looking for ...'
'You wanna do it, then?'
'No! Thanks all the same ..

I closed the door and moved away fast, down the corridor, turned left ... right ... aha I Now, this must be it. Gingerly this time I opened the bedroom door. The room was in darkness but from the light that shone in from the hall I could see I'd done it again. The bed was there all right - but occupied by such a tangle of limbs and torsos it was impossible to tell how many people were there to the nearest dozen. Heads grew out of crotches, hairy male legs appeared to issue from female bodies. It was a right royal rave-up! And the things they were doing!

'Sorry, man, no more room.' a regretful voice told me. 'But try next door - they're two short.'

'Thanks, but..

'Maybe tomorrow - come early, bring a friend.'

'Thanks very much.'

'You're welcome.'

I quickly closed the door. Now I really needed a fag - but where was that room?

On again, every damned corridor looking like the last one. I turned a corner and there was the same door combination again. I approached the bedroom, listened at it. No sound. I knocked. No response. Maybe this was it!

I turned the knob, pushed the door open a crack. 'Anyone in?' No reply. I went in.

It wasn't the right room, there were no clothes on the bed. The bathroom door was part open and the shower was running - then I heard the giggling. I took a step towards it, intrigued, and the big wall mirror came into view - and so did the big Negro lad and his bird, going at it heavens hard under the spray, laughing like loons, bless 'em. Well, it's better than making war.

I crept out, leaving them to it, and closed the door. Well,

stap me, where *was* that damned changing room? One more try and then I'd have to find Delphi and find out from her.

I started off again, feeling like the only bloke on New Providence not getting his oats at that moment. I turned yet another corner and there they were again - cupboard and bedroom door.

I knocked, loud and clear.

A female voice answered. 'Yes, who is it?'

'Er ... is that the changing room?'

Two voices, male and female, laughed.

'Sure is!' she called. 'We just this minute changed!'

'May I come in?'

More giggling. 'Sure - why not! '

I opened the door and marched in. Holy Jezus - *they* were at it! Well, not so much *at* it as having a breather - the bird sitting astride the bloke, both of them having a smoke.

'Hi,' she said, giving me a wave.

'Oh...!'

'Hey, you leavin'?'

'I ... I'm just looking for my clothes ... my cigarettes,' I stammered, turning away.

'You want a cigarette? They're on the dressing table - help yourself.'

'Well ...'

Dammit, I *needed* one.

'Well, thanks very much .. .'

Facing away, I sidled over to the dresser, snatched a fag, lit it with shaking hands and made a bee-line for the door. 'Thanks very much! '

'Hey,' she called to the closing door. 'Would you do something for us?'

'Wh ... what is it?'

'There's a camera over by the cigarettes - would you take a snap of us ...?'

I was off. My God, I was surrounded by the flower kids! All for one and one for all!

Afraid now to try any more rooms I headed for the main staircase, determined to find Delphi - but finding, instead, the Contessa who appeared at the bottom of the stairs as I ran down them.

'Well, hi, again,' she smiled, frowning a bit. 'How's it going?'

'Well, I'm afraid I've lost Delphi ...! Have you seen her?'

'Not since last time with you. Gee, that's too bad. She's a nice girl, huh?'

'Yes, very nice.'

'You ... really like her?'

'Very much.'

'Mmm ..Her eyes were drifting all over me as she talked, and I mean *all* over me. 'Say,- did you ever do any weight trainin' any time?'

'Er, no ..I gulped, feeling naked under her prying gaze. 'Never.'

'Mm ... you've got a nice body, kid.'

'Th ... thank you.'

'Sure. Well, I'll be seein' you. Tell you what - try the pool area, you'll probably find Delphi down there. And if I see her I'll tell her where you're lookin'.'

'Thanks very much.'

"Don't mention it - I'd like to see you two t'gether again.'

I could feel her eyes on me all the way to the bottom. Now, what was she up to? Was she looking for a bit of slap and tickle herself? I hurried out of the house and headed for the bar, finding myself confronted by my freedom-loving barman again.

As he spotted me his eyes opened wide in mock amazement. 'Now, don't tell me you gone an' drank *all* that booze a'ready! Man, have *you* gotta juice problem. Now I suppose you want anuther of them shots?'

I shook my head. 'Nope - I want a Contessa Special - my nerves are shattered.'

His face fell apart. 'Now yuh're talkin', baby. Ah just knew you'd come around to our way o' thinkin'.'

Humming happily he poured about a pint of neat voddie and added a toothful of tonic, then placed it before me with ceremony.

'There yuh go, friend - an' no more drinkin' outta damp glasses, yuh'll get your death of cold.'

'Thank you.'

I picked up the drink, took a sip, shuddered, walked off

towards the pool and almost ran into her. It was the Valkyrie, Horsebox Helga, heading straight for me, madder than hell.

'Hey - kom here, you Eenglisch fink, I'm gonna *keel* you!'

Oh, bloody hell. I took a huge swallow of the voddie, bashed the glass down on the nearest table, and *ran* - round the pool, through the dancers, jumped over the sun-loungers, dodged around the diving tower and fled for the bushes, Hellcat Helga right behind me all the way, screaming oaths and promising death and destruction every step.

'Kom here, you Britisch bum! I'll break your head ...! Kill you three times ...!'

Into the bushes I plunged, dodging this way and that, Helga still close behind me, crashing through the undergrowth like a rampaging rhino.

'Kom back here, you svine! I keel you for running away!'

Like hell you will, love. On I plunged, heart thundering, blundering blindly through the thicket without a clue where I was heading. Suddenly ... silence! Not a sound. It was eerie. She was stalking me! For a long, heart-thudding moment I stood in utter silence and listened, the dense dark bushes close around me. Then - a faint rustle over to my right! I crept left, ears straining, eyes straining, crabbing sideways round a huge, looming bush ...

'Gotcha!'

A hand shot out of the bush and grabbed my wrist. I staggered back, tripped over a root and fell, dragging the body out of the bush with me.

She fell on top of me, clamped her hand over my mouth, whispered in my ear. 'Sssh! It's me! Don't make a noise!'

It was Delphi!

'Sssh!' she hissed. 'She's drunk - she'll kill us both!'

As shock subsided I became aware of the intimacy of our positions, of her near-naked body pressed against mine, and aware of the fact that she was making no move to get off! And as the moments ticked by I realized to my delight that she was fully aware of where she was lying and had no intention ' of getting off.

'I ... think she's gone,' she whispered in my ear.

I listened ... and shook my head. 'No - she's still there.'

'I can't hear anything.'

'I've got super-sensitive hearing.'

'You have ...?'

I nodded. 'I'll let you know when she's gone - you'll have to take my word for it. She may be there for hours, you know - she's a very determined woman.'

Her grin told me I'd been rumbled. 'You ... enjoying yourself down there?'

I tightened my arms around her, relishing the feel of her body. 'I'm having a whale of a time. You feel wonderful.'

'So do you. It's like lying on a big, warm raft.' She gave a sexy wriggle and chuckled. 'Anyway, why was she chasing you? What have you been up to?'

'Me? I got roped into that damned fishing game and she hooked me out - brought me here. I didn't know what was going on.'

She giggled. 'And you didn't fancy her?'

'In a word - no. I ran away. She's a very scorned lady.'

'What would you have done if I'd fished you out?'

'You were there?'

She shook her head. "No, I don't dig that scene. When I choose a fella I like him to like the idea. But you didn't answer my question ...'

'I... would have enjoyed that very much.'

'You would?'

'And if you don't stop wriggling around like that I'm going to disgrace myself.'

'Feel free.'

'Oh?'

'Listen ...' she pecked me on the lips with her soft mouth, 'How would you like a nice quiet drink ... some music ...'

'Oh, would I.'

'I know a place - come on.'

Taking my hand she led me through the bushes to the beach and down to the water's edge.

'It's not far,' she said, slipping her arm round my waist as we paddled.

'Hey, what happened to you,' I asked her. 'When I came out of the changing room you'd gone.'

'*I'd* gone! You were in there so long I had to go to the bathroom - and when I went back *you'd* gone.'

'Yes, I'm sorry about that - I was a bit smashed, took a long time. I was very miserable when I found you'd gone. I thought you'd changed your mind.'

'Were you? That's nice.'

'After I escaped from that German maniac I went back into the house to get my cigarettes but I couldn't find the changing room. You'll have to show me where it is. But, boy, I found a few other things in some of the bedrooms instead of cigarettes.'

'Oh,' she laughed, 'what sort of things?'

'Half the population of Nassau being extremely friendly with the other half. What sort of parties does the Contessa throw?'

'That sort,' she grinned. 'She's a great believer in free love.'

'Obviously.'

'And ... how about you ...?' she asked, peering at me whimsically, 'do you believe in it?'

'I go a bundle on it.'

She chuckled. 'And wouldn't you say this was the perfect place for it... a tropical island on a warm, moonlit night...?'

'Super-perfect.'

'Tobin, do you fancy me?'

Out it popped, just like that. 'I ...' I croaked, 'of course I fancy you.'

'Good,' she said, smiling to herself.

'Where ... exactly are we going, Delphi?'

She looked up the beach, nodding to a row of houseboats moored at several jetties along the beach. 'There.'

'Do these belong to the Contessa?'

'Yes - all six of them. She uses them as annexes to the villa.'

'Have you got one?'

'Yep - the first one.'

'All... to yourself?'

She laughed. 'All to myself. The Contessa's very generous.'

'You work for her, I take it.'

'Yes.'

'Doing what?'

'Oh, sort of ... general duties. I do a hundred little jobs for her.'

'Nice job?'

'Wonderful,' she chuckled.

We'd reached the first jetty now and Delphi led the way on to it and jumped down on to the deck of the houseboat. At close range it was just a large box, its exterior giving no clue to the luxury that I found inside. Delphi opened the door and switched on the lights, revealing a beautiful living room, simply but luxuriously furnished, with a tiny bar in one corner.

'Hey ...' I exclaimed.

'Ain't it something? Come in, close the door. What would you like to drink?'

'Vodka tonic?'

'Sure. Ice?'

'Perfect.'

While she made the drinks I wandered around, taking a look.

'You're first time on a houseboat?' she asked.

'Yes. I'm very impressed - it really is a house!'

'Better,' she smiled. 'When the view becomes tiresome you can pull up anchor and sail off.'

She came round the bar with the drinks then went to a cassette rack and slipped in something very dolce vita.

'Delphi ..

She turned to me, moving to the Latin beat. 'Mm?'

'Do you mind if I ... ask you something?'

'Oh ... that sounds serious. What is it?'

'D)o you ... *please* ... have a cigarette - I'm in agony.'

She laughed. 'Sure - they're on the bar, help yourself. Light one for me, too.'

Willowing to the gentle bossa nova she opened an inner door and went through. I lit the cigarettes and followed, discovering we were in a bedroom almost entirely furnished with a large, gorgeous double bed covered in white silk.

'My, my ...' I said from the doorway.

'More inviting than a sandy hollow with Helga?' she laughed, sliding on to the bed and placing her drink on a side table. She patted the bed at her side. 'Come here.'

I got rid of the cigarettes and lay down beside her, my heart hammering. It started slowly, knowing we had all the time in the world with no chance of interruptions. I rolled over her and kissed her, lightly, but suddenly she wanted more. Her mouth was hot, her tongue adventurous. She surged against me, thrust into me, bringing me up like O'Flaherty's flagpole.

Then she broke away, gasping, 'Hey ...'

'Mm?'

'This is gonna be fun.'

'Yes, it is.'

'You like it that way?'

'It's the only way.'

'Sure,' she chuckled. 'Y'know, I reckon you can fly when you put your mind to it...'

'Well ...'

'You in the mood for flyin' now, baby?'

'Yes.'

'And *so* am I. I want a wild an' woolly knock-down-drag-out session with you, boy ... a full-blooded, anythin' goes free-for- all! What d'you say?'

Her bubbling enthusiasm made me laugh. 'Sure ... why not?'

'O.K.'

She broke away, swung off the bed, headed for the door and closed it, then pulled down what appeared at first to be a roller blind with drawings on it.

'Ever seen one of these before?' she asked.

I peered at it. 'No, what is it?'

'It's a horoscope chart. What sign are you?'

'Er ... Scorpio.'

She chuckled delightedly and stabbed the chart with her finger. 'One of my favourite signs - but it says here Scorpios are "Cautious". Are you cautious, baby?'

'Depends on the occasion.'

'How about right now?'

I laughed. 'Not at all right now.'

She moved back to the bed, leaving me a clear view of the chart, and what I saw hit me under the heart.

The chart was divided into twelve panels, three across and four down, and each of the panels represented a birth-sign, beginning with Gemini, followed by Libra, then Leo and so on. In each of them was a black silhouette drawing of a very loving couple thoroughly enjoying one another in a certain sex position. In Gemini, for instance, the silhouette lady, a lovely slender creature with perfect breasts and long, flowing hair, was on her knees, apparently looking for something under the bed, and the silhouette gentleman was right behind her, obviously helping her to look for it!

In the top left corner of the panel was the sign of the Gemini twins and the word 'Gemini', and at the bottom, under the drawing, the word 'Superior', indicating the character trait of Gemini people - (though on second thoughts it could equally well have been the artist's opinion of the position!).

The 'Pisces' character trait was that of 'Provider' - and the silhouette drawing left no doubt as to what the bloke was providing ! One of the more conventional poses, this - the lady flat on her back, legs in the air, the fella between them, giving her his all.

'Aries', the ram, was portrayed as 'Fearless', and a right old fearless ram it was going on, too, with the bird doubled over as though playing leapfrog and the gent looking as though he'd chickened out on the leap at the last second and run into the back of her.

In 'Leo' the characteristic 'Friendly' was abundantly appropriate, since they were both killing themselves laughing, he sitting on a stool, she on his lap, facing him, legs over his shoulders, impaled to the navel.

In 'Taurus', the 'Creative', the position was well worth a gasp for its arduousness - he kneeling upright and holding her upside-down in front of him, his face hidden from view between her shapely thighs. Creative? Yes, a lot of imagination had gone into this one - and a lot of training. Not at all easy.

'Aquarius' was denoted as 'Humanitarian' and highly appropriate, too, since she was on top giving the poor lad a well- deserved rest. Very thoughtful.

'Capricorn' was similar except she was facing the opposite way with her back to him, the trait 'Aware' obviously indicating their awareness of need for change.

'Sagittarius' was 'Active' and you couldn't fault that! The lad was kneeling upright again, clasping his love to him, her thighs binding him in a scissors-grip as though she was swarming up a telegraph pole - which she was.

'Virgo', the 'Ingenious', truly deserved the epigraph. I'd never thought of using a piano stool for that ! Our boyo was kneeling upright on it and the girl was using him shamelessly and to everyone's delight.

'Libra' indicated 'Professionalism' and the dedication was there for all to see. Quite out of the ordinary this one, and a little solo bonus for the bird since she was getting all the treatment at the hands - and tongue - of our hero.

'Cancer' claimed 'Versatility' and there was little room for argument here. More of the piano stool in this one and jolly comfortable it looked, too - the lady sitting on his ... well, lap, facing away from him.

And last but really the most was our 'Scorpio' the 'Cautious'. In this panel they looked as though they'd knocked off for a minute for a lie down and a bite to eat - out of each other. All very French and Vat 69, as they say.

Delphi had been sitting at my side, hugging her knees and watching me explore the chart, smiling mischievously.

'Well!' she said, raising a brow.

'Huh huh,' I nodded. 'Is ... that what you ...?'

'Huh huh,' she nodded.

I cleared my throat. 'Well, then ..

'You want to finish your drink?'

'I think I need it.'

As I reached to the bedside table for my glass she moved, slid off the bed, slipping her fingers into my swim trunks and taking them with her. Off came her bikini, quick as a blink, then, naked as Truth, she climbed on to me, wriggled up until we were face to face.

'Drink,' she demanded.

I fed it to her and she sipped, then began to back slowly away. 'You ... reckon you can stay the course?' she teased.

'Well ... it won't be for the want of trying.'

'Betcha don't.'

'*That* sounds remarkably like a challenge, madam. Be warned

- I shall go down figh ... hey! where are you going?'

'Down,' she chuckled.

'Nobody's fired the starting gun yet ...'

'Call it a ... preliminary skirmish.'

'Delphi, you're taking ad ... *vantage* ... hey! ... ooh! that's sneaky ... Whoops! you're spilling the drink ...!'

'Throw it away.'

I leaned sideways and got rid of it on the table.

'Scorpio, hm ...?' she was saying.

'Yes ... November the ... wow!'

'Great - Scorpio will do beautifully for starters. Come here.'

'D... Delphi...?'

'Mmmm?'

'D ... Do we need *all* these lights on ...?'

'Yes, I want to see you.'

'Well, sure, but... oh, boy ... that is fantastic .. .'

I forgot the lights ... forgot time ... forget everything but the project in hand. I never did get to know what *her* birth sign was but it wouldn't have mattered anyway - *all* the signs applied to her character. She was Superior, Friendly, Ingenious, Fearless, Active, Aware, Humanitarian, Creative, Provident and Versatile (Wow!) - and, yes, she was even Cautious (jumped on the dressing-table stool to make sure it would hold us both). *And,* through her dedication to perfection, could also be termed Professional.

And I'll tell you what else she was - at least until the very end - she was insatiable. A glutton! If I hadn't seen it with my own eyes I wouldn't have believed it possible for a bird to go through the roof so many times.

'OOOOHHHH!!' Up above me (now in Aquarius pose) she let out a bellow, mouth wide, eyes screwed tight, then with a sob and a limp laugh collapsed on me, gasping, 'Ohhh ... *baby!*'

'I ... don't ... believe it,' I panted. 'That ... was number ten!'

'Oh, baby ... baby ... what's ... left... now?'

I shifted position and glanced round her at the chart. 'Gemini... and Pisces.'

'Wonderful. Gemini for me ... it's my favourite ... then Pisces is all yours ... and, boy ... you deserve it. You've done ... phew! ... terrifically well to hold on ...'

'*I've* done well! What about you?!'

'Boy, I need a drink .. .'

She rolled off me and drank thirstily. 'Oh, that's better ... how ... long have we been at it?'

'About an hour and a half.'

She uttered a groan. 'Feels like a week. How're you feeling?'

I laughed. 'Fine.'

'You sure are. Well... you ready?'

"When you are, ma'am.'

'O.K.... here goes Gemini.. .'

She was away almost instantly. 'Oh, my God ...! That's fantastic ...! Fabulous ...! Craaazy ...!' It was going to be a big, fast finish. 'Oh ... my GOOOODDD, I'm there ...!'

'Already ...?!'

'Can't help it ...! it's this damned position! Here I G-O-O-O ...! OOOOHHHHHHH!'

A convulsion racked her. She drove her fingers into the pillows, crying, 'Oh ... oh ...!' and beat at the pillows, then suddenly she was gone from me and was lying on her back, arms outstretched, reaching for me. 'Pisces ... now ... quickly!'

I stared down at her, stunned by the urgency of her need, by her awesome capacity.

'Now!' she demanded and pulled me down desperately, exploded yet again almost at the moment of penetration and this time taking me with her in a devastating release.

'You DID IT ... YOU DID IT! ' she yelled, laughing deliriously, tugging my hair, kissing me all over the face, hugging me hard. 'Right through the goddam chart! '

'The credit's ... all ... yours ... Delphi ...' I panted. 'Twelve times ...! '

'No ... no ... I couldn't have done it without you ... oohhhh,' she groaned.

'Are you all right?'

'N-o-o-o, I'm numb ... dead ... finished ...'

'Is it any *wonder?*'

'Ohhh ..her arms flopped to the bed. 'Come and lie down..

We lay there for quite a while, floating in torpor, nerveless, thoughtless, saying nothing, then in a sleepy drawl she smiled, 'How're you feelin', lover?'

It was an effort to open my lips. 'Like ... I've just swum in from England.'

'Man ... you really go.'

'*I* really go! '

'Well, it was all your doing ...' She shook her head slowly. 'Right through the chart ...' then chuckled huskily. 'Hey ...?'

'Mm?'

'Let's do it again, hm ... ? - in reverse order.'

'Ohhh ... Delphi ..

She laughed weakly. 'Relax ... you know I've *gotta* be kidding.'

The sudden muffled ringing of the telephone in her bedside cupboard frightened the life out of me. I shot up, heart thumping. Delphi gave a groan and rolled over, opened the door, lifted the receiver then fell back against the pillows. 'Yeh ...?'

The exchange was brief, the female voice on the other end sounding urgent. Delphi's contribution was, 'All right, I'll tell him,' then she put back the receiver and rolled into me. 'That was a message for you.'

'For me! '

'You're wanted at the villa. Some guy named Stud Ryder is looking for you.'

'Stud...?'I frowned. '

'Apparently he's got something important to tell you.'

'Stud...' I repeated, suddenly concerned. What had the daft bugger been up to, now? 'But ... how did he know I was here?'

'He didn't. That was the Contessa.'

'Oh? But how did *she* know...?'

She grinned. 'She must have guessed I'd bring you home.'

'Oh. Hell, I wonder what Stud's got to tell me that's so important ... ? '

She touched the end of my nose. 'There's only one way to find out.'

'And leave you?'

'You can come back. It does sound kind of important.'

"Yes ...' I said with concern. 'Stud's terribly accident-prone, something could've happened to him. He wouldn't try to contact me unless it *was* important..

'Well, then, you'd better go and see what it's all about.'

'Are you sure you don't mind?'

She laughed and lay back against the pillows. 'No, I don't mind. You really fractured me, baby ... I'm goin' to sleep.'

'Well, all right.... I'll be back.'

'And I'll be here - in body if not in spirit. Don't bother to knock - just walk right in.'

'O.K.'

I got off the bed, pulled on my trunks, then leaned over and kissed her. 'I won't wake you - I'll just creep into bed.'

'You do that,' she smiled, almost asleep.

' 'Bye ...'

She raised a limp hand and let it flop. ' 'Bye, lover.'

I closed the door quietly behind me.

On the way back along the beach my concern for Stud grew. It had to be something serious for him to come looking for me. What *had* the idiot been up to?

On I trudged along the cold sand, alone with the dark ocean and the riding moon. How unreal it all seemed now. Was this really me ... walking along a Bahamian beach at four in the morning? Had I really just left Delphi Orme? Did she exist? Did Stud ... or the Contessa? Or was it all a dream?

No, it was real enough - there was the proof, our footprints in the sand, leading inland to the thicket of bushes. I stopped and gazed around me, at the endless ocean, then up towards the black loom of bush a few yards away ... and then a disturbing realization struck me - the house was silent! There wasn't a sound! No voices ... no music ...

My scalp crawled and I shivered with a premonition of danger. Something was wrong! There ought to be lights over there - from the house if not from the pool. Even if it had grown too cool or too late for outdoor sport there should have been lights and noise from the villa!

Suddenly the route through the bushes was a frightening prospect. Fear urged me to turn tail, to run back to Delphi. Huh! I could see me doing that, too. Please, Delphi, I'm frightened of walking through the bushes - will you come with me? No ... I had to do it solo.

Urged now by masculine pride I took a few steps up the beach towards the blackness of the thicket, every nerve in my body protesting, every muscle turned to jelly. With dry mouth and thumping heart I plodded on ... then suddenly I was there
- on the verge of utter darkness. I stopped ... listened hard, straining to pick up the smallest comforting human sound, a laugh, a cough, something...!

There was nothing. I took another step - and entered the tunnel of terror.

Ten yards ... twenty ... on I went, treading stealthily, afraid to make a sound, afraid of looking left or right in dread of what I'd find, every nerve twitching in expectation of an imminent and awful shock as someone - or *something* - leapt out of the blackness.

Thirty yards ... forty ... my heart pounding with every tiny snap of twig or swish of branch ... then, suddenly - up ahead !
- a faint gloom of greyish light! I was almost through! I quickened my pace ... broke into a trot ... a run, crashing now through the bushes, careless of pursuit, knowing that when I reached the patio I'd be safe. Only ten yards to go!

Just a few more strides!

As I ran out of the bushes the lights hit me, blinding me, shocking me to a terrified standstill. Then the noise! The music exploded, loud, strident, joyful ... and a million people swept towards me, laughing, shouting jubilantly, hands outstretched, reaching for me.

'Bravo! Bravo! Long live the King!'

It *was* a dream! I'd gone mad, bonkers, potty!

'Bravo! The King ... The King!'

A hand smote me between the shoulders. 'Well done, old sport!'

'Damned good show!'

'Crazy, baby ... !'

'Man, you sure showed the opposition!'

Shocked, I stared at them. They were *all* mad! They were all loonies! Hands seized me ... hoisted me high ... and from up there the scene became even more nightmarish - a sea of upturned faces, grinning, winking, shouting, laughing ...

Then off I went on a forest of arms, round the pool in triumphant procession, to the diving platform, then, tilted precariously, I was borne aloft ... up and up and up, the faces diminishing, replaced by the moon and stars.

On the topmost platform they put me down, urged me forward towards the dreaded edge.

'Sit, your Majesty!'

Down I went, legs over the edge. I peered down, wished I hadn't, the bright turquoise tank lay a thousand feet below.

Then suddenly ... silence.

The music stopped ... the murmur of the crowd died away. I heard a scuffle of feet behind me and turned. Three men, clad in long, flowing capes, came to rest and bowed ceremoniously to the crowd. Each held something in his hands. The man on the left carried a silver orb - shaped like a monstrous pair of testicles; the man on the right held a sceptre - a long silver rod in the shape of an enormous erect penis. And the chap in the middle was holding aloft a silver crown.

Now, down below, a drum began to roll, its rippling beat

sinister in the silence. The three men stepped forward. The orb was thrust into my right hand ... the sceptre into my left ... then finally the man with the crown came up behind me, raised the crown on high and proclaimed in a thundering bellow, 'AS JUSTICE IS DONE ... WE CROWN RUSS TOBIN ... KING ... DICK! !'

Plonk! The crown came down on my head, light as a feather, made of plastic.

'KING ... DICK! ! ' roared the crowd.

Then, with a thump in the back, I was hurtling into space.

Down ... down ... down ... through a nightmare kaleidoscope of whirling stars, moon, and chanting crowd the pool flew up to meet me. SSPPLLAASSHHH! ! In I went, feet first ... down ... down ... down ... Clouds of bubbles rushed past my face ... then the orb ... the sceptre ... streaking for the surface. Then I was streaking after them, lungs bursting, and as I shot through the crowd began to roar, 'KING DICK! ... KING DICK! ... LONG LIVE KING DICK!'

A million hands reached down to me ... others scooped out the orb and sceptre ... people dived in, held me up, propelled me to the side, Then I spotted him - Stud! He was standing on the steps, bellowing at me, hand outstretched, waving me in. Shrugging off my supporters I swam over to him and climbed out.

The crowd pressed in, slapping me on the shoulders, congratulating me. One sexy-looking creature growled like a dog and winked, 'Well done, champ! '

'Thank you,' I grinned.

I turned to Stud, surprised to see his expression grim – as severe as all the others were elated. He grabbed my arm, 'Come on, get out of here! '

'Uh?'

'Come *on!* '

As he pulled me out of the crowd the orb and sceptre were thrust into my hands and the crown was plonked on my head.

'LONG LIVE THE KING!'

'Stud ...' I protested, frowning at him.

'Man, will you get outta here! ?'

'Well, sure ... but what happened? Did I win something or something...?'

'Ha!'

He urged me away, his hand firmly under my arm, towards the house, passing the bar en route. The friendly barman was leaning on it, grinning and shaking his head.

'Man, Ah just *knew* it - you wus in training' all the time! Well, no more Contessa Specials fo' me - Ahm on English pub trebles from now on! '

'Quite!' I called, not knowing what the hell he was talking about.

'Come *on*! ' growled Stud, yanking at my arm.

'Stud ...' I frowned, 'where are we going in such a flamin' hurry?'

'Home.'

'What...?'

'Just as fast as you can get your clothes on.'

'Well... why?'

We almost ran into the house and there, in the hall, seven million people broke into a rousing cheer when they saw me. 'It's the King! LONG LIVE THE KING! Yeh, *real* long! '

Stud pushed through them, dragging me in his wake, up the stairs and into a bedroom. It wasn't the original changing room but my clothes were there with Stud's.

'Hurry up - get dressed! ' he pleaded, locking the door tight.

'Stud...'

'Look - will you do yourself a *big* favour and just get dressed?! '

'Well, sure, but.. .'

'Later. Trust me! '

'Well, O.K....'

I threw my clothes on with all speed, hastened by his panic, and in a brace of shakes we were creeping down the corridor like a couple of thieves.

'This way!' he hissed, peering round a corner. 'I know an

exit?

'But ... shouldn't we say goodnight to the Contessa?' I whispered.

'No need - I said it for you.'

'Oh. But Stud ... there's a girl.. .'

'I know there's a girl. Skip the girl - *believe* me! '

'Eh?'

It was all extremely puzzling but his tone brooked no argument and I knew I'd get an explanation in the car.

We reached a staircase and descended. Stud in the lead, we went along a hall and finally came out of the house at a side exit that led into a small garden. Now we broke into a fast walk, turning and twisting and suddenly coming upon the car park, much to Stud's relief.

Ducking low and moving fast we crossed to the car and fell into it. Stud started the engine, backed up, threw it into forward gear ... and as we moved off, a farewell committee of some fifty cars all hit their horns and lights, pinning us in their beams like specimens on a slide.

BA ... DIDDY ... BA ... BA! went horns. 'LONG LIVE THE KING!' went the chant. And BAAARRROOOMMM! went the Mustang down the drive at ninety, screeched to a halt at the main gate. 'Open up! ' yelled Stud, then tore through the part-open gateway, flattening the accelerator to the floor.

We were half-way home before he slackened speed, bringing it down to a mere hundred and forty.

'Phew!' he gasped. 'Got a cigarette?'

I lit one and passed it to him. He dragged on it fiercely, shaking his head. 'And they say the innocent shall inherit the earth. Tobin, after tonight, you own the lot - lock, stock and barrel.'

I laughed at him. 'Why, for Pete's sake?'

To tell the truth I was now reaching the stage of such perplexity it was fast becoming daftness. Something terrible must have happened, I knew. I'd obviously done something that had shocked him to his boots, but somehow I didn't care. All I knew was that I'd been crowned king in some crazy game and chucked off a diving board, and I couldn't see much in that.

'You have no idea, do you?' he said ruefully, his expression grim.

'I don't even know what you're talking about.'

He sighed. 'And I just don't know how I'm gonna tell you.'

'Hell,' I laughed. 'Is it that bad!'

'Worse.'

'Eh? Is it... something I *did?*'

'Huh!'

'Stud ...' I sighed, 'at the moment I am wallowing in a mire of utter bewilderment. It's like going to sleep in one place and waking up in another. I just haven't a clue what it's all about. All I know is ... that I got a telephone message that you wanted to see me and I...'

He shot round. 'Eh?'

'Mm?'

'*What* message that I wanted to see you?'

I gaped at him. 'The ... you mean you didn't ... you hadn't ... oh Christ, what *has* been going on. Stud, I was with a bird ... Delphi Orme ... and ...'

'I *know* about that...'

I stopped. 'You know ...? Look, Stud, for God sake ...'

'I'll have to tell you,' he said miserably, biting his lip. He nodded to the crown on my knee. 'Take a good look at that thing ... a *good* look.'

He flicked on the interior light. I picked up the crown, held it to the light, and saw there was printing on it. I began to read ... and with each word my bewilderment turned to burgeoning horror. These were the words:

'For SUPERIOR ... INGENIOUS ... ACTIVE ... CREATIVITY. For PROFESSIONAL ... CAUTIOUS ... AWARE ... PROVIDENCE. And for FRIENDLY ... FEARLESS ... HUMANITARIAN ... VERSATILITY we crown bearer KING DICK!'

'The ... chart!' I gasped.

He nodded grimly. 'The chart.'

'But...' I stared at him, 'how do *you* know...?!'

'They all knew, Russ ... every one of them. It was a set-up - a contest. There were six houseboats on the beach - right?'

I nodded, mouth-open.

'Well ... in each boat there was a loving little trio - a man, a woman ... and a chart.'

'My ... God! ' I gasped. 'And ... everybody *knew?*'

'The works.'

'But... the crown ... why was I...'

He gave an embarrassed cough. 'Well, you ...' he faltered, . you were the only one to ... go right through the chart.'

'But ...' I shook my head, still bewildered, 'how did they get to *know I?*' I had the answer before I'd finished the question and it mortified me. 'Delphi! She ... must have told them when she answered the phone ... in code or something ...'

Stud was shaking his head, his face a picture of misery. 'No, man ..

'Well, how else...?'

'Russ, I'm trying to tell you but it's damned difficult. Delphi didn't *need* to report the results - everybody already *knew* them.'

'But, how ..

'Hell, man ...' he groaned, 'you were on *television!* '

My chin hit the floor. Blood flooded my face. I heard his voice saying, 'There must have been closed-circuit cameras all over that room - in every houseboat ...'

'The lights ...' I murmured. 'She wanted the lights kept high..

'Man, everyone saw everything ..

'Stud ... did you ... see ...'

He shook his head, 'Only the last minute or so. I was with that red-head - in the villa. We were taking a breather when we heard a commotion out in the corridor. I went to look and found a crowd around one of the bedroom doors. One of the fellas called me over and said, "Come and take a look at this guy, he's gonna win hands down! " I squeezed through and saw what they were looking at - six monitors, one for each houseboat. It took me a few seconds to realize what was going on ... and when I did, well, it really shook me. I couldn't believe it was you ... couldn't believe you'd do it on television, like that. Then a guy said "He's gonna win the crown for sure" and I asked him what crown and he said "The King Dick crown - the champ's crown. He doesn't know it, but in about ten minutes from now he's gonna be crowned king and pushed off the top board into the pool." Then I asked him why you didn't know it and he said "Because none of them poor dopes knows anything. They don't even know they're on TV." '

I closed my eyes and gave a groan.

'Well, I flipped,' Stud went on, 'and just as I was wondering how I could find you to warn you the screens went blank and everybody moved out to the pool. There wasn't a thing I could do - except get you away from there as fast as I could..

'My ... God,' I gasped. 'Two ... hundred ... people ..

'A lousy, low-down, stinkin' trick.'

'I'll sue her! There must be something I could get her on - invasion of privacy ..

'Well..' he shrugged.

'You don't think so?'

He shook his head. 'She's a mighty powerful woman, Russ..

I nodded. 'And I'm in a foreign country ... and she's going home in a few hours.'.

'Well, that's one good thing - and most of those people will be going with her. You won't have to face any of them in the casino.'

'Sure.' I heaved a sigh. 'Well, that's one to chalk up to experience. Huh! Russ Tobin - star of houseboat, boudoir and television. Oh, boy ...'

He looked sidelong at me, his severity now softening a little in a wry grin. 'Was she ... worth it?'

I smiled, catching his humour. 'She was really something, buddy. And ... how did you make out?'

He answered with a broader grin and swung the car on to Paradise bridge.

He stopped outside my hotel, yawned and rubbed his eyes. 'Me - I'm going to skip the beach and sleep until eleven, I'm on at noon. Geez, what a prospect.'

'I'll spare you a thought - around four - when I wake up.'

'You're a good man, Tobin. Well... goodnight, your Majesty.'

'Ryder...'

'Ha! Don't worry, I'll keep it quiet. There'll be no repercussions, you'll see. See you tonight?'

'Sure. Goodnight, Stud.'

In the elevator weariness hit me and on buckling legs I entered the room. Wincing at the coming dawn, I pulled the curtains and flopped down on to the bed to take off my shoes. Then the telephone rang, shatteringly. Stud, I thought - playing games.

But it was not Stud.

'Tobin,' I said.

'Hi.' Her voice was a deep-throated purr, a blatant sexual caress. 'Is that... King Dick?'

My pulse erupted. 'Who is this?'

'You don't know me ... at least, not yet. But you certainly could if you felt inclined ... right now, if you wanted to.'

Oh, boy ... here we go again.

'Were you ... at the party?' I croaked.

'Hm mm. Are you ... busy now? I'm only just across the bridge. I could be there in three minutes.'

'Well, I'm ... very tired .. .'

She gave a velvet chuckle. 'I'll bet. Listen ... I don't dig that scene - not the TV bit ... but the action was something else again. I've ... got a proposition for you - one I *know* you'd enjoy. Let me talk to you ... tomorrow?'

'What's ... your name?' I asked.

'Tonie - short for Antonia.'

'Did I see you there? What do you look like?'

'I'm terrific.'

' laughed. 'Are you blonde or ...'

'Red ... five seven ... and built. Believe me.'

'I believe you. Tonie ... what's the proposition?'

'Tomorrow. Where shall I meet you?'

'Paradise Beach?'

"What time?'

'Say ... two?'

A pause. 'O.K. - two o'clock.'

'I'll be wearing ...'

Her laugh cut me off. 'I *know* what you look like - remember? Sweet dreams, baby ... and get lots of sleep.'

Huh, fat chance. I smoked four fags, wondering what this 'proposition' could be, before finally dropping off - and then was wide awake again at eleven, wondering the same thing.

I found out at two.

It was unbelievable.

CHAPTER EIGHT

Well, there I was, spreadeagled on a sun-lounger in my best tiger-skin swim trunks and airline pilot's sun-glasses, trying to pretend I didn't give a damn whether she turned up or not.

Nevertheless I was getting severe eyestrain from squinting sideways towards the beach entrance looking for her.

Ten past two and still no bird of her description had come through the turnstile.

Two fifteen: a gorgeous blonde with enormous boobs and a come-hither walk approached, smiling cheekily. I shot up, returning the smile, preparing to speak. The she waved - to the guy right behind me, a bloke with biceps like coconuts - and walked past. I pretended a fit of coughing had made me sit up then I lay down again.

Two twenty. Damn it, she'd stood me up. Perhaps she'd had a few Contessa specials last night and in the sober light of day had been mortified at what she'd done.

Two twenty-five. I must have dozed off because the hot sand trickling on to my chest and filling my navel woke me up. I shot up. My vision was filled by a wondrously flat and naked belly, brown as boot polish. I looked up exchanging the turn for a breathtaking pair of knockers straining to burst out of a pale green towelling bikini bra.

'Hi,' she smiled down. 'It is you, isn't it? Maybe I'm doing this to the wrong guy.'

'R ... Russ Tobin,' I stammered, struggling to get up, but she eased me down and squatted on the adjoining sun-bed.

'Tonie Burnet,' she smiled, leaning forward to take off my

sun-glasses, then inspect me, head on one side. 'Yep, it's you. Hi.'

'Hi, yourself,' I laughed.

She was gorgeous - not wildly beautiful but handsome in a sun-tanned, windswept way, very attractive. Her hair was a bright copper colour, long and shiny, falling around her shoulders, catching the sun when she moved. Her eyes were jade green and worldly-wise, her mouth a lover's dream.

I fancied her like mad.

Full of self-possession she stretched out on the sun-bed, opened a small towelling beach bag, took out a pack of Chesterfields, shook one out, snapped a light to it and closed her eyes.

'I'm kinda late, huh? Did you think I wasn't going to turn up?'

'I was beginning to have doubts,' I said, watching her turn rise and fall as she breathed. She had a wonderful body.

'Problems ... always problems.'

'Man-type?'

She laughed. 'What other kind are there?' She sat up suddenly. 'There's a bar over there, let's have a drink.'

'Great idea.'

A creature of sudden impulse, she was up and away before I could get off the lounger. I strolled after her, determined she wouldn't make me hurry to catch up, but such a female ploy was not in her mind at all. As suddenly as she'd started, she stopped ... and looked out to sea, offering an exciting profile in the sun. When I reached her she turned and gave me a quick smile, then slipped her arm through mine and gave me a squeeze, as though happy to be with me.

'Great day, huh?'

'Yes,' I laughed, tickled by her manner, suddenly very happy to be with her. 'Wonderful.'

We started towards the bar. 'Where do you come from, Tonie?'

'Oh ...' she gave a shrug. 'New York ... Chicago ... San Francisco.'

Her tone was off-hand - as though the subject was

unimportant and she had no wish to pursue it. A complex girl, I was discovering - one moment warm and gay, the next so independent as to be unreachable. No questions, she was telling me. Let's just spend the day, have fun, live now.

Which was fine with me.

We got to the beach bar and straddled a couple of stools. 'Well, what would you like?' I asked her.

'A Bloody Mary - lots of ice.'

'That sounds terrific.'

I ordered two and as the waiter departed she turned to me with playful eyes. 'Were you surprised to get my call last night?'

I'd been wondering how, in the hot light of day, she was going to reintroduce the subject. I should have realized by now it would just pop out like that - no hesitation, no embarrassment. Her directness excited me.

I smiled, fighting the lump in my throat. 'Yes, I was - because I'd been assured there'd be no repercussions from the party since most of the guests would be going home today with the Contessa. You didn't arrive with her, I take it?'

'No, I didn't. Tell me, were you ... shocked by what I said?'

'Shocked? No. Surprised ... and excited.'

She looked at me. 'Were you?'

'Of course. You sounded *very* sexy.'

'I wanted you.'

Again her directness left me quite breathless.

'Tell me about the ... performance,' she went on, twiddling a beer mat. 'You didn't know you were being televised, did you?'

'No - how did you know?'

'You didn't look the type.'

"Yet you still made the call?'

She grinned. 'Sure - I saw what I wanted and went for it. You could only say no.'

She was quite incorrigible.

The barman arrived with the drinks, tall glasses packed

with ice. Tonie raised hers. 'Well, here's to it.'

'To anything in particular?'

'To whatever you need.'

'I'll drink to that.'

The ice-cold vodka and tomato juice slid down like a knife blade and a moment later the glow began. 'What a great way to eat lunch,' I said. 'Would you like an English cigarette?'

'No, I'll stick with mine, thank you.'

As I gave her a light I studied her closely, captivated by her style, her personality, her uncompromising sexuality, feeling quite overwhelmed that she'd wanted me and, because she was here, still wanted me. I knew instinctively it wouldn't last long, perhaps just this one brief day, but that every moment would be accounted for. It was going to be quite a day.

'Thank you,' she said, taking the light. 'Are you on vacation here?'

'Yes ... just taking a look at the world.'

'An investigator of life.'

'It's the only way to travel. Look what it brings - yesterday I didn't know you existed and to-day I'm drinking lunch with you. I think it's lovely.'

'How come you got mixed up with that circus last night?'

'I was charmingly seduced into it.'

'And thoroughly enjoyed it.'

'Of course.'

'I could tell. That was spontaneous fun - not a performance for TV. Did you like her - the coloured girl?'

'Delphi? Of course.'

'You wouldn't have done it if you hadn't?'

'Couldn't have done it. I don't see sex that way.'

'What way do you see it?'

I shrugged. 'As a love affair - at least a "like" affair ... and a "respect" affair.'

'Go on.'

'Well ... what's the alternative? Two rutting animals and a very nasty aftermath. If I can't lie happily with her afterwards, I don't do it.'

'Not ever? Not even when you're drunk?'

'I don't get that drunk.'

'Oh,' she smiled.

'No,' I grinned, 'that's not immodesty - it's a fact of life. When the world starts to spin I have to quit until it stops - crawl away somewhere and sleep. I'd make a lousy drunken lover.'

'Don't we all. Tell me ...' she sipped her drink and carefully set the glass down, turning it thoughtfully, 'do you like me?'

'Very much.'

'And are we going to make love?'

She looked up quickly and laughed. 'You've gone quite pale.'

'I... don't doubt it.'

'It's nice ... I like it. Don't lose it - ever. Come on.' She drained her glass and swung off the stool. I followed, shaking all over. As we walked back to the sun-beds to collect my beach things she again hooked her arm through mine and hugged it, then traced a finger over my shoulder. 'You have very nice skin.'

'Thank you, so do you.'

'Skin's very important, isn't it?'

'Very,' I grinned. 'If it wasn't for skin your bones would fall out.'

She laughed.

'Tell me something,' I said. 'Is a man's skin important to a ~-"T ?'

She frowned. 'Certainly - why shouldn't it be?'

'Oh, some women say a man's looks aren't important - it's the fella underneath that counts.'

'So it is - but if we can get both, so much the better. We're human, too, you know,' she smiled.

'So I noticed.'

I picked my things off the bed and pushed them into a holdall. 'Will you tell me something else?'

'What is it?'

'Why me?'

'Why you ...? - because you and that girl were having fun.

I *envied* her. I think if I'd known where you both were I'd have joined you. Does that shock you?'

I shrugged. 'Nope. I'm flattered.'

'Now let me ask you something ..

'Fire away.'

'Are we going to stand here talking all day?'

I laughed. 'No ma'am, we're not.'

After the heat of the beach the room was deliciously cool. As we entered, Tonie went to the curtains and drew them against the glare, darkening the room.

'Would you like a drink?' I asked her. 'I can manage a Bloody Mary.'

'Yes, thanks.'

While I poured the drinks at the dressing table, she lay full length on the bed, sighed contentedly and closed her eyes. Her reflection in the mirror stirred me .. . golden brown, almost naked, her hair spilled across the pillow.

'I'm teasing myself,' she murmured, 'knowing the afternoon is all mine ...' then, with sudden concern, 'it *is* all mine, isn't it? You're not going anywhere?'

'No, I'm not going anywhere.'

She relaxed again. 'That's wonderful.'

I took the drinks over and sat at her side. She opened her eyes and took the glass, smiling with amusement. 'Your hands are shaking.'

'Not only my hands - everything's going.'

'Me, too.'

'Really? You look very composed.'

'I'm not. I'm very excited inside. It's a wonderful feeling, isn't it - knowing you're going to make love to somebody ... knowing it's going to happen.' She looked intently at me. 'I'm very happy I wasn't wrong about you - more than you know.'

'Oh?'

'We ... all have fantasies, don't we ...?'

'Sex fantasies, sure.'

'Well, mine need a man like you. I can't believe you're turning out so perfectly ... it's too good to be true.'

'Well ... I'm glad,' I laughed. 'Will you ... tell me what your fantasies are?'

'Do you have them?' she asked, avoiding the question.

I shrugged. 'Sure.'

She sipped her drink. 'What kind?'

'Oh ... making love to a particular girl ..'

'How? And where?'

'All sorts of places ... all kinds of ways,' I laughed. 'How about you?'

She hesitated, stared at her drink. 'They ... might shock you.'

My heart gave a lurch. 'Oh?'

'I ... wouldn't want to spoil anything.'

'You think it might?'

She shrugged. 'I don't know. You might just laugh.'

'Why not try me?'

She hesitated again, still staring at her drink. 'Tell me ... do you think a person ... well, I'll put it this way ... I've discovered certain things about myself ... certain ways of doing it that give me incredible enjoyment, you know ...?'

'Yes, I know.'

'And seeing the fun you had with that girl ... I thought you...'

She was having a lot of trouble, so I helped her out. 'What do you want me to do?' I asked her.

'Don't laugh, will you ? ' she said seriously.

'No, of course I won't.'

'Well, I want you to ... tie me to the bed ...'

I waited. 'Is that all?'

'No ... then I want you to rape me.'

My vision blurred.

She went on quickly, excitedly, now the worst was over. 'I want you to pretend you're a burglar ... breaking into my bedroom while I'm asleep ... and I wake up ... scream ...'

'Hey, hold on,' I laughed, 'we'll have the cops breaking down the door!'

She shook her head. 'No, I won't really scream, just pretend - and you can gag me! Then you *rip* the bedclothes off and find me naked. You ask me where the jewels are hidden and I won't tell you ... so you tie me to the bed ... arms and legs wide apart ... and then you rape me. Will you do it?'

'Well , I...' I laughed.

'Oh, *please*! I want it very much.'

Well, Tobin, I thought, there's got to be a first time for everything.

'You will, won't you! ' she said excitedly, touching my hand.

'I can see it in your face.'

'Well, I'm ... just trying to adjust to it. I mean, what can we use for ....' I felt so damned silly asking, '... for rope ... and a gag..

Eagerly she jettisoned the drink on the side table and reached for her beach bag ... and from, it pulled four length of silk cord and a white handkerchief.

I laughed. 'Boy, you came prepared.'

'I *knew* you'd do it for me,' she said excitedly.

A remarkable change had come over her since we'd entered the room, and especially in the last few minutes. The toughness, the slick self-assurance had disappeared. Now she was an excited girl, anticipating a party, and I knew that no matter what she asked me now, I wouldn't have the heart to refuse her.

'Well,' I said, 'we can certainly give it a try.'

'You won't be disappointed, I promise,' she said earnestly.

'It'll be *very* exciting.'

'I'm sure it will,' I laughed. 'O.K., what d'you want me to do?'

'Go into the bathroom ... take the ropes and gag with you - oh, and this ...' she reached into the beach bag again and brought out a torch. 'Every burglar has one of these ...'

'During the day?'

'Oh, it isn't day - it's dead of night. Four o'clock in the morning'

'Four o'clock ... right.'

'Now ...' she paused, looked at me imploringly, 'please use your imagination. Really act it up ... really *be* a burglar breaking into a wealthy woman's apartment. There's a fortune in jewels somewhere in here and you know it - that's what makes you so ... ruthless ... so *brutal,* understand?'

'Ye ... yes,' I croaked. 'Ruthless and brutal ...'

'Right - off you go. Give me a couple of minutes to get to sleep, then ... break in!'

'Right.' I swallowed the drink in one - I was going to need it - then picked up the equipment and stood up.

'Don't forget now - ruthless and *brutal,*' she reminded me.

'Right.'

I crossed to the bathroom, feeling a right narna, I can tell you. Still, it was all good experience. Huh, I was going to be bulging with it by the time I left Nassau the way things were going - and there was still the States to come yet!

I went into the bathroom, closed the door and sat on the bath, pondering developments since I'd set foot in the John F. Kennedy airport two days before. Two days! Is that all it was? Felt like a bleeding month.

Anyway, it was better than flogging sewing machines in the pouring rain.

Right, now, I had to put my mind to this, it was a challenge. You are now a burglar, I told myself - a nasty, scheming, determined, ruthless, brutal, sex-crazed feef, about to break into that gorgeous, wealthy bird's apartment and filch her baubles.

But what if she wakes up? '

Too bad. She'll get hers. I'll ... I'll gag her ... tie her to the bed - and then filch her baubles.

I reckoned by now I'd given her enough time to get to sleep - after all it *was* four in the morning. So - here goes.

I opened the door a crack and listened. No sound but the soft hum of the air-conditioning. I slipped into the darkened hall ... and listened again. What was that! Thump ... thump ... thump. Your heart, you fool. I was as nervous as a real burglar! Quite ridiculous.

Slowly I scanned the room, dimly picking out the dressing table, the bed ... the mound *in* the bed. Aha! She was fast asleep. Now, think - where would she keep her sparklers? In the dressing table ... the bedside drawer?

I'd try both.

Switching on the torch I advanced on the dressing table, now as fully immersed in the part as any self-respecting method actor. God help her if she wakes up, I thought ruthlessly, brutally. Keeping an eye on the mirror for signs of movement behind me, I began opening drawers. Now ... let's see what we'd got ... socks ... shirts ... Socks and shirts? Of course - it was *my* room.

Right, nothing there. I flicked the torch across the room to the bedside drawer. Yes, much more likely. I tip-toed across the room, reached the bed - then froze! She stirred! ... turned on to her back ... then settled again, one arm flung languidly above her head, her golden hair trailing across the pillow.

I played the beam on to her face ... then down the slender mound of her body, excitement knotting my stomach. A damned good-looking girl ... alone ... in bed ...

Forget her. There was a fortune in ice somewhere around her and with ice you can buy all the good-looking broads you want - any type, any number, any shape, colour and inclination.

I turned my divided attention to the first drawer and eased it open. The damned thing squeaked like a castrated mouse!

She stirred at the sound. I snapped off the torch. The bedclothes rustled. 'Wh ... who's there? Is that you, Al?'

Silence. My heart was hammering wildly. Surely she would hear it!

'Al ...?' More scared, now - suspicious. 'Is ... that you?'

A rush of bedclothes I She was getting out ! This wouldn't do. She might run for the door ... call for help! I flicked on the torch, hit her full in the face. She screamed - a choked, terrified scream - and yanked the bedclothes to her chin.

'Shut up! ' I hissed. 'One more scream an' I'll blast you! '

She gasped, eyes wide with fright. 'Who ... are you? Oh, my God ...!'

'Shut up! You've been hit, lady - I'm turnin' the joint over.'

'A burglar! '

'Well, I ain't the gasman.'

'What... do you want?' she gasped.

'The ice ... the stones. Where are they?'

'They're not here ... they're in the bank!'

'You're lyin'.'

'I'm not!'

'Listen to me ... I'm ruthless and brutal - and if you don't tell me where they ...'

'I'll tell you *nothing* - I'm not afraid of you. The police are right next door ... I'm going to scream ...!'

She drew a breath and opened her mouth but my hand was across it fast. 'Right, lady - you asked for it!'

I threw the torch on the bed, tugged the hanky out of my swim trunks and got it over her mouth, quite loosely, really, but she was pretending she couldn't make more than a grunt.

'O.K., that'll fix *you*. And you may as well shut up, nobody's gonna hear that pathetic squeak. Now - just in case you're thinking of running for the door ..

I grabbed the bedclothes from her clutching fingers and pushed them to the bottom of the bed, the sight of her unbuckling my mind. She *was* completely naked. With a cry she fell backwards, staring at me in terror but parting her long, slender legs to help me *a* bit.

'Er ... right,' I stammered, fumbling a length of cord from the waistband of my trunks. Looping it around her right ankle I dropped to my knees and tied the other end to the bed leg, wondering how in hell, short of knocking the bird unconscious, anyone ever tied a bird up to rape her. I mean, if she'd wanted to she could have been off the bed and out of the door while I was messing around on the floor. Maybe that was the answer - they never wanted to!

'O.K., sister - next leg.'

I tied that leg, then both wrists to the top end of the bed, and stood back to survey the effect. I'll give her one thing - she put on a lovely performance, writhing and groaning, eyes flaring with anger and fright. And what a sight! *I was* fast losing interest in the dramatics, I can tell you.

'O.K.,' I sneered, 'now I'm gonna loosen the gag and

you're gonna tell me where those stones are - or else ...! '

I leaned over her, quaking at the closeness of her naked breasts, and untied the handkerchief.

She shook it away and spat, 'Or else what?'

'Or else, lady ...' I growled sinisterly, covering her body with a threatening leer, '... I'm gonna *rape* you.'

Her eyes widened. 'No! not that ...! ',

'Sure, that.'

'Oh ... my God ...! ' she gasped.

'It's up to you - if I don't get the ice - you get raped.'

'No ...! I'll *never* tell...! '

'O.K. ...! ' I shrugged. 'Have it your way ...'

'No ...! ' she cried out.

I switched off the torch, plunging the room into darkness, kicked off my swim trunks, climbed on to the bed and stood between her legs. Then I switched on the torch.

She gasped anew, eyes huge with terror. 'You can't ... ! You're too big ...! You'll kill me! '

I sneered at her. 'It's up to you, sister - you gonna change your mind?'

'Never! Do what you will - I'll *never* tell! '

I dropped to my knees and she cried out, arched her body, trying to escape, shuddered at the first touch of my fingers on the inside of her thigh. 'No ... no! You can't... you can't...! '

'Oh, but I *can.*'

She was trembling, really straining against the ropes.

'You have a wonderful body ...'

'Dear ... God ... dear ... God .. .'

'Tell me where the stones are! ' I hissed.

'No... no!'

Slowly I reached higher, torturing her with every creeping inch. Her legs were like iron, rigidly braced ... my fingers lanced through her cute little heart-shape of curly golden hair ...

. 'You ... bastard! ' she spat.

'Names won't get you anywhere, lady - only information. The stones ...! '

'Never!'

I moved quickly over her, not touching her, looking down upon her averted face ... 'Tell me!'

'NO!'

I plunged, took one vibrant breast in my mouth. She went berserk, thrashed and fought, but to no avail.

'The stones!' I gasped.

'No ... no!'

'Right ...!'

I hung above her for the briefest moment, giving her one last chance ... then dropped and entered her.

Her eyes flew wide ... then she began to move beneath me, to bump and grind, staring up into my face with an expression of disbelief. Then the movement began to grow ... to build ... blossoming and swelling until she was bucking and bouncing clean off the bed, taking me with her, throwing me high. 'OHHH ... OHHH ... OHHH!' she began to cry - a whimper, a forlorn agony, it, too, building as her climax came. Louder ... louder ... now a shout, 'OHHHH! OHHHHH!!' and suddenly she was there in a stupendous climax that creased her face in a mask of pain 'Oh, my ... GOD!! what have you *done* ... what have you done!'

'You,' I laughed, collapsing on her, kissing her face, finished with the histrionics now. 'And don't you *dare* tell me where those stones are - ever!'

Then she was laughing, too, chuckling with pleasure, shaking her head and gasping, 'What a performance ... *what* a performance. You should ... take up acting, you know ... you really had me frightened back there.'

'Huh!'

'I'm not kidding! You looked quite terrifying standing up there!'

'Oh, that part.'

'Yes - that part! It was the torchlight! You looked ten feet tall ... *and* eight feet long ...'

'Mm, I must remember that - carry a torch all the time.'

She collapsed beneath me. 'Oh, *boy,* that was ..she shook her head, then turned and looked at me. 'Did ... *you* enjoy it?'

'Eh?' I grinned.

'I mean ... *all* of it.'

'I had a wonderful time. I'm a real ham at heart.'

'Is it ... the first time you've done anything like that?'.

'Hm mm.'

'You were fantastic. You deserve an Oscar ...'

'I've ... had my reward.'

She sighed contentedly. 'And so have I. There's ... just one *more* thing I'd like you to do, though ...'

'Oh, what's that?'

She smiled. 'Untie these ropes? I'm getting cramp ...'

'Ha, sure.'

I lay with her then - lazed away the whole, hot afternoon, dozing and waking, hearing the distant beach sounds, enjoying each other's warmth. But when I finally woke, she was no longer there. The room was dark and empty. I sat up quickly, thinking she'd gone, experiencing alarm ... but then I heard a sound from the bathroom and lay back.

She came out a short while later, dressed in a green floral frock she must have had in the beach bag.

'Hi,' I said and made her jump.

'Oh, you're awake - did I disturb you?'

'No, I just woke up.'

'I have to go, Russ.'

'Go? Where ...?'

'Back to Nassau.'

'So early? I was going to take you to dinner ...'

'No, really - I must get back. Thanks all the same.'

'Then, I'll *take* you back ...'

'No,' she said quickly. 'Really, it's all right.'

She came to me, combing her hair, and sat on the bed. 'It was wonderful,' she smiled. 'Thank you.'

'And I thank you. Are you sure you can't stay?'

She reached for my hand. 'Yes, positive.'

'Am I going to see you again?'

'Do you want to?'

'Well, of course I want to. How about tomorrow? I've got two weeks here and no plans at all.'

She nodded and smiled. 'All right. Will you be on the beach again?'

'I can be on the beach again.'

'Same time?'

'Same time, same sun-bed.'

'All right... I'll be there.'

She moved close and kissed me, intending it to be a fleeting farewell kiss, but it quickly got out of hand. '

'Hey! ' she panted, breaking away. 'I've got to *go* ...'

I patted the bed. 'Come back in here.'

She glanced down and tutted, raising a censorious brow. 'Look at you - that's disgusting.'

'It's all your doing.'

'Do me a favour ...' she patted the sheet affectionately, 'stay

like that until tomorrow.'

'All right.'

'I've ... got plans ...'

'You have?'

'You'll see.' She got off the bed and headed for the door, saying over her shoulder, ' 'Bye, Tobin ... whoops !'

I was right behind her. She swung round, startled, holding me off. 'Now ... you just get back into bed ... ! '

'One last kiss.'

'No I I'm not letting you get near me ... you'll destroy my will-power .. .'

'Just one ...'

'No ...! ' She felt behind her for the doorknob, opened the door, slipped outside. 'G'bye ...! '

'G'bye! '

She closed the door, then opened it again quickly and looked me up and down. 'Stay *just* like that - y'hear?'

And with a laugh she was gone.

I returned to the bed, smiling to myself. Ah, sweet mystery of life ... how good it could be when the chemistry was right.

I was making the bed when the phone went. It was repercussion number two, though the voice was Ryder's.

'Tobin,' I announced.

'Aha - the man's awake.'

'Stud! How're you feeling?'

'Fucked.'

'Me, too.'

'You! I'll bet you've been in bed all day.'

I chuckled. 'Well, most of it. Listen ... have there been any repercussions from last night - any chat around the casino?'

There was a telling pause. 'What are you - psychic or something?'

'No, Church of England - why, what's happened?'

'There's been a guy asking for you - came up to me in the bar a few minutes ago ...'

'Oh ...? Who was he?'

'I don't know. He was a Chinaman.'

'A ... a *Chinaman!*'

'Yes ... smartly dressed - lounge suit ... but he didn't look quite right in it, know what I mean?'

'No.'

'I mean ... well, he'd look more at home in a uniform ... chauffeur or something - dig?'

'Dig - go on.'

'Well, he sidled up, gave me a big grin ... apologized for the intrusion - all very polite ... they're kinda like that, aren't...'

'Stud, will you get *on* with it?'

'I'm *getting* on with it. I'm painting the picture for you. Anyway, he said, "I understand you're friendly with a Mr. Russ Tobin ... I wonder if you could tell me his present whereabouts?" Well, being a naturally suspicious bastard - especially after last night - I played it kinda cool ... told him I didn't know where you were but said I thought you were sightseeing ...'

'Dead right,' I said. 'I was.'

'Hmm ...?'

'Skip it.'

'Tobin ... what have you been up to?'

'Ha! you'd be surprised.'

'Like hell, I would. Come on - give ...'

'Tell you later. Hurry up! - tell me what this bloke said, man ...'

'Well, he asked me if you were going to be in the casino tonight and I said quite likely. Then he said, "Fine, I'll see him later, then - but if you *do* happen to speak to him in the meantime, ask him to make sure and be here ... because I have an invitation that could prove not only very interesting but also very profitable for him." '

'Wha-a-a-t?' I gasped.

'That's what the man said - "interesting and profitable."'

'Good God, what could *that* be all about?'

'I shudder to think. Mighty intriguing, though, hm?' he grinned.

'Yeh - mighty.'

'And *then* .. '

'There's more?'

'And then, old buddy, he asked me what time *I* finished at the casino - and when I asked him why he wanted to know he just grinned and said maybe *I'd* get an invitation, too! So I told him midnight and he said, "Good ... good," and buzzed off.'

'Hey, Stud ... what's going on? It must have something to do with last night, hm ...?'

'I'd lay money on it.'

'Stud ... I don't like it.'

'Well... you did come out here to take a look at life.'

'Yes - but not death. Sounds mighty fishy. He's probably a front-man for a blue-movie mogul.'

'That ... did cross my mind. Well ... there's only one way to find out.. .'

'Mm,' I said doubtfully. 'Right now I've got sixth-sense prickles it's something very rude - like maybe another Tobin TV Spectacular ...'

'You can always say no, son.'

'Mmm. What do *you* think we should do?'

He hesitated. 'Well ... at least we can talk to him - no harm in that. It's this ... "profitable" bit that kind of intrigues me.'

'All right - we talk. I'll be over about ... what?'

'How about dinner? I get a break at ten. Nothing profound - a quick steak in the Bahamian Club - O.K.?'

'Sound thinking, Watson - I need the sustenance.'

'Tobin - what *have* you been up to?'

'Me ...? Nothing at all. I've ... just been playing charades all afternoon, that's all.'

'Char ... have you flipped?'

'Just the once. See you at ten ... tata.'

To ... bin ...!'

I put the phone down on him and headed for the bathroom, pondering this Chinaman ... I mean - a *Chinaman*! Good God, what was I getting into this time? Fearful visions filled the mirror while I shaved - of an opium-filled room and rows of ghostly white faces watching Tobin perform at knife-point ... of Tobin shackled to a plank, being mounted by a succession of drug-crazed women ...!

Nah, don't be so ridiculous. I thought. It's probably nothing at all - nothing more than ... than ...

You know, try as I might, I could not think of any possible solution that added up to nothing. 'Interesting ... and profitable.' No matter *how* you apply that phrase it always remains ... ominous.

I shook the thought away. Well, heck, we couldn't get into much trouble just *talking* to the fellow ... *could* we?

At nine thirty I took a cab to the casino, dressed to kill in an Italian-cut midnight-blue suit, blue silk shirt and tie and I may as well have worn dungarees.

It wasn't my clothes she was interested in.

CHAPTER NINE

There was no getting away from it, the casino was a *very* exciting place. Maybe when I'd seen it as often as Stud had it would begin to lose some of its glamour, but so far it had never failed to thrill me the moment I walked through its doors. Tonight, as always, I felt its immediate effect - a coercion to feel grander, more important ... a compulsion to add just a touch of the old 007 swagger to the walk.

I spotted Stud on roulette and sauntered over. As I approached, sixth sense made him glance round and he gave me a wink and a be-with-you-soon nod, so I wandered round the other tables until he joined me.

'Hi,' he said, 'you look mighty spruce. Expectin' a big time?'

'Mummy always said dress up - you can always take them off.

How're you feeling?'

'Well, I *was* feeling knackered until this Chinaman business. He's revived me. What the heck can it be?'

'Obviously something to do with last night.'

He nodded. 'Got to be. How else would he know you? Hey - you're not famous or anything, are you ... not Viscount Tobin of Twickenham - travelling incognito?'

'No ... don't think so. Has he been in tonight?'

'Not a sign. Listen, d'you fancy that steak? I've only got forty minutes.'

'Sure - I'm starving'

As we moved off towards the Bahamian Club he gave me a leer. 'O.K. - what's all this crap about charades?'

'Huh! *I* thought you said there'd be no repercussions

from the party.'

His brow shot up. 'Why - what happened?'

'Son, I hadn't even got me boots off last night before the telephone rang ..

'No kidding! Who was it?'

'A pussy cat who'd been at the party and seen the lot - *and* fancied the same. Wanted to come over right then.'

'Good God. And of course you said no!'

'That's what I said - no.'

'Ha!'

'I'm not kidding! Stud, I was *shattered*'

'Yeh, I guess you were,' he said seriously.

'But ...' I grinned.

'I had a feeling there'd be more.'

'She came over today - at two o'clock.'

'Yeh!' he beamed. 'What was she like?'

'Fantastic.'

'Yeh?'

'Incredible ... unbelievable !'

'You seeing her again?'

'Yes, tomorrow, same time.'

'Has she got a pal?'

I shrugged evasively. 'Maybe ... maybe not.'

'Russ ... old buddy ...' he put his arm round my shoulder. 'Don't you agree that we have been put on this earth to help each other ... Russ, old friend, hm? Don't you go along all the way with that Christian principle? And did I mention that the steaks were on me tonight, hm ... hm?'

'I'll see what I can do,' I grinned.

As we entered the Bahamian Club Stud had a word with the maître d', requesting speed, and within five minutes we were seated before two incredible steaks.

'All right,' he said, slicing into the succulent sirloin, 'this is the way I see it. I think he's a chauffeur or something - delivering a message.'

'Who from?'

He shrugged. 'Not the foggiest.'

'Mmm ... mighty queer.'

'And *that* thought had crossed my mind, too.'

'Eh?'

'Well ... who knows what sort of kinks were at the party last night? It's a possibility. *Anything's* a possibility! There are some mighty peculiar folk around these pans.'

'You're telling *me* I ? After the Contessa I'll believe anything. So - we listen to what he's got to say.'

'Sure, why not?'

'*But* ... how do we know he's telling the truth! ? I mean, I thought I was going to a perfectly respectable party last night.. .'

'We don't know,' he admitted. 'But, whatever it is ...' he shrugged, 'Well, it can't kill us ...'

'Oh? I have your firm assurance on that, do I?'

He gulped. 'No.'

'You're a great comfort, son.'

'Aw, well .. you only live once.'

'How true - but I did sort of plan on doing it for a bit longer, know what I mean?'

'Have no fear - I'll be right behind you.'

'Quite. I need a drink.'

'By ... golly, I thought you'd never offer.'

It was eleven o'clock when he came. Stud, back on roulette, gave me the nod that he was coming up behind me but I didn't turn round. With severe palpitations I calmly watched the game and a moment later he was at my side.

'Mr.-Tobin ...?'

I turned, pretending surprise. He was a happy-looking little fellow, stockily built and of uncertain age, not, I thought, altogether Chinese. Smiling genially, he gave Stud a slight bow of recognition, then turned to me, saying in perfect English, 'Please forgive this intrusion. Mr. Ryder has undoubtedly told you I was here earlier ...?'

I glanced at Stud who was straining his ears to hear. 'Yes, he told me.'

'My name is Wray. I wonder ...' he glanced towards the Gallery Bar, 'if you'd care to join me in a drink - it would be easier to talk there.'

His jovial grin was so infectious I felt compelled to smile back at him. 'Er, yes ... all right.'

'Thank you - I won't keep you long.'

With a nod to Stud I walked off with Wray, my heart thudding with apprehension. Weird it all was, but I had to find out what it was all about.

'A beautiful room,' he gestured, small-talking us to the bar.

'Yes ... it is.'

'Is this your first visit to Nassau, Mr. Tobin?'

'Yes, first time.'

'You're ... from England?'

'Yes, London.'

'Ah, I was in London last year - a very beautiful city. Here ... I'd like to show you .. .'

He plunged a meaty hand inside his dark grey jacket, withdrew a leather wallet, extracted a photograph and handed it to me. A lone, diminutive figure stood huddled deep in a heavy overcoat before the towering gates of Buckingham Palace, beaming at the camera as he was now beaming at me.

'Buckingham Palace,' he explained proudly.

'Yes, that's the palace, all right. Taken last winter, I presume?'

'No - July.'

'Of course.'

I handed the snap back to him.

By the time we'd reached the bar I was feeling more at ease with him. The photograph had humanized him, removed much of his disquieting mystery. He was really a very nice little fellow.

At the table I offered him a cigarette which he took, signalling the waitress as he accepted a light.

'What would you like to drink, Mr. Tobin?'

'Vodka tonic, please.'

'Vodka tonic and a fresh orange juice,' he ordered, explaining to me after the girl had departed, 'I enjoy a drink but not on duty ... madam does not permit it.'

Very neat. The whole scene in one.

'Oh?' I said, the excitement starting again, knowing now

that Stud's guess about him being a chauffeur had been very close. 'And who is madam, Mr. Wray?'

'Mr. Tobin ...' he began, hesitantly, ignoring the question, feeling his way, 'this is a matter of some ... delicacy ... and I can only hope you will be good enough to hear me fully before coming to any conclusion or decision ...'

I nodded, smiling at him. 'All right - I'll listen.'

'Thank you.' He leaned closer, lowered his voice, began earnestly, 'Mr. Tobin ... I have been asked to present an invitation to you ... and to Mr. Ryder, too,' he added quickly, 'though, to be perfectly frank, the invitation *is* directed essentially to you. The invitation is ... well, put simply, my mistress would very much like to meet you. She would like you to visit her home - this evening if at all possible. She is holding a small ... "soiree" - just a few select guests - and would be honoured if you - and Mr. Ryder - could attend.'

My heart was thumping so hard it was shaking the table. What a blooming turn-up! There was no doubting from his tone that the 'soiree' was a lot more than just a friendly little get-together for a few drinkies and peanuts! He'd done it very subtly, telling me an awful lot without actually saying anything, but it was going to be the Contessa's party all over again or I was Stud's uncle!

I was glad the waitress arrived just then because the interruption gave me a chance to get my voice under control and swallow a belt or two of Russian courage, after which I found the nerve to ask him, 'And who is your mistress, Mr. Wray?'

He hesitated again, setting down his drink before answering. 'Mr. Tobin ... as I've said it is a matter of some delicacy. My mistress is a lady of considerable social standing, considerable wealth. She wondered if you would be understanding enough to forego names until a little later - as a precaution against ... well, any unfortunate gossip. She was sure you'd understand.'

'Has she, now?' I grinned, feeling the voddie begin to knock the edge off the nerves. 'Your mistress knows me?'

He gave an amused half-smile. 'Rather better than you

might imagine.'

'Oh? Mr. Wray, I'm blessed - or cursed - with a fairly lively imagination ... tell me, could the information about me have come from someone like the Contessa Gabrielle Da Vichi, for instance?'

His expression did not change. 'I ... really couldn't say *where* madam received her information, Mr. Tobin.'

'All right ... it doesn't matter. And what time does this "soiree" start?'

'As soon as Mr. Ryder finishes work - that is provided you wish Mr. Ryder to accompany you.'

'Oho, I do, Mr. Wray - provided, that is, that I decide to go myself.'

'Of course.' A mysterious, Oriental smile now. 'He can be assured of an equally interesting ... though perhaps not quite so "profitable" evening as yourself. He will be made very welcome.'

'Look,' I frowned, 'what exactly do you mean by "profitable"?'

He shrugged eloquently. 'Perhaps in many ways - spiritual as well as practical. My mistress is not an ungenerous lady.'

Anger stirred in my breast but I thought to myself - cool it, Tobin - don't get all proud and huffy, not for the moment. Hear him out and *then* tell him to get stuffed.

'I see,' I said impassively. 'And where does your mistress live, Mr. Wray?'

'On a small island ten miles east of New Providence ...'

Eh! Oh, my God ...

'An island ! '

'There will, of course, be no problem regarding transportation,' he went on unconcernedly. 'There is a very fast boat at your disposal. I shall take you both myself.'

'*And* bring us back?'

He laughed, surprised. 'Well, naturally - whenever you like.'

'Mmm,' I went.

He frowned. 'Does the prospect of a sea trip bother you, Mr. Tobin?'

'Not if it's a *return* sea trip, Mr. Wray.'

His frown deepened. 'I'm sorry, I don't...'

'It's all right ... I was just reminded of something.'

What I was reminded of was the one-way boat ride I'd taken with the lovely - and lethal - Caroline Courtney out to the luxury yacht 'Candy King' in Palma Bay - and of the near disaster that befell me aboard *that* kinky craft. And if I had to stop investigating life this moment and go back to sewing machines I didn't want *that* experience again!

'Everything will be just as you wish, I assure you,' he assured me earnestly. 'The boat will be at your complete disposal during your stay, however long - or short - it may be.'

'Mmmm,' I said again.

'Mr. Tobin ... if there is anything about the invitation that troubles you, please tell me and I'll try to put your mind at rest.'

I didn't answer.

'Perhaps ...' he went on anxiously, reaching again into his jacket for the wallet, '... perhaps you might care to see a photograph of madam? Perhaps you are concerned that the ... company ... might be a little, shall we say ... *mature* for your tastes. That being so, I hasten to assure you that none of the other guests will be any older ... or in any *other* sense more mature ... than madam herself.'

He consulted a snap he'd taken from the wallet. 'This is madam - taken in her drawing room just the other evening ...,' he passed the photograph to me. 'In my opinion, a very accurate likeness ...'

I've no idea what I expected - perhaps someone like the Contessa - a faded beauty, trying to look madly girlish for the camera. But if I'd sat there contemplating possibilities for a year, I would never, even in my wildest imaginings, have dreamed up such a breath-taking creature as the girl in the photograph. She was incredibly beautiful - a sloe-eyed, olive-skinned doll, fragile, exotic and immensely chic, peering cheekily at the camera behind a swathe of tumbling black hair, stirringly sexy, radiating eastern promise.

The outrageous beauty of her face - her small, slender nose, her wide, sensuously full and sinfully inviting mouth, her warm, languorous eyes, held me hypnotized, breathless for many moments before releasing me to explore her slender, full-breasted body, draped in a sleeveless evening gown of rich silk, revealingly open at the neck to show a hint of firm, full breasts. A living doll.

Finally, *I* got round to noticing the room she was standing in. It was richly furnished with antiques, hung with oils and pulsing with money - a *lot of* money. The home of a *very* wealthy woman.

Releasing the breath I'd been holding since taking the photograph from Wray, I looked up at him and found him smiling. 'A very beautiful woman, you might agree, Mr. Tobin? She is Philippine - like myself.'

'Mr. Wray ...' I groaned, handing back the snap.

'Sir?'

'Aw, come on, now ... this doesn't make any *sense* .. .'

'Sir?' he frowned.

I snorted. 'Look ... what would a woman like her want with a chap like me? I'm way out of her *class,* man. She could have the handsomest, richest men in ...'

His eyes seemed to cloud over, as though he'd withdrawn behind some protective shield, and when he spoke his tone was now more formal, more deferential. 'I really wouldn't know, sir - and it's none of my concern. I'm merely carrying out madam's instructions.'

I knew I'd get nowhere along this tack so I took a big swallow of voddie and tried to analyse the situation. It really was quite unbelievable - these things just didn't happen! And yet - neither did things like the Contessa's party! I was wishing Stud was with me to at least lend some semblance of reality to the situation.

'Look .. .' I said hesitantly.

'Sir?'

'What happens now - if Mr. Ryder and I do decide to come?'

'I have a car waiting outside. We will drive over the bridge to the yacht harbour and board the boat. We will be at the island in about twenty minutes - half an hour at the most.'

'And ... how long does madam expect us to stay?'

'As I said, sir - you need stay only as long as you wish.'

'And you will bring us back when we say so?'

His manner stiffened a trifle. 'That was - and still is - my assurance, sir.'

He was getting a bit narked, bless him, and I could understand it. If he hadn't been on official business he wouldn't have given a no-account like me the time of day.

'All right,' I said, 'I'll have a word with Mr. Ryder. Will you wait here?'

'Certainly, sir.'

I got up and walked across the casino to Stud's table, finding him dealing to only one client - a drunk who was half asleep. I mouthed, 'Can I see you?' to him and he waved to a replacement croupier and came over.

'Well,' he grinned, 'what gives with Ho Chi Min?'

I groaned. 'Oh, Stud ... you won't believe it ...'

'Christ, here we go again.'

'You were right on the button - he *is a* chauffeur - of a boat! We've been invited to some wild-sounding shindig on an island ten miles east of New Providence ...!'

'Eh?'

'No kidding. This chap Wray works out there for some *incredible-looking* bird he calls madam but he won't tell me her name. Says she's big in the social register and doesn't want anything slipping out before we get there.'

'Well... how d'you know she's incredible-looking?'

'Wray showed me her photograph! Stud - she's a living doll! A Philippine - really *gorgeous*! She ..

He was frowning heavily. 'Hang on a minute ... ten miles east of here ..

'You know something?'

'Well ... it may not be the same island - there *are* seven hundred of them around here - but this Philippine bit is too much of a coincidence for it not to be. There's one about ten miles out owned by a ludicrously wealthy Arab oil tycoon who's got a beautiful Philippine wife. The villa was featured in a Bahamian magazine last year - incredible place - makes the Contessa's look like a potting shed ... and his wife was featured in the article ...'

'What was she like - small...?'
'Yes, very slim ... petite ... big boobs.'
'Long black hair ... wonderful face?'
'Fabulous.'
'It's *got* to be her!'
'Oh, my God ..
'Oh, hell ...'
'Oh, boy ...' His frown deepened, irritably. 'Look, what did Wray *say*, f'Godsake?'

I hesitated. 'Well... I... don't quite know how to put it...'
'Try words, man - I've got to get back to the table.' 'Well, he ... sort of intimated that it was *me* she was inviting ...'

'Well, of course, it's you. If it's got anything to do with last night it's *got* to be your party.'

'Yes, but he did say you'd be made very welcome, too.'
'He did, hm?'
'D'you reckon that's it - because of the Contessa's party?'
'What else?'
'Nothing else. Stud ... I'm scared.'
'Me, too. Sounds a bit...'
'Yes, it does ... ten miles from home ... across the sea! Wray insists the boat's at our disposal - that he'll bring us back any time we want, but...'
'You didn't believe him?'
'No, it's not that exactly - but he *is* only the hired help, isn't he? What if someone else has other ideas when we get there?'

We looked at each other, swapping indecision.

'Well...' he said, 'what d'you think?'
'AH my instincts are screaming "Don't go! " '
'But...?' he grinned.
I sighed. 'Stud ... she is the most fabulous-looking bird. I'm very tempted ... just for the experience.'
'And it *is* a beautiful villa ...'
'Only one thing really disturbs me ...'
'What's that?'
'Why me? A bird like that..
'Oh, don't let that worry you,' he advised sagely. 'They all fancy a bit of rough from time to time.'
'Thanks a bucket.'

'No, you know what I mean ...'

'Sure,' I grinned. 'And you're right. Compared to her husband I ... oh, Jesus - now *there's* a thought - hubby ... Abu Ben Moneybags! Where does *he* fit into this ...?'

'Sixteen to one he doesn't. I'll bet he's somewhere on the other side of the world drilling for his next million.'

'Mmm ... it's hairy all the same, son. I've got the hackles about this one.'

'Well ... if that's the way you feel - tell Wray to go to hell.' He sighed despondently. 'Sure would be a great pity, though ... I mean, if hubby *was* on the other side of the world ...'

'Stud ...' I said, brightening, 'look at it this way - what's *wrong* with us going? I mean, all we're doing is accepting an invitation to a little soiree, isn't it?'

'Tobin, is your memory really that lousy? Wasn't it through accepting an invitation to a little soiree last night that...'

'Yes, granted - but last night I barged in with my eyes closed. Tonight will be different.'

'You reckon?'

'Aw, heck, Stud, I don't know ..

'Look ... why not toss for it?'

'Hm?'

'We can't make up our minds, so why not toss for it?'

'Hmmm.' I thought about it. 'O.K., why not?' I took a coin from my pocket. 'Right - heads we go ... tails we don't.' I flipped, flattened the coin on the back of my hand and cautiously uncovered it.

'Well..' I sighed, 'that decides it. It's heads - we go.'

'Oh, boy .. .'

I put the coin away. 'I'll go and tell Wray.'

'All right ... I'll join you in the bar at twelve ... and have a big stiff one waiting for me, I'm gonna need it.'

'I'll order two - quadruples.'

I left him and walked back to the bar, wondering just what I'd let us both in for this time - and also wondering whether I'd ever have the nerve to tell Stud - if things did go wrong - <u>that</u> the coin had really come down 'tails'.

Well, serve him right. He ought to know better than

gamble.

CHAPTER TEN

On the stroke of midnight Stud left the roulette table and joined me in the bar where I had a quadruple adrenalin-and-Coke waiting for him. He swung on to a stool and sank half of it in one gulp, gasped, put down the glass and reached for a cigarette.

'Well,' he said, 'had any second thoughts?'

'Second, third, fourth and fifth - but I always arrive at the same conclusion - either we go and find out what it's all about or stay here and forever wonder what we've missed.'

'Check - then we go. Boy, I needed that.'

He plonked down the empty glass and we got off the stools. I was a couple of belts ahead of him and feeling very nicely, and by the time the voddie I'd just finished made its presence felt I wouldn't be giving too much of a damn what was happening. It really is the only way to sail.

Wray was waiting for us outside the casino, seated at the wheel of a black Cadillac nine blocks long. When he saw us he leapt out and bowed us into the back seat with a beatific smile. Maybe he was on bonus if he got us to the island.

In two minutes we were over the bridge and running along the yacht harbour quay, and there, at the foot of one of the jetties, Wray stopped the car and apparently abandoned it.

'This way, gentlemen!' He started off along the jetty.

The harbour was quite a sight in the moonlight, a forest of masts, a plethora of motor cruisers. Some way along the jetty Wray stopped and jumped down on to the after-deck of a splendid fifty-foot cabin cruiser that had the name 'Lazy Lady' painted in gold across her stem.

'Careful, now,' he said solicitously, offering a hand. 'Sit here if you like - or go down below into the cabin if you wish. But I think you'll have a more enjoyable ride up here.'

Taking his advice we sat on the cushioned bench-seat in the stern. Wray quickly cast off the two stem mooring ropes then climbed up into the cockpit which was open to us but roofed over and protected on both sides by a canvas awning.

He swung his squat body on to the pilot's seat, worked levers then pressed *a* button and the twin engines roared to life, settling instantly into a deep-throated, sweetly grumbling rumble that sent a shiver of excitement through me.

Stud turned to me and grinned. 'Well... it's too late now.'

I nodded. 'It might be worth it just for the ride in this.'

Wray eased the huge boat away from the jetty then turned out into the main channel that would take us past sleeping Nassau. Here we were just puttering along and I could almost sense a straining impatience in the mighty engines to open their shoulders and go.

In a few minutes we were passing very close to two docked cruise ships. They towered above us, blazing light, and people on the rail waved to us. Then finally we were clearing the harbour and nosing out into the open sea.

Wray turned to us, grinning like a schoolboy. 'Hold tight, now - here we go! '

Down came the levers. The boat shuddered with sudden shock. The engines erupted in crescendo roar. Stud and I were pressed back into the seat as the bow came up and the tail went down, biting deep, and then we were away! flying hell-bent across the top of the ocean, trailing a wake of boiling white water and spawning a tidal wave that would've swamped Nassau if Wray had cut loose in the harbour.

'Yyyyiiiiipppeee! ' yelled Stud, thrilling to the speed, the wind in our faces, hair flying, ripping across the flat black water under a high full moon. It was a crazy breathtaking chase and in no time at all the island loomed, a sharply-rising mass of black rock against a paler sky. And there - at the summit of a sheer cliff face a hundred feet and more above us - was the villa, lit dramatically to impress, a majestic beacon guiding us in.

Wray cut the engines and drifted into a flat platform of rock, a natural landing stage. Expertly he brought the boat to rest with scarcely a bump or rub, then jumped ashore and quickly made it fast to two iron bollards embedded in the rock.

'This way, gentlemen ... I trust you enjoyed your ride?'

'Terrific,' we laughed.

We followed him across the quay to the rock-face. On the right was a staircase, cut from the rock and railed in, but we didn't have to climb eight thousand steps. There was an elevator - naturally. Wray pressed a button ... the metal doors slid open ... and we stepped into startling luxury.

The walls of the car were covered in jade-green velvet and hung with gilt-framed mirrors, and there were velvet-covered bench-seats to ease the journey. As a further comfort, soft, romantic music came from speakers in the roof, relaxing the soul, setting a mood.

Stud rolled his eyes and gave a silent whistle of disbelief, as impressed and excited as I was.

Up we went and the doors opened, revealing a sight that left us open-mouthed. Before us stretched a garden terrace, magnificently landscaped with trees, flower beds, ornamental pools and spilling fountains, lit by a hundred concealed lights to create a mystical grotto of shape and shadow.

Beyond this garden rose two more terraces - the first containing the swimming pool and a cluster of coloured umbrellas and sun-beds, and on the upper-most terrace stood the villa itself - a vast, white, two-storeyed Spanish hacienda with pale blue shutters and little sun-balconies.

'Man, oh, man ...' gasped Stud, shaking his head. 'How the other half lives.'

'Follow me,' smiled Wray, starting up towards the second terrace.

We did follow him, gawping round us like a couple of hicks on their first visit to the city, muttering wows and ahs and would you look at *thats!*

We caught up with Wray at the portico-ed door and he

turned, inviting us to take a look back the way we'd come. The view was staggering ... the descending terraces, the illuminated turquoise pool, the mysterious gardens beyond that, and finally the backdrop of the ocean, bathed in moonlight, stretching endlessly away, silent and magical.

Stud sighed yet again and shook his head.

'Rather ... reminiscent of home, really,' I said. 'On a clear day you could see the village duck-pond from our house.'

Wray rang the bell and the door was opened instantly by yet another Philippine - an aged gentleman in a white uniform and red sash. Silently he bowed us into the hall, a glittering marble place ablaze with light from a huge crystal chandelier in the high, ornate ceiling. Towering gilt mirrors adorned the walls, antique furniture abounded, but the eye was predominantly captivated by the grand sweeping staircase, built of pale green marble, that rose to a galleried landing.

It was all incredibly rich, incredibly grand and altogether too bloody much. I wanted to turn tail and run right then. I just didn't belong.

'Hot-damn! ' I heard Stud gasp behind me, and knew he was feeling the same.

Wray left us and approached a pair of tall white-and-gilt doors on our right. He knocked and went in, closing the doors behind him, but before I could exchange a word with Stud the doors opened again and he beckoned us in, beaming a smile.

I glanced at Stud. 'Ready?'

He swallowed hard, straightened his bow-tie and nodded. And in we went.

The room was an Aladdin's cave of treasure, a Versailles of antiques, furniture, carpets, paintings, porcelain, books. It was the room I'd seen in the photograph ... and there, standing by the fireplace, regarding me with much the same expression as I'd seen in the snap, was the lady herself.

There was only one word to describe her quizzical smile - devilish.

Now she left the fireplace and moved languidly towards us, floating across the room in a swirl of green silk, so incredibly beautiful - an exquisite, fragile thing, supremely feminine. I was seized by a sudden urge to hold her, crush her to me, to taste her lips, bury my face in her tumbling hair, and yet at the same time I was terrified of her.

'Hello,' she smiled, including Stud but concentrating on me.

'H.. .hello,' I stammered, throat constricted, stomach in knots.

'Mr. Tobin, isn't it.' She took my hand in hers, smiling teasingly, seeing my confusion and thoroughly enjoying it.

'Yes ...' I croaked and cleared my throat. 'Russ Tobin.'

'My name is Malinda,' she said, her voice low and warm. 'Thank you very much for coming.'

'It's ... my pleasure, ma'am.'

Laughter wrinkled her nose. 'Ma'am ... I like the way you say that - but call me Malinda.' She turned to Stud. 'And this is Mr Ryder.'

He grinned nervously and muttered, 'Stud ... Ryder ... how d'you do.'

'Stud,' she repeated, compressing a smile. 'How ... unusual.' She turned to face the room. 'I'd like you both to meet a friend of mine.. .'

Now, for the first time, I realized there was someone else in the room, concealed in the depths of a wing-backed chair. A blonde head appeared. A tall, lithe, marvellous-looking girl in a white cat-suit uncoiled herself from the chair and came over at her indolent leisure, not smiling but certainly looking - at Stud. She was a complete contrast to Malinda, rangy, deeply tanned, a sand-and-sea and don't-give-a-damn-for-anything creature, sexy as hell.

'Hi,' she said, raking Stud with violet eyes.

'This is Jane,' explained Malinda. No surnames. 'Jane, this is Russ Tobin ... and Stud Ryder.'

'Hi,' she said again, smiling a little now as though the evening was beginning to interest her. 'I guess you'd both like a drink?

'I'll get them,' Malinda said to her. 'You and Stud put some music on. Russ ... you come and help me?

Unbelievably she hooked her arm into mine and led me

to a cocktail cabinet. Her closeness, the feel of her flesh intoxicated me. I felt heady, quite dizzy. I was her slave. She could have done anything with me - poisoned me, stabbed me, thrown me over a cliff and I'd have enjoyed every, excruciating minute of it.

'What would you like?' she asked, releasing my arm.

'Well ... we usually drink vodka and tonic ... if you've got it... but anything, really .. ?

She smiled gently. 'You're very nervous, aren't you? Don't be, I won't bite?

I laughed. 'No ... I... it's just that..'

'Just what?'

'Well ...' I glanced around the room, 'all this ... and you ... it's all a bit overwhelming?

'You mustn't *let* it overwhelm you ...'

'And also a bit puzzling?

She turned away from me, smiling to herself, and began pouring the drinks. 'Is it ... really so puzzling?'

A meaty calypso beat suddenly pervaded the room and from behind me I heard an 'Ole! ' from Jane. I turned and found her wriggling her fabulous chassis at Stud, arms in the air, clicking her fingers. 'Come on, let's go - let's get some life in this joint! '

Then Stud was away, swinging his hips and clicking his fingers.

'You see Malinda said behind me, 'your friend doesn't seem too overwhelmed.'

I turned to her. 'No, he ...'

She was smiling that smile again 'Here, drink this, it'll help you relax.'

I took a sip and almost choked. We were back on Contessa Specials again.

'Make yourself at home,' she said, waving at the room. 'It's only furniture.'

I grinned. 'Sure.'

'I mean it.' She took a step towards me, fixing me with a meaningful eye. 'And, Tobin ... I'm a *woman* - not a china figurine. I may be skinny but what there is is all flesh and blood - understand?'

I flushed beneath her gaze. 'Yes ... of course.'

She smiled suddenly. 'O.K. - so relax, enjoy yourself ... and let me enjoy you.'

'Right,' I smiled.

She shook her head. 'You fooled me, you really did.'

'Oh?'

'I was told you were the quiet type but ...' she smiled, 'I didn't think there were any shy men left.'

'Er, who told you I was quiet?' I pressed her. 'Were you at the Contessa's party?'

'No.'

She turned away and called down the room, 'Drinks!' then turned back to me, 'But I know all about it.'

'You and the rest of the Bahamas apparently.'

'Well, if you *will* exhibit your prowess on television ...'

Well, there it was. I couldn't believe it - a woman like her. Why? Boredom? O.K. - but why me? Heck, the session with Delphi hadn't been super-human, just a happy fusion of like- souls. A hundred men in Malinda's world would be just as capable of ... and there, of course, lay the answer - in anonymity. A 'bit of social rough' as Stud had so complimentarily put it. No names - no chance of scandal.

Well, well... Russ Tobin and the fabulous Malinda Whatever- her-name-was, joined together in holy fun-lock. The thought stirred me enormously. There was no need for any more guess work. 'It' was it !

'Who ... told you about the ... TV thing?' I asked her.

She smiled secretively. 'Oh ... a little bird. It's a very small colony, you know - and we don't have much to amuse us. Such moments make news. I just *had* to see what you looked like - at least..

'And...?'

'You're not at all what I expected. You're much nicer.'

'Thank you. But ... there's one thing you may not know ...'

'Oh ... what's that?'

'I didn't *know* I was being televised.'

A slow smile plucked the corner of her lovely mouth. 'Oh, I knew that ... Had it been otherwise I assure you you wouldn't be here now.'

I nodded, returning the smile. 'I'm very glad of that.'

She broke away and looked down the room at the other two. The music had now changed to a slow smooch and I was a bit amazed to see Stud and Jane locked together, lost in each other. A very fast transition.

Malinda turned to me, smiling, 'Don't you think it's awfully crowded in here?' She held out her hand. 'Come - I want to show you something. They can take care of themselves.'

We left the room by a smaller doorway and entered a hallway with a much less imposing staircase than the main hall. Up the stairs we went, in silence and not slowly. At the top she took me quickly along several corridors until we emerged on to the galleried landing I'd seen from the main hall and here she stopped at a pair of ornate white-and-gold doors, just short of the marble staircase.

She opened one of the doors and went in. I followed. Then she closed the door behind me, putting us in absolute blackness.

'Wait,' she murmured.

I heard a click and expected a light but nothing happened, not immediately. Then, slowly, the lighting came - not *a* light but an entire system of lighting, beginning as the merest glimmer, then growing, theatrically, to reveal a room of stunning Arabian splendour, adorned with silks, festooned with cushions, its floor carpeted in white fur, its bed an acre of white fur raised on a dais against the far wall.

The walls, covered with silk, were hung with many paintings - oils, water colours, drawings and etchings. The ceiling was one vast pink mirror. And to the left, forming a part of the room though divided from it by the flimsiest curtaining - the bathroom. No, not a *bath* room - a *pool* room ... its sunken green marble tub large and deep enough to hold a dozen swimmers. Unbelievable.

I gasped and Malinda chuckled.

'How's your drink?'

'Mm ...?' I'd forgotten I was holding the glass.

'Bring it over here.'

She went to the wall to the right of the bed and touched a button. A panel slid back, revealing a cocktail cabinet and, beneath it, stereo equipment.

As she took my glass she said, 'Find something nice and relaxing. I think you're still a bit up tight.'

'More stunned,' I laughed. 'What an incredible room.'

'Yes, I suppose it is. But like everything else, one gets used to it. What have you got there?'

'Julie London?'

'Just right.'

She took the cassette from me and slipped it into the deck, punched a button, and Julie's velvet caress began bending my mind.

I sipped the drink (another Contessa Special but I was past caring) and Malinda kicked off her shoes and walked towards the raised bed, saying, 'Take yours off and walk barefoot in the fur - it's scrummy ... and while you're at it - take your coat and tie off, maybe that'll help.'

I put down the drink and did as I was told, saying to her, 'I'm sorry if I still appear all stiff and formal - but it's getting better, I promise.'

'I don't care if you're stiff ... and formal,' she called, putting her drink down on the bedside table, then she turned and flung herself onto the bed, luxuriating in the deep fur pile, running her fingers through it, grabbing handfuls of it, calling to me, 'Come on, Tobin ... run! Dive into it! *Feel* it!'

She was suddenly just a girl, wallowing in sensual play, all social reserve abandoned, out for kicks and firing the green flare for action. She was no longer untouchable - she was a bird! A gorgeous, giggly, lovable ...

'Here I come!' I called and took a running, flying dive on to the bed.

She was on me with a whoop, tickling me, ripping at my shirt buttons. 'Come on ... get this damned thing *off*, you ... stiff... formal ... Englishman ...!'

'No ... hey! stop! ... oooh ... oww!'

Ping! Away shot a button.

'I'll teach you ... how ... to ... relax, you ... great ... British

... stiff!'

'Owww! Oooohhh!' I was helpless. I'm so ticklish I laugh when I dry myself. Now the shirt was off - torn from my back. 'My shirt...!'

'Screw the shirt ... I'll give you another one!'

'Hey ... *now,* what you doing?'

'Taking your goddam pants off, what d'you think!?'

'Malinda, you ca ... hey! Oohhh!'

Slap went the belt ... zzzip went the zipper ... then she shot off the bottom of the bed, caught hold of each leg and ... heaved! Wwwhhhooosshhh! went the trousers. Then she launched herself at me.

"No ... hey ...! you can't!'

'The hell I can't ... gimme those shorts!'

The shorts were off, flying across the room, and she was kneeling at my feet, bosom heaving, staring gleefully at me, that devilish look in her eye again.

'Now, Malinda ...'

Suddenly she stood, reached behind her and dropped the gown to the floor. She was naked.

With a mischievous smile she stood there, posing for me, allowing me to feast my eyes. 'You ... like, mister?'

'I... like very much, lady.'

'Good!'

She plunged, straight between my legs, then wormed her way up, covering me, kissing me all over, neck, ear, chest, sucking my nipples. I was helpless, crying for mercy, trapped between her delicious warmth and the silkiness of the fur.

Suddenly she stopped, raised herself and looked down. 'Oh ...!' she said, pretending surprise.

'What's the matter?'

'That... thing - what is it?'

'Haven't you ever seen one before?'

She shook her head, eyes innocently wide. 'Never. What does it do?'

'Keeps me balanced. If it wasn't for that I'd fall over backwards.'

'Is that all?'

'As far as I know.'

'Mmmm' ..she said thoughtfully, then slowly got off me and lay at my side, propped on an elbow, studying Here closely. 'Funny thing, isn't it?'

'Very.'

'Do ... all men have them - or just you?'

'No, just me - at least in this model. They do come much *smaller*, but... HEY ! '

She pounced. Into her hot, sweet mouth I went. She probed, tickled, teased and toyed, driving me potty for several incredible minutes, then suddenly she stopped and with an impatient moan swiftly mounted me, grinning down at me, gasping small apprehensive breaths and gnawing her lip as she descended, as though lowering herself into ice-cold water. A moment's pause, eyes closed, savouring the sensation, 'Ohh ... that is *wonderful !*' and then she began to rock, using me, spreading wide to take every vestige of me, suddenly, with a gasp, beginning ... building now ... breaking from a canter into a gallop ... now into headlong, breathless flight, eyes wide, mouth wide ... 'Ohhh ...! OhhhHHH!' and then a loud, full-blooded, 'OHHHHH!!' a shout that echoed round the room. And on she rode for a moment longer, slowing now, head dropped forward on her chest, racked by a shudder ... then another ... and then with a drawn-out groan she fell forward and collapsed across me, chuckling warmly, moaning softly.

'Enjoying yourself?' I whispered.

'Yes ... yes ...' she said excitedly. 'It was wonderful ... !'

'And what would you like to do now?'

She looked up quickly, eyes bright, then suddenly rolled from me, right across the bed, and reached out to a bookcase. In a moment she was back, holding out to me ... a vibrator.

'Will you?'

'Sure. I've heard about these things ... what are they like?'

She closed her eyes ecstatically. 'Incredible!'

'All right,' I grinned.

'But not here.'

'Oh ... where?'

She flung an arm. 'In there ... in the bath!'
I laughed. 'O.K.'
She kissed me quickly. 'I think you're beautiful - come on.'

I sat on the side of the bath watching her prepare it. She started the water by pulling down the heads of two golden swans and was lost to view immediately in billowing steam as the water gushed in under tremendous pressure. Now she reappeared, moving towards an array of bottles standing on the side. There were crystals, salts, lotions and oils and happily she went from one to the other, dribbling in a drop of this, throwing in a handful of that. Clouds of colour eddied through the water, banks of bubbles rose and perfume filled the room.

Already there was a foot of water in the bath. She dipped in a toe, then slipped over the side and began splashing around, mixing the lotions, forming great cloud-banks of bubbles.

'Come and help!' she laughed, shouting above the roar of the cascading water.

I dropped in, the water now coming to mid-thigh, playfully warm. She splashed over to me, flung her arms around my neck and kissed me. 'Thank you!'

"What for?'

'For being fun!'

"Well, thank you, too!'

Wwwwhhooossshhh! She scooped up great handfuls of suds and threw them in the air, then took another lot and plonked them on my head ... then, with a giggle, scooped up a third lot, plopped them on the end of Hercules and collapsed laughing.

'He looks like an ice-cream cone! ... Hey ...! *that's* a thought!'

'Malinda ...!'

She came in quickly, blew off the suds and swallowed me. 'Hey ...!'

With a laugh she left me, dived into the waist-high water and struck out for the taps.

Silence.

'Phew!' she went, lying down and floating on her back. 'Terrible noise but nice and fast. Coming for a swim?'

I joined her in a float around the pool, holding her hand. 'Oh ... this is the life, Malinda ... your own indoor, hot-water pool ...'

'Enjoying yourself?'

'I am having the time of my life ..

She broke into a giggle.

'What now?' I asked.

'You ...' she chuckled, pointing. 'You look like a submarine with its periscope up.'

She came to her feet and began massaging me with soap suds.

'Hey ... you'd better stop that ... or there'll be a few more bubbles in here.'

'Well?'

'No, I've got other plans.'

'You have?'

'Yes...'

I dropped to my feet and made for the side and the vibrator. 'You're sure these things are waterproof? I'd hate to electrocute us both.'

'It's waterproof.'.

When I turned she was at the steps that led down into the pool, floating again on her back, her elbows resting on a step, head back. I crossed the pool, switched on the vibrator, and began at her feet, making her toes twitch, making her chuckle. Then slowly I began moving up her leg.

Just above the knee I touched a spot that made her explode with laughter ... but by the time I'd reached mid-thigh the laughter was gone and she had begun to stiffen in anticipation.

Very slowly I trickled the softly-humming vibrator up the inside of her thigh. She began a low moan and her breathing became erratic. And now the tenure began. Slowly I crept closer ... closer ... probed the rounded tip of the phallus into the junction of one thigh then moved it up and around her pubic mound and down the other side ... then away ... so near and yet so far ...

'Don't ... keep me too ... long,' she gasped, eyes closed, frowning.

'I'm in charge,' I said, now withdrawing it down her leg, prolonging the agony.

'Oh, no! ' she groaned.

'At last I have you in my power ..

'You swine! '

Quickly I brought the throbbing tool back along the inside of her thigh. She jerked ... opened her thighs hungrily. Closer ... closer ... now touching ... probing ... beginning to penetrate. A sob ... a cry, 'Tobin! ' then an all-consuming gasp as in it slid. She cried out and flung her legs together, squeezing hard, bracing her thighs like girders of steel as the first climax engulfed her. Her tortured cry echoed through the marble room, plaintive, so tortured I thought I must be hurting her - and yet *she* was controlling the vibrator, holding it captive.

Now I knew the stories I'd heard about these things were true. I'd scoffed at the rumour that one woman had had fifty- four orgasms with one, but the way Malinda was now quickly reaching her second I believe it possible.

'Ohhhh ... GOD! ' she was crying, her exertions splashing water out of the bath, then suddenly, 'Russ ...! '

'Yes, love?'

'I want you! Now ...! '

She dropped to her feet and flew up the steps to the bed, trailing buckets of water. 'Quickly ! '

I ran up after her, amazed by the turn of events. On to the bed she dived, her face buried in a pillow. 'Quickly ... quickly! '

'I'm coming ... I'm coming! '

'Yes, you must... you must! '

I was on the bed in a trice, realizing that no matter how wonderful those mechanical things were, they would never replace the feel of a real live man.

'Oh, that's ... fabulous!' she was crying, tearing at the pillow. 'Oh, Russ ... I'm cccooommmiiinnnggg ...! '

'Sooo ... aaammm ... IIIIII ...! '

By the great balls of St. Bude ... I felt someone had pulled *my* six-inch bath plug out.

Gasping for breath we collapsed in a great wet heap, laughing and groaning and breaking into chuckles of laughing, finally calming.

'Well! ' she gasped, 'I feel well and truly ...'

'Yes,' I panted, 'me, too .. .'

'Oh *brother*..

The sudden knock on the door sobered us like an ice-cold shower. We froze literally stiffened, stared at one another,

mouths open, listening. The knock came again, more insistent this time. She touched my arm, a gesture of assurance belied by the alarm plainly written on her face. 'Y ... Yes?' she called. 'Who is it?'

A nervous cough, then a muted, diffident voice, 'It's Wray, madam ... may I see you for a moment ? '

Malinda frowned, obviously troubled. 'Just a minute.'

'What is it?' I whispered.

She shook her head and slid off the bed, ran to a wardrobe cupboard, slipped on a negligee, then moved quickly to the door. Something was wrong, I could feel it. She opened the door a crack and spoke with Wray, their conversation conducted in terse, tense undertones, and the little I caught scared me witless. But before I could make a move to get off the bed Malinda had closed the door, snapped the lock and was heading back to me, eyes wild with fright.

'It's my husband! He's here! '

'Here!?'

'Downstairs! He's arrived! It's impossible! He's ... oh, my *God,* he *can't* be! He telephoned me this morning from New York ...! He ...'

A second knock on the door, frantic, panicked, all but finished me. Malinda gasped, spun round, ran to it, called through the door, 'Yes?'

'It's Wray, madam!'

She fumbled with the lock, pulled the door open. Wray murmured something. Malinda uttered a small, desolate cry and slammed the door.

'He's coming up! ' she gasped, hurrying back to me.
'Oh, God!'
'Quick - under the bed! '
I leapt off it, dropped to the floor.
'Your clothes! ' she cried, 'Hide them ... hide them! '
I scrambled to my feet, flew round the room, snatching up shirt ... trousers ... shorts like a man chasing tenners in a hurricane. Demented, sick with panic I dived for the dais, wriggled under the bed and clung to the rear wall, gathering my clothes around me. My sainted bloody aunt, what a turn up! Bang! One of my shoes shot under the bed and clouted me on the head.

'You'll get us both murdered!' she hissed.

Mounted on the dais, the bed was too high off the floor for comfort. I could see the entire room and the bottom half of Malinda as she flew around in flat-out panic, hiding the two glasses ... picking up her gown ... her shoes. Then she raced for the bath, snatched up the vibrator, ran back and hid it in the bookcase.

'Don't make a move until he's gone to his own room!' she whispered breathlessly. 'Don't dare *breathe* or he'll kill you ... kill *both* of us!'

I felt sick. I wanted to die. How did I get into these terrible messes? Why couldn't I stay put in my own back yard? God, if I ever got out of this alive I'd take the first plane back to Cheshire and never move out of that stultifying little village again - ever! A quick flip in the hay with a local buttercup and to heck with the jet-set, they were too flaming dangerous.

The knock on the door brought a plaintive gasp from Malinda. He was here! I backed even harder against the wall, trying to get behind the plaster, feeling sure he could see right under the bed.

'J ... just a moment! ' Malinda called, her voice thin and quavery.

I watched her progress to the door. She paused, collecting herself, then opened it.

'Ahmed! Wray just told me ...'

Great little actress. Voice wondrously controlled.

'My dear ...' His voice was deep, richly resonant, slightly accented and not too friendly. He came into the room. All I could see were the trousers of a dark blue, pin-stripe suit and a pair of highly polished black brogues but I could tell by the way he put his feet down he was enormous. He took a few steps towards the bathroom, then turned.

Malinda, closing the door, said lightly, 'I was taking a bath, Ahmed. What happened?'

'Happened? Nothing happened, Malinda - I simply decided to come home. The deal was completed more quickly than I'd expected and ...' his voice changed, became gentler, more caressing. 'Look ... don't let me keep you from your bath, my dear...'

'No, no ... it's quite all right.. .'

An oily chuckle. 'But I insist. You know how it pleases me to see you bathe.'

'I ... I'd finished, Ahmed. I was just ...'

He moved towards her, stopped close. 'It has been a long, hard week, Malinda. I shall be staying here for three or four days to take a rest before the Ankara meeting.'

'That's ... nice.' She sounded dead bloody miserable.

'And I shall expect my beautiful wife to ... help me relax.'

'Of ... course, Ahmed.'

'So ... continue your bath ... and I shall join you.'

Oh, hell. If he got in the bath he could see right under the bed!

He moved close to the bed, his feet only inches from my nose, and sat down, the sag almost touching my head. Off came one shoe, then the other, then his socks. He stood up ...

'Carry on, my dear, I shall join you.'

'No ... I'll... wait for you, Ahmed.'

Now, what was Malinda up to? Was she planning something?

He dropped his trousers, stepped out of them, stooped to pick them up. Huge brown hands appeared, smothered in rings ... a strangler's hands, big as meat plates! A pair of voluminous blue shorts descended. It was like a marquee falling down. Then he was walking away, towards Malinda.

More and more of his legs appeared, finally his arse ... it was enormous - like two sides of smoked bacon.

As he reached Malinda she side-stepped and moved round him, came quickly to the bed, slipping off her gown as she came, then threw it on to the bed so it hung down to hide me. Wonderful girl.

I couldn't resist a peek at Ahmed, though, so, very carefully, I adjusted my position until I could squint round the negligee.

My eyes popped. He was *bloody* enormous ... a belly on him like King Farouk and jowls to match ... three hundred pounds if an ounce and every dram of it revolting. How in God's name, I wondered, could a bird like Malinda marry a bloke like that, even for money?

Now she appeared in view, such a tiny fragile thing compared to him, making the union seem even more obscene. As she walked towards him he turned dark falcon eyes on her and devoured her inch by inch. 'I've missed you, Malinda ... missed the sight of you bathing ..

'Really?' Her reply was cool, her manner off-hand. 'Surely there were plenty of ... distractions in New York to keep you from being *too* lonely?'

His lips twisted in a crooked smile. 'There is only one Malinda ... that is why she is my wife - and all the others are, as you say, distractions.' He began to walk down the steps, holding out his hand to her. 'Come ... you shall wash me.'

She didn't take his hand but slipped into the pool from the side, her face expressionless, and collected a sponge and soap from the tray containing the lotions. Ahmed ducked beneath the water to wet his shoulders then turned his back towards her, and while she lathered the vast expanse of flab he spoke to her.

'And what have you been doing to amuse yourself?'

She shrugged. 'Swimming ... sailing ... Jane has been over for a few days.'

'Any parties?'

'Yes - Elliott's ... the usual crowd.'

'Any ... lovers?'

My heart tumbled.

'Yes, ten,' she sneered.

'Ten!' He barked a laugh, wobbling like a jelly. 'Malinda, I know your capacity for sexual enjoyment is prodigious - but ten!'

Slowly he turned to her, smiling down at her with a narrowed, lecherous gaze. 'But not too exhausted to enjoy an eleventh, I trust...'

Oh, Christ, he was getting randy!

He reached out for her hand, his eyes burning into her, and slowly drew the sponge down to his genitals.

'That is ... very soothing, my dear ...'

After a minute of this he suddenly swept her into an embrace, crushing her against his belly, kissing her passionately. And she hated it. I could see her straining against him. After a while he released her, breathing heavily, eyes glazed, mouth loose. Ducking quickly to wash off the soap, he took her hand and led her up the steps. He was bringing her to bed!

What made me glance behind me at that moment, I don't know - perhaps I was subconsciously searching for a way out - but thank God I did! Out there, eight feet from the bed, half-hidden in the deep fur pile - snake! A snake? It's your bleeding tie, man!

Ahmed would see it! Bound to! He couldn't miss it!

I shot a glance towards him. He'd stopped momentarily at the top of the steps, having a quick grope while she dried him. I backed up, flat to the floor, and began wriggling out ... and out ... I was clear of the bed, right out in the open! I grabbed for the tie ... grabbed a handful of fur ... lunged again and got it! I turned ... began wriggling back ... but, my God they were coming! They were on me! Nearing the bed!

'Ahmed ...' It was Malinda ... she must have seen me! 'I've got something in my eye - could you ... ?

'Of course, my dear ...'

Wonderful, *wonderful* girl.

While his back was towards me I snaked back up the plinth and under the bed then lay like a corpse, not daring to breath.

'Thank you ... it seems all right now ...'

Then they were climbing on the bed.

Ahmed's great weight brought the springs down to

within an inch of my backside and the back of my head. Pinned face-down against the fur I felt a sudden surge of panic. I was stifled, trapped, smitten by claustrophobia. I wriggled sideways, this way and that, but it made no difference. Everywhere was fur ... fur ... fur ... It was like being entombed with a bleeding polar bear.

Up above I heard a snuffling begin, like he was kissing her, and the thought revolted me. What was she feeling, I wondered - knowing I was only inches away listening to this lot? Poor kid, I felt sorry for her, having to put up with that. I wanted to climb out and drag him off, pull her away and run like hell with her and who was I kidding? She'd murder me for doing it. She'd made her choice. It was either Butterball and his billions or somebody broke but beautiful and she'd chosen the money. So...

The great bulge suddenly shifted above me and the bed creaked like it was about to collapse. That was all I needed ! I heard Malinda give a stifled groan and Ahmed croaked, 'Am I too heavy, my dear?'

'No ... heavier than usual,' she gasped.

'I... can't get it in, Malinda! '

'It's in, Ahmed.'

'It is? You're ... very wet tonight, my dear.'

'That's ... because you excite me so much, Ahmed.'

He gave a delighted chuckle and I was having another one underneath.

The bulge began to bounce, the first one catching me unawares in the back of the neck. I wriggled sideways and thank God I did because the next one would have flattened me like a flounder.

BOOM ... BOOM ... BOOM! Now he was really going to town. The springs were taking hellish punishment, almost hitting the floor, and I was almost out in the open to avoid their lethal plunge.

On and on he went ... BOOMTITTY ... BOOMTITTY ... BOOM. I couldn't believe that tiny fragile bird was able to take so much punishment. Then, suddenly, 'Malinda ...! Ooooh ... Aaaahhh ... UUUUUHHHHH! ! '

Ahmed had blown his gasket. He gave a couple of shudders and collapsed, breathing like an asthmatic dray horse.

'Was that good, Ahmed?' she enquired. She could have been talking about dinner.

'Wonderful, Malinda.'

Could this be the same bird who'd been tearing the pillows to pieces a few minutes ago and having multi-orgasms in the pool?!

The bulge began to shift, moved to one side and settled. A long, long silence followed, and suddenly Malinda's hand dropped below the bed. She wiggled her fingers at me and when I reached out and caught them she gave my hand a squeeze, reassuring me, perhaps telling me that he was falling asleep and that everything would be all right.

Then her hand disappeared again.

Now, what was I going to do if he *did* fall asleep? He might stay there all night! Well, there was only one thing for it - I'd have to try and escape while he *was* asleep - and that meant I had to get my clothes on.

I gave him another few minutes, listening hard for his first snore. But none came. His breathing got heavier and more regular - and neither of them had spoken for a good five minutes - but there was no snoring.

Well, I'd have to take a chance, I couldn't lie there all night doing nothing, so very gingerly I turned on to my back and began disentangling my clothes. What a mess - trousers inside out ... one sock up the arm of my jacket ... the shirt in tatters ... Finally I got them in some semblance of order and then I began.

Ha! Ever *tried* getting dressed under a bed - a *sagging* bed, not daring to touch the bulge suspended a couple of inches from your nose? Come to that - ever tried getting dressed under a bed?

I was yanking my trousers up over my hips when one hand flew off and hit the blasted bulge. I froze, appalled!

'WWHHAAA ...!'

It was Ahmed!

'What is it, Ahmed?'

'I ... *felt* something ..

'Something?'

'... hit the bed ...'

A consoling laugh. 'You were dreaming - you jumped. Go to sleep.'

'Ohhhmmm ... mmmmmm ..

Snuffle ... sniffle ... settle.

My heart was thumping like a drum. Sweat was pouring off my face. It must have been a hundred and forty under there.

Now I knew what those poor devils felt like in the war - digging escape tunnels. I was suffocated. Anything would have been better than this - even discovery! Well, almost.

The contortions I went through getting those clothes on! But at last, looking like something just savaged by the Jersey hunt, I was ready. Now I had to let Malinda know!

Wriggling sideways, I cleared the bed and gave the fur coverlet a little tug. Nothing happened. I gave it another, stronger one. And still nothing happened. Beautiful - now *she'd* fallen asleep!

I wriggled out a few more inches, got my head and shoulders clear, but still couldn't see her. Only one thing for it - I'd have to touch her!

But what if Ahmed was awake ... and saw a strange hand rising like a cobra above the bed? Smitten by indecision I lay suspended, my hand almost to the top of the bed, and at that moment Malinda's head shot into view and frightened the bloody daylights out of me.

She gasped. I gasped. She glanced at Ahmed, then mouthed at me, 'What are you *doing*. ?'

'I'm dressed!' I mouthed back. 'Can you put the lights out?'

'Uh?' she frowned.

'Can ... you ... put ... the ... lights ... out?'

'Oh!'

She nodded ... disappeared from view again and I slid under the bed in case Ahmed woke up.

Her legs appeared and very stealthily she slid off the bed, then tip-toed across the room to the light control. The lights began to fade ... down ... down ... reaching the merest glimmer. Through it I saw her pry open the door ... look along the landing ... then she was waving me out.

Out I slid and got to my knees. Oh, the sheer *luxury* of kneeling up! There lay Ahmed on his back, mouth open, legs wide apart, his great belly rising and falling like a beached whale. Slowly and with infinite caution I backed away, keeping an eye on him, and reached Malinda.

She slid her arms around me and gave me a hug, whispering with sincere concern, 'How *awful* for you! '

'It was beautiful,' I whispered back, managing a stiff grin.

'Go down to the quay - Wray will be waiting for you. He'll take you back.'

'What about Stud! ?'

She shrugged. 'He'll be with Jane.'

'Where?'

She pointed to the right. 'Five rooms along.'

I nodded.

'Go on - hurry! '

'O.K.' I kissed her on the lips, then sneakily on the breast.

'Hey ... I ' she giggled.

' 'Bye, love - take care.'

'And *you!* '

She rose on tip-toe and kissed me. 'Thank you for a lovely evening.'

'And thank you! '

She opened the door, peered out, then beckoned me through. 'Careful, now! '

'Sure. 'Bye!'

I slipped past her on to the landing, looking left and right, and the door closed silently behind me.

Phew! Shaking all over I breathed a stupendous sigh of relief. What a nightmare! Well, from here on it should be easy ... collect Stud ... make our way down through the gardens ... find Wray and we'd be flying home.

Ha!

How little I suspected then that the *real* nightmare was just about to begin!

Tobin In Paradise

CHAPTER ELEVEN

But for the sombre tocking of the grandfather clock way down in the main hall the house lay in sepulchral silence. The chandelier had been turned out, and the galleried landing, which stretched away endlessly to my right, slumbered in sinister gloom. Funny though it may seem, the last thing I wanted to do right then was wander along it looking for Stud's room. The first and only thing I desired was to get the hell down that staircase as fast as my boots would carry me, out through the front door and down to the quay, but of course I couldn't leave Stud behind, unaware of Ahmed's arrival, as he may well have been. Wray *might* have told them but I couldn't count on it, and the thought of Stud banging on Malinda's door next morning and shouting 'Come on, Tobin, get your trousers on, I'm on duty at twelve!' didn't bear thinking about. Or at least Ahmed opening the *door* didn't bear thinking about.

So ... girding my sagging loins and gritting my rattling teeth I started off, hugging the wall, silent as a shadow. Five doors along, Malinda had said ... I reached the first one, at the top of the staircase, and stopped - listening for any sound from either the room or from the gloomy hall.

Nothing - save the ponderous tock of that damned clock. I crept on, reaching the middle of the gallery, the hall directly beneath, and paused again, at the second door.

Not a sound.

Huh huh. On I went ... but had taken only a couple of steps when the sound began. Wwwwhhhrrrrrrrr ...

I shot round, looked back, turned again, perplexed, terrified. What was it? Where was it coming from? What the hell *was* it? Then ...

Boooommmm ... Booommmm ... Booommmm ... Booommmm.

That bloody clock struck four. The noise! It echoed through the hall and up along the gallery. I flattened myself against the wall, wincing at every booming explosion, certain it would wake everyone in the house, planning my escape when the first door opened ...

But none did. Slowly the echo died away ... and the house returned to its eerie, graveyard silence.

On quaking legs I staggered on, passing now into deeper shadow as the balustrade gave way to solid wall. Door number three was negotiated ... then four ... and finally I reached number five.

I put my ear to it, not a sound from within. I released a weary sigh. Now what? I couldn't knock in case it was heard - and so ...? I gripped the knob, turned it, gave the door a gentle push. It opened! I peered through the crack ... into a total blackness. Not a vestige of light. *Now* what?

I was trembling, nerves rubbed raw. I opened the door wider, popped my head in. Quiet sounds of breathing reached me. He was in there all right.

'S ... Stud! ' I hissed, barely hearing it myself. 'Stud! ' a touch louder. No response and not surprising. If he'd been working *half* as hard as I had, nothing short of a thump in the ear would wake him.

Well, there was only one thing for it - a thump in the ear. I slipped into the room, closing the door behind me. How much can the human heart take, I wondered, standing there in the absolute blackness, my poor old ticker banging away like I'd just carried Ahmed from the quay. God, what an eerie experience it is, standing in a strange black room with two people asleep somewhere out there, knowing you've got to wake them in the darkness. You've got to lean over them ... touch them ... What would their reaction be? Fright? Would Jane scream? Would Stud? ! And even if *they* weren't frightened, *I'd* be scared witless!

Aha! My eyes were now adjusting to the darkness and a vague patch of light had appeared over to my right! It

Tobin In Paradise

would be the window, curtained against the moon. Another few moments and I began to see the faint outlines of the room. There ...! Ten paces in front of me, its pale silky coverlet reflecting the meagre moonglow - the bed!

I tried a hoarse whisper. 'Stud!'

Someone stirred! A male voice chuntered in sleep. But which side of the bed did it come from?

I took a couple of steps closer, feeling ahead of me for obstructions ... then some more steps ... finally reached the end of the bed. Now I could see two vague mounds - but which was Stud?

'Ssssss!' I hissed. 'Stud!'

A masculine mutter emanated from the mound on the left!

I tip-toed to it, bent closer. 'Stud .!'

No response.

'Psssttt... Stud!'

A movement!

'Stud ...!'

'Mmmmnnnnnxxxxcccczzzz..

'Stud - wake up!'

He gave a start. 'Mmm ... wha ...?'

'Stud - it's me - Russ! Wake up, man!'

'Wha ... who ...?'

'It's me - Russ! Wake up, for Chrissake!'

A pale shadow shot up. 'Wha ...?'

'Stud - we've got to get out of here! Put the light on, man!'

Pause ... then panic! He shot sideways, fumbled for the bedside light, knocked something heavy off the table ... click! The light blinded me. I shut my eyes ... opened them ... and died!

It wasn't Stud! It was a naked, hairy monster ... a thug, a heavy, a gorilla with a broken nose and a countenance of crumpled concrete! And the guy next to him ... just waking up'... could've been his ugly brother!

I gasped.

'And who the hell are you?' croaked Broken Nose.

I was rooted, frozen petrified - staring down at the thing

161

he'd knocked off the table and which was now resting against my left shoe - a revolver!

'Assassin!' yelled the second bloke, whipping back the bedclothes.

Eh!

That did it. With a flick of my foot I sent the revolver skittering under the bed and hit the door in two bounds. I yanked it open, slammed it shut and fled, yelling 'STUD! STUD! ' as I hared along the gallery. 'STUD! I yelled again as I fell down the stairs eight at a time. I bounced off the banister, threw myself round the turn, stumbled across the hall and got a hand on the doorknob as the cry rang out from up above.

'RUSS!'

Stud was peering myopically out of the door of the *fourth* bedroom, boggle-eyed, frowning heavily.

'STUD ... GET BACK! RUN FOR YOUR LIFE! '

At that moment the door of the fifth bedroom crashed open and the two gorillas, in dressing gowns, came thundering out, heading fast for the stairs, Broken Nose waving the revolver in the air. 'STOP RIGHT THERE OR I'LL SHOOT! '

That did it for Stud. With a gape and a gawp he shot back inside the room and slammed the door. And it sure as hell did it for me. I was out through that door before you could say death, tugging the door closed behind me, out into the moonlight and across the terrace for dear life.

Incredibly, even in the madness of flight some reason prevailed. Not in a straight line, you fool - they'll pick you off before you reach the pool! Cut left ... right ... well, *which!* Left... left...

I was half- way across the terrace when the door clattered open and Broken Nose bellowed, 'STOP OR I SHOOT! '

Oh, sweet Jesus ...

My mind was stark confusion. I couldn't think! Panic drove me on, legs pumping, breath hissing. Any second now he'd shoot, I knew! I could hear the crack ... feeling the scalding lead smack into my spine ... the pain ... the searing agony ...!

Suddenly I was plunging into a bed of bushes, high, thick, blessedly dense shrubs. I belted through, careless of what lay beyond, heedless of injury, driven by the voices close behind. On I crashed, fighting away the branches, kicking them down, backing into them and forging through. Then suddenly I was through! In front of me now - a low, stone wall, waist-high, marking the end of the terrace - but beyond it a ten-foot drop down to the terrace below! Without hesitation I climbed up, turned on to my stomach, lowered myself and dropped. Crump! I landed, staggered back, tripped over the coping of a flower bed and fell on my ass in the daisies. Up again, propelled by the shouts from the bushes above and on into nightmare flight through the flowers, across the open terrace, reaching another wall. Beyond this - impenetrable darkness! A forest!

This time I did hesitate, appalled at the prospect of dropping into it, but a moment later came the shout, 'STOP!' and I was over the wall before the echo died, dropping down, landing awkwardly on a treacherous slope, slithering and sliding down the severe pitch and into the first line of trees. I slammed against a solid trunk that stopped me dead, then down again, slithering from tree to tree, using them to stagger my rushing plunge, and then I hit the bank of treeless shale and away I went! Whhooosshh! Hurtling into blackness on my backside, I slid, bounced, bumped and rolled twenty ... thirty feet ... then crashed to a halt against a wall of boulders, feet first, thank God!

I lay there panting, bewildered, shocked. There was no ache, no pain - only an all-pervading panic. I had to get away! I scrambled up, tripped, stumbled along a gulley of small loose stones, going heaven only knew where - but going!

On and on, the dense blackness of the forest soaring above me to the left, a low bank of trees on my right. Suddenly the bank petered out and in its place a wall of tumbled boulders — huge things, six feet high. I climbed between them, squeezed around them and came upon a tiny clearing of sand. Cover! And a place to rest.

I collapsed in a heap, lungs heaving, my breath raucous in my parched throat. I could hear, nothing else, see nothing. My sight was blurred by the thunder of my heartbeat. Dear God, how terrible to be hunted. I strained to listen for sounds of pursuit but knew I wouldn't hear anything until my breathing calmed and my pulse ceased its gargantuan thump.

Gradually it did calm and then the sound came to me - the sea! Close behind me! I'd come all the way down to the beach! Well, at least that was something ... for where the sea was, Wray was ... Wray and the 'Lazy Lady' and a chance of getting back to Nassau.

Wrapped in a cocoon of shock I sat with my back against a boulder, shaking my head. It was all too unbelievable ... me, Tobin, sitting on a beach in the Bahamas ... being chased to the death by an Arab oil tycoon's bodyguards or whatever they were ... having just made wild, wild love to his wife ... then hidden under his bed listening to *him* make love to her ... nah, it really couldn't be happening. It was all a dream ... a nightmare of stupefying realism ... like the trickle of stones that was now falling down the slope on the other side of these boulders!

I came into a crouch, prepared for instant flight, my nerves shrieking at the scrape of shoes in the loose shale not a dozen yards away. Then ... silence. I could feel him looking round, peering among the boulders, feeling for vibrations, gun held at the ready. Now he moved again, cautiously, undecided which direction to take, then, having decided, he came on - between the boulders and straight towards me!

I crouched lower, sick with fear, trying hard to look like a boulder. What would they *do* to me ...? What terrible Arab tortures would be mine? Disembowelling ...? Castration ...! I will make sure, Tobin, that you do not cuckold any other man ... swish! Here lying on the floor ...

He was coming on ...! - stepping from boulder to boulder! A blur of movement entered the edge of my vision. There he was ... up above me ... standing on the boulder not ten feet away ... searching the beach ... now turning slowly towards me ...!

'STUD!'

'YYYYOOOOWWWW!!'

He leapt two feet in the air and disappeared backwards.

'OWWW!' he yelled.

I scrambled up, heart bursting with relief, leaned over the boulder. He was flat on his back, trousered legs in the air, naked to the waist and sockless.

"YOU!' he gasped.

He rolled over and got to his feet, looking one hell of a mess, streaked with dirt, quite bewildered.

'Tobin ... what the *hell* is going on! Who were those two bloody maniacs with the gun ...!'

'Sssh! be quiet! Climb over here, man.'

He climbed over, dropped down into my 'hide', and we squatted.

'Listen ...' I whispered, 'we've got to get off this island - got to find Wray ..'

'But *why*, man - what the hell's been going ...'

'Ahmed came back! Walked right in on ...'

His face creased in a frown. *'Ahmed?* Who the fu ...?'

'Ahmed, old son, is Malinda's bleeding husband!'

He gaped.

'Quite. He was supposed to be in *New York* - he phoned her from there this morning! Then changed his tiny mind and came home - almost caught us at it..

'Good God ...!'

'And if Wray, bless him, hadn't given us two minutes' warning he *would've* caught us at it!'

'Holy mac ... but how did you get away?'

'I didn't! I had to hide under the bloody bed!'

His chin hit the sand. 'Wha ... while he was in the *room!?*'

'Not only in the room, mate - in the bed! Arrived home all randy and couldn't wait to whip her into the hay!'

His eyes became saucers. 'Wha ... after *you'd* just...?'

'Yes - after I'd just ... and *how* I'd just.'

A small whimper escaped from him as the outrageousness of the situation struck him. It forced a grin from me which got him going and suddenly we were chortling with laughter, trying desperately to keep it quiet.

'Ssshh!' I laughed, finger to my lips. 'Those two gorillas

can't be far away ...! '

That sobered him. Wiping his eyes, he whispered earnestly, 'And who were *they, for* God sake! ? '

'I don't know ... bodyguards, I should think.'

'But ... where did you run into *them?*'

'In your bedroom ..'

'Eh?'

'Well, what I *thought* was your bedroom. Malinda told me you and Jane were five doors along the gallery and I barged into the darkened room to warn you Ahmed was home and woke *them* up instead! She must've meant five doors including hers or something, I don't know. Anyway, how did you get away?'

'Fast - and out of the goddam window! I was climbing out when I saw you haring across the terrace like your ass was on fire, heading this way, so I followed.'

'And where was Jane?'

'Fast asleep! Out for the count.'

' 'Well, she won't be now - and neither will Ahmed! He'll be very wide awake ... and on the hunt for a couple of assassins! '

He frowned. 'But surely to God Malinda will tell him who we are ...?'

'Don't count on it, son. She's in a very dicky position, isn't she ... ? - no pun intended. If she tells him who we really are there's a good chance he'll boot her out - or do her in. He looks quite capable of it. She's got an awful lot to lose, Stud ...'

'Yeah,' he said glumly. 'So where does that leave us?'

'Right up it - without a paddle. Our only hope is Wray. Malinda told me to make for the quay ... that Wray would be waiting there for us. But that, of course, was before all mayhem let loose. I've got a sneaky feeling that Ahmed will be keeping a beady eye on *that* avenue of escape.'

He nodded, beginning to think it out. 'Yeah, he must be wondering how we got on the island in the first place ... where we moored the boat. And that means ...'

'They'll be searching for it. Hey, you didn't hear any dogs by any chance, did you?'

'Dogs? No.'

'Thank God for that, that's all we need.' I turned to look at the eastern sky. The dawn was beginning and in another hour our cover of darkness would be gone. Then they could hunt us over the tiny island at their leisure.

'The way I see it,' I said, 'we've got two choices - we either move now and try to find Wray - or we dig a big hole and lie low until tonight.'

'Hey, I don't fancy that - what about my job? I've got to get back, man ...!'

'O.K., then ... we go and find Wray.'

'At the quay?'

I shrugged. 'I wouldn't know where else to look.'

'O.K....' he gestured, 'after you.'

'Thanks, pal.'

'You're welcome.'

CHAPTER TWELVE

Moving at a cautious crouch along the sand, hugging the wall of boulders, we quickly encountered a thrusting shoulder of cliff-face that reached almost to the sea. Beyond this shoulder, I felt, we would see the quay - perhaps a hundred yards or so away. And so, expecting trouble round the bend, we edged silently along the shoulder and just before the end I dropped flat and wriggled forward to take a look.

Gradually the land on the other side was revealed to me, and as it appeared I realized that in my demented flight down through the trees I'd come much further from the house than I'd thought. The quay was not there. I was looking at a small sandy bay, perhaps a hundred yards wide and almost totally enclosed by the towering eighty-foot cliff-face, its far boundary appearing to run into the sea, although it was impossible to see in that light. The quay must obviously lie beyond *that* bend.

'Can you see it?' whispered Stud.

I backed up. 'No - it's a small bay. We'll have to cross it. The quay must be further on?'

'Let's have a look.'

He wriggled forward but in a moment was scuttling back, all excited. 'Did you see it I '

'What?'

'The boat! Moored off-shore ! '

'No!' I gasped. 'Where ...?'

Now we both wriggled forward. Sure enough - there it was, a tiny motor-boat bobbing at anchor not fifty yards from us, its stem now swinging towards us as we watched.

Stud peered at it and slumped a bit. 'Oh ...' he said, despondently.

'What's the matter?'

'The outboard motor - it doesn't look very big ... maybe five horse. It's only a little run-about, Russ?'

'Well? Couldn't it get us back to Nassau?'

'Hell, it's ten miles, man?

'Well, won't that thing *go* ten miles ...?'

'Yes ...' he said hesitantly. 'If there's enough gas in the tank, but..?'

'But what?'

He gave a sigh, not at all happy. 'It's the sea ... it's calm enough right now - but if a wind got up ...'

'How long would it take us - if it stayed calm?'

He shrugged. 'Two hours.'

'Mmm ... so if we started out right now we could at least be out of sight before it gets really light?'

'Yes,' he admitted. 'But, Russ, these little plodders aren't meant for the open sea ... they're for puttering around just offshore. If we hit any kind of current we'd stand still!'

My spirits dropped. 'O.K. Well ... we'd better cross this bay. We'll creep around the foot of the cliff, they shouldn't be able to see us in this light.'

'Right.'

I started off, Stud close behind me, at first on hands and knees until we'd rounded the shoulder and then at a crouch, hugging the cliff-face like limpets, eyes glued to the cliff-top and the two shoulders.

In five minutes we were nearing the far shoulder's edge and again went to ground, ten yards from the end - because the shoulder *did* reach into the bleeding sea I

'Now what do we do?' whispered Stud, peering with some dismay at the black water.

'Well, I know what *I* do,' I said pointedly, taking off my shoes and socks and rolling my trousers to the knee.

'You're a good man.'

'Here - hold these.'

Feeling like Uncle Bert at Blackpool I gingerly stepped into the cool, dark water, searching ahead for nasty rocks and things as I shuffled towards land's end. Suddenly the beach began to drop alarmingly. Ten feet to go and already I was up to my knees. I turned, grimaced at Stud who shrugged helpfully. What the hell, I thought - my trousers were ruined anyway. I shrugged back at him, took three more steps and disappeared up to my waist! Aw, screw it...

Swimming now, I reached the end of the shoulder and began edging around it, pulling myself along on the rock, craning for first sight of the quay. And there it was! And there, also, sitting on one of the iron bollards, smoking a fag and gazing out to sea, was number two gorilla. No boat, no Wray - just Legs Diamond.

Having seen more than enough I was just about to return to Stud when a voice stopped me - a tinny, radio-transmitted-type voice. Then Legs reached down and picked up a walkie-talkie and answered it, though I couldn't hear what he was muttering.

Well, that was that! I swam back to Stud and squelched out of the water.

'We've had it,' I said, crouching beside him. 'The boat isn't there but one of the gorillas *is* and he's chatting into a walkie-talkie ..

'Hot damn! They're searching for us - probably using the boat. Well, *now* what do we do?'

I shrugged. 'It's back to square one - we either lie low ... or take a chance in that run-about before it gets too light.' I turned and looked again at the eastern sky. 'I reckon we've got about half-an-hour - no more.'

'Yeah,' he said glumly.

'Stud, how are you on navigation?'

'That's no problem. We just head straight out and when it gets light we'll be able to see New Providence. I don't know where we'll land but at least it'll be New Providence.'

'Well... what d'you think?'

He heaved a sigh, giving it consideration. 'The weather *looks* pretty settled ...'

'Sure.'

'Ah, but don't let it fool you. The wind can whip up any

time.'

'Oh.'

'Still ... two hours. It'd be a fair risk ...'

'And I say let's take it.'

He considered a moment longer, then nodded. 'O.K. - let's go.'

We crept back around the bay, clinging to the cliff until we'd almost reached the far shoulder, then, leaving the safety of the rock-face, we struck out across the open beach, walking backwards, watching the cliff-top.

Slop ... slop ... we were in the sea. Stud reached the boat first, swung the stem towards him and inspected the tiny outboard. He unscrewed the petrol cap and stuck his finger in.

'Not bad,' he muttered. 'About half full.'

'My, this is our lucky day!'

'Go on - get in!'

I swung a leg aboard and hopped in. It really was very small - about eight feet long and three feet wide - no more than a ship-to-shore painter for flat calm waters.

Stud climbed in and purposely rocked it, testing its stability.

'Well?' I whispered.

'Lousy.'

'Thanks.'

'Just pray the wind stays at zero for the next two hours.'

'Our Father, which art in Heaven..

'Now to start the little bugger ..'

Left hand on the motor, right hand gripping the pull-cord, he took his stance, braced his legs ... and pulled.

Cough ... cough ... cough a-n-d cough ... cough ... cough.

'Come on, you asthmatic armhole,' he cursed.

A-a-n-n-d-d ... cough ... cough ... cough. Stop ... fiddle ... fiddle ... prime ... prime ... and ... cough ... cough ... cough ... splutter!

A splutter!

'Come on ... come on, baby,' he pleaded. 'Just this once ... just for Stud and Russ.'

Cough ... splutter ... splutter ... cough ... choke.

'You ... bloody bas ...'

'Stud! Don't hurt its feelings!'

He heaved a long despondent sigh. He was getting worried. *He* was getting worried!

Yank! Splutter. Yank! Splutter. Yank! Cough ... cough. 'Oh ... bloody ... buggerin' ... screwin' ... fornicatin' ...

'HEEYYYY!! YOU DOWN THERE!!'

The voice boomed off the cliff-top. Stud and I spun round in horror. There he was - Broken Nose! - racing along the top towards the end of the shoulder, going like hell.

'Stud!' I gasped.

'Jesus Christ!'

Yank ... yank ... yank ... yank! His arm pumping like a piston but the damned, dead, damp, dumb, dud, doped motor refused to fire.

'Stud ... !' I pleaded.

'OH ...! you dirty, rotten, stinkin', filthy little .. .'

'Stud ... did you turn on the petrol?!'

'Of *course* I turned on the ...' He stopped, stared at the motor, then dropped to his knees peering closely at the petrol switch and let out a howl of agony. 'No ...! I turned the bloody thing OFF! It was already open ...!'

Snapping the tap switch he shot to his feet.

'YOU TWO DOWN THEEERRREEE!' Broken Nose was almost at the shoulder's end. STAY WHERE YOU ARE OR I'LL ...!'

ZZZZZIIIIIZZZZZZZ!! The gallant little motor zizzed into life.

Stud plopped down on the stem seat. 'Get the anchor up - quick!'

I scrambled forward, yanked on the nylon rope and up she came.

Plop! Plop! Two strange splashes at the side of the boat threw water on to my arms. Then came the delayed staccato cracks from the cliff top. I swung round ... gaped up. Broken Nose was pointing down at us - both hands clasped together.

'Get down!' yelled Stud, throwing open the throttle.

'He's *firing* at us!'

Ping! Something ricocheted off the anchor blade.

'Get DOWN!' yelled Stud.

Firing ...? Bullets ...? *Real* bullets ...?

Zzzziiippp ... thuck! A square inch of fibre-glass shot out of the side of the boat and flew into the sea.

I gaped at Stud. 'Stud ...! He's ... FIRING AT US!'

I hit the deck, cowered beneath the shallow bulwark ... and now Stud was down beside me, one arm raised, holding the throttle open, keeping us pointing out to sea.

'The mad bastard!' I gasped, 'he can't *shoot* at us! I mean .. 'Man, he's *shooting* ...!'

Ping! Another slug crashed into the engine casing and whined off into the sea. Splut! Another one slammed into the bow platform.

'He'll *murder* us!' I protested.

'Keep down ... keep down ...!'

'Are you *kidding ?.*'

The brave little motor was zizzing away getting nowhere - and yet it must have taken us out of range because there was suddenly no more shooting. Either that or B-N had run out of bullets. As a precaution, though, we gave it another couple of minutes before risking an eye over the bulwark.

'He's gone!' I panted.

Stud looked up, furtive until he'd made certain, then resumed his seat in the stern. I took the middle one.

'Here ...' he said, handing me a shaking cigarette.

'Mad!' I gasped, taking a light from him. 'Stark ... raving ... homicidal..

'Yeah,' he agreed, inhaling smoke hungrily. 'But don't forget - he does think we're assassins!'

'He thinks *we're* assassins!'

I glanced at the motor. 'Stud - is this the fastest this thing will go?'-

'The most,' he nodded. 'Flat out - wide open.'

I winced. 'Are we *moving?*' I looked towards the shore. I could still see it - even in this light. 'By ... golly, we must be doing all of ... ooh, four miles an hour.'

'Nearer five, I'd say.'

'Really? That much? Well, son ... what's going to happen

now, d'you reckon?'

'Well,' he sighed, 'seein' as how the game is well and truly up - I reckon the sea will be swarming with heavies any minute now.'

I looked towards the east. It was getting mighty light. 'Another fifteen minutes ...' I muttered disconsolately.

'No more than that.'

'Couldn't I ... paddle or something - help that flamin' thing along a bit?'

'Sure.' He nodded to the emergency paddle in the bottom of the boat. 'Every little helps.'

'Well, it's better than just sitting here - contemplating imminent death.'

I got the paddle out, turned round and plunged it in the sea, knowing after a minute that all this was doing was getting me tired arms.

'By ... golly, that's made a difference! ' exclaimed Stud. 'Man, just look at that bow-wave ! '

'Very funny,' I sneered. I was tired already. How *did* those chaps in 'Hawaii Five-O' do it? 'Stud ...' I said over my shoulder.

'Yes, Russell?'

'I'm too young to die.'

'Oh, I don't think they'll kill us.'

'You don't?'

'Nah - rip out a finger nail or two ... break a leg, sure - but...'

'Will you stop! O.K., well, if they don't intend killing us - what was that gorilla doing back there - waving us goodbye?'

'Nah, that was just a fit of pique because he couldn't get at us. If he'd caught us I honestly believe he would only have pistol-whipped us ... smashed in a tooth or three, but he wouldn't have killed us.'

'Stud ...

'Yes, Russell?'

Why don't I ever listen to my own sixth-sense and ignore suspicious propositions from mysterious Chinamen?'

'Well, Russell, it's because you're a lecherous, low-down,

no-good, randy-minded bastard to whom the prospect of an exotic, glamorous and forbidden piece of ass is totally irresistible.'

'Oh. I wondered what it was.'

'Hey ...'

'Mmm?'

'How was it, by the way?'

I pulled the stupid paddle out of the water and turned to face him, grinning at the memory. 'Out of this world, Stud.'

'Worth all this trouble?'

'Every damned inch of it. And how about *you?*'

His teeth gleamed in the coming dawn. 'To a standstill. That bird simply does not *know* the word "enough".'

'Ah, well...'

'Yeah, a night to remember.'

'Stud ...' I frowned. 'Is that motor making a ... funny noise - a deeper sort of ...'

He listened, also frowning, then his eyes shifted one degree to port, over my shoulder, and his mouth dropped open. I whirled - and saw it. They were coming! The 'Lazy Lady', as yet a blur in the grey light but unmistakable, was bearing down on us, if the roar of her engines was anything to go by, at around eight thousand miles an hour. We could hear above the pathetic putter of our own egg-beater the power-driven, deep- throated wwwuuuzzz ... wwwuuuzzz ... wwwuuuzzz as the boat buffeted the waves.

Fear clutched my heart. Somehow *I* just *knew* they were going to ride us down - smash clean through us ... hurl us into the air, a tangle of bloody, severed limbs and cartwheeling carcasses.

'My God ...! ' gasped Stud, 'they're *heading* for us ... they're going to *hit* us ! '

We were helpless, defenceless ... there was nothing to do, nowhere to go! Now they were on us! Only a hundred yards away and coming on at terrible speed ... fifty tons of roaring death bearing down at more than forty knots!

'Russ ...! ' yelled Stud, coming to his feet, cutting the motor. 'We've got to jump!'

I got up, wobbling wildly, ripped off my jacket ... my

shoes ... and then ...

WWWWHHHHOOOOSSSSHHHH!!

At no more than twenty yards' range the thundering cruiser swept suddenly to port, loosing at us a monstrous tidal wave as lethal as the boat itself.

'JUMP!!' yelled Stud.

Out we went - into the face of the rushing green wall of water. Biff! I was hurled backwards, carried down, tumbled and tossed like a sock in a washing machine, then spewed back to the surface. Gasping and choking I broke through, only to be slapped in the face by another huge wave. Blinded and choking, I thrashed and kicked wildly, fighting to stay on top. Then a hand grabbed me by the hair, holding me up. It was Stud, coughing and spitting himself.

'You ... all ... right?' he gasped.

I managed a nod. The water was calming a little. Stud coughed and spat again. 'The ... crazy ... *bastards!*'

'Wh ... where are they ...?'

'They're ... coming ... back!'

Now the roar began, reaching us not only through the air but through the water, a fearful rumbling that made the ocean tremble. And then they were on us again ... then sweeping away! The tidal wave boiled over us, swamping us, smashing us down. I kicked frantically for the surface ... was hit again by another wave and then another! They were circling us - hitting us from every angle, hitting us continually, creating powerful currents and counter-currents all around us. It was a maelstrom, dragging us down ... down!

I caught a glimpse of Stud's frenzied arm, heard his cry, but was helplessly caught in the whirlpool that was hurling me round. I was fighting for my very life, clawing to stay on top, knowing that in a very few minutes I was going to drown. I couldn't last much longer ... my strength was going ... my legs ... arms ..'. the whole damned thing was just too ... big!

Then, with astounding suddenness ... silence. Everything stopped. The ocean ceased to boil... the boat was gone. I could see ... and hear - hear Stud's wretched coughing behind me. I turned and saw him, twenty yards away, clinging to the overturned hull of the run-about, more dead than alive.

'S ... Stud' ' I croaked.

He flopped a feeble arm at me. J started to swim, my arms dead-weight, too desperately tired to lift out of the water, finally grabbing for the boat with a desperate lunge. And there we clung, coughing up salt water, gulping air.

'Are you ... all right?' I gasped.

He nodded, managed a bleak smile. 'Not bad.'

'Good. Any ... chance ... of turning this thing over?'

'Yes ... I'll have a go ... in a minute ... the crazy bastards ...'

'Wonder why they didn't pick us up?'

He shook his head. 'I dunno. Maybe the girls told Ahmed who we were ... when they heard the shooting.'

'Yes ... I'm sure they would. They couldn't let Ahmed go on thinking we were assassins. Boy, I'm freezing to death ...'

'Come on ... let's try and flip this thing over. I'll get on top ...'

Three times he got half up then fell back into the sea, but the fourth time he made it. Then, kneeling up, he reached into the water, got hold of the bulwark and fell backwards, taking the edge with him - and over it went. A few minutes more and we were sitting in the boat, shivering while Stud inspected the motor.

'What d'you think?' I asked him, teeth chattering. 'Any water get in?'

'O ... Only one way to find out.. .'

He yanked the cord. Would you believe the damned thing started first time?

Stud sagged with relief, collapsed on to the seat and set course for New Providence, now a thin black line on the pale pink horizon.

'All in all,' he grinned ruefully, 'a very interesting night.'

'Extremely - and not in the least expensive. I personally have only lost the jacket of a one hundred and fifty dollar suit ... in the pocket of which was a hundred dollars in cash ... a pair of fifty dollar shoes ... a shirt ... tie ... socks ...'

'Huh huh,' he nodded, 'that's about my tally, too. Er,

forgive me for bringing it up, old boy - but wasn't it supposed to be a "profitable" evening as well as "interesting"?'

'Oh, but it *has* been profitable, Stud. We've profited *enormously* by the experience! I mean, just think of the satisfaction you'll get next time a Chinaman approaches you with an interesting and profitable proposition, in telling him to take his proposition, four handfuls of rice balls, six fried prawns and a chopstick and thrust them up his ..

'Ssssshhh!' His eyes were wide, staring wildly.

'Wha ..

'Listen! '

I did listen ... and there it was again - the distant roar of that goddam boat! I whirled round, followed Stud's appalled gaze. There it came, rushing towards us in a plume of spray. Well, this was it. If they threw us into the sea again it would be the end, we didn't have the strength to fight that maelstrom any more.

Like zombies we came to our feet, half-crouched for the dreaded impact of the first gigantic wave, the plunge into the wild water. I shut my eyes, fearing and hating the sight of the flying white hull. It was here ... on us! Less than a hundred yards before its vicious turn!

Its sudden deceleration, the diminishing of its terrible roar startled me. I opened my eyes. Now only thirty yards away it was drifting benignly towards us - and up there in the cockpit, peering down at us, his expression heavy with concern, was Wray!

He drifted closer, called out, 'I'll throw you a line from the stem! Tie it to your bow! '

Moments later he was helping us up the ladder and on to the deck. 'Go down below,' he urged us. 'There are some towels and brandy.'

He followed us down, fussing around us like a mother hen. We took our sodden clothes off, wrapped ourselves in warm towels, then sat at the dining table with two inches of brandy in balloon glasses, beginning to feel a touch more human.

'Quaint people you work for, Mr. Wray,' remarked Stud,

not entirely without rancour. 'I reckon your boss is very lucky not to have two murder charges looming.'

Wray shook his head. 'Terrible ... terrible. I was watching the whole thing through glasses - they went much too far.'

'Who were they?' I asked. 'Ahmed's bodyguards?'

He nodded. 'Yes, they travel everywhere with him. There has been more than one attempt on his life - he's ... very concerned with Middle East politics.'

I raised a brow at Stud. 'Well, I reckon we were lucky to get out of the house alive if they thought we were assassins.' I turned to Wray. 'One thing puzzled us - why didn't they pick us up instead of trying to drown us?'

'Well ...' the severity of his expression softened a touch, 'you have Miss Jane to thank for that. My mistress was, of course, in a very ... difficult position ...'

'Of course,' I said. 'We anticipated that.'

'At first the ladies thought it better to say nothing - expecting you to find me and get safely away. But when they heard the shooting and later learned you were about to be picked up in the boat, they decided to act. Miss Jane admitted that *she* had invited both of you to the island ... that you were *both* her lovers ..'

I gasped at Stud. 'Did Ahmed swallow it?' Stud asked.

'Yes ... eventually. That was when he called off the 'Lazy Lady'... a trifle late for your comfort, I'm afraid.'

I frowned. 'But ... if Ahmed was satisfied with the explanation, why didn't he have us pulled out of the water? Why leave us floundering with an upturned boat?'

Wray's mouth tightened. 'He's a strangely perverse man, Mr. Tobin. On this occasion he chose to allow the "immorality" of the situation to anger him. It was his way of showing Miss Jane his displeasure.'

'Really.'

Ha! That was rich - coming from a man who'd just admitted numerous 'distractions' in New York to his wife! Ahmed wasn't perverse - he was perverted!

'And what will happen to Miss Jane?' Stud asked. 'Will there be any trouble?'

Wray's smile was highly amused. 'No, no trouble. Miss

Jane can more than look after herself.' He turned to me. 'Mr. Tobin, my mistress deeply regrets what happened and is aware that you must have suffered considerable personal loss ...' his eyes flickered briefly to the pile of rags drying in front of a heater, then returned with a twinkle of amusement to me. 'Clothing, perhaps ...?'

I grinned and shook my head. 'No, nothing, Mr. Wray. Thank her for the thought, but tell her ... yes, tell her *nothing* was spoiled. All right?'

He nodded, understanding what I meant. 'I will tell her with pleasure - and thank you. Now ... where can I take you both?'

'Can you drop us on Paradise Beach?' asked Stud. 'It won't matter if we're only wearing trousers, they'll think we've been swimming.'

Wray nodded. 'Surely, I can put you ashore in the painter.'

Within half an hour Stud and I were standing on the deserted beach, waving Wray off in the run-about, then we turned and trudged up the beach towards the hotel.

'Oh, *man* ..Stud groaned, 'I am *shattered. I* am not going to stir a muscle until five to twelve.'

'And I ...' I said, stifling a gigantic yawn, 'am not gonna do likewise until nine tonight... ! '

'You wanna bet, Tobin?'

I looked at him, 'Hm?

'You wanna bet, old buddy?'

What d'you mean?'

'Russell has forgotten, hasn't Russell?'

'Forgotten *what?*'

He gave a fiendish chuckle and slapped me on the back. 'You have company at two o'clock, old bean - remember?'

I stopped, gasped, gaped at him. 'Tonie! Oh, my ... *God..!*'

'And, buddy,' he laughed, forcing me on up the beach, 'just forget what I said about her having a friend for me, huh? The lady's *all* yours.'

With a despairing groan I staggered after him on legs of rubber. I was exhausted ... *dying* from lack of sleep! This had to *stop!* I couldn't go on! Not another bird would enter my life for the rest of my stay! I was *determined!* I would spend my nights sleeping - solo! - and my days lazing in the sun. I would banish all women with the fervour of a misogynist monk ... turn queer ... lock myself in the loo if necessary ... BUT NO MORE WOMEN!

And so, dear friends, it came to pass.

Well, almost.

Actually it was three nights later that I spotted her in the casino ... tall and tanned and lovely, graceful as a colt, long shining red hair reaching to her tiny waist. An absolute must.

Her name was Frenzy.

Hot *damn,* I was in it again.

CHAPTER THIRTEEN

'Cheers, old buddy,' Stud raised his illicit rum-and-coke. 'And here's to celibacy.'

'By golly, I'll drink to that.'

It was ten o'clock and we were sitting up at the Gallery Bar during one of his twenty-minute breaks, enjoying the view and gloating over our fifty-three-hour-and-fourteen-minute abstinence. Nary a bird had darkened our portals for three whole nights and the rest had made new men of us.

Sun, sea, sand and buckets of sleep had been our wholesome diet since, in Stud's case, Wray had dropped him on the beach, and in my case since Tonie had closed the bedroom door on a near-corpse, and two fitter and more sun-tanned Adonises you could not hope to meet.

Muscle-hard and resolution firm, we glowed with health and that radiant sense of well-being that derives only from a job well-done, a difficult mission accomplished, a target well-and- truly attained and who the hell was I kidding? I was climbing up the bleeding wall.

'Who needs them, that's what I say,' Stud stated emphatically *'Who?'*

'Who indeed,' I replied, forcing my eyes and mind away from a gorgeous little bottom in suede hot-pants bending over the next table.

'Aah, I should have done this a long time ago,' he was going on. 'Man, I feel marvellous ... full of vim and vigour ... strong as a bull.'

'Amen to that,' I muttered, tearing my attention from a stupendous pair of boobs at the bar.

'How can you possibly call walking around in a state of

total exhaustion pleasure? What *joy* is there in waking up every morning smoked-out, drunk-out and fu...'

'Quite.'

'Full of remorse? It's a fool's paradise, Russ - an idiot's ... an idiot's ... Jeezus, would yuh *look* at that...?'

She was suddenly there, playing the slot-machines, sauntering from machine to machine, popping in quarters with languid abandon. She was wonderful ... a long-legged, red-haired tom-boy in tight white trousers and a green floral blouse open one button too many for any fella's peace of mind - let alone one who's been in purdah for three nights. The old ticker started its terrible tattoo and I knew for certain my new-found resolutions had gone for a loop.

'Tobin ..Stud's tone was brutally censorious.

'Uh?'

'You're ogling!'

'Huh huh,' I nodded, mind swimming.

'You're abrogating our pact... !'

'Hm mm.'

'Sliding down the slippery slope of sensuous surrender ...!'

'Huh hmm.'

'But, hot *damn,* she's lovely !'

'Gorgeous.'

'The face of a randy angel..

'I must go to her ..

'Steady!'

'I must, I must!'

'Then go, damn you ... and find out if *she* has a friend.'

'But... our pact?'

'Screw the pact.'

I was right behind her at the change desk as she whipped a ten-dollar bill from her breast pocket and asked for quarters. Her body, so very close, was a fiercely magnetic thing, drawing my hands compulsively towards it. I ached to touch her, hold her, stroke her gleaming copper mane. As she moved away from me I slapped a ten-buck note on the counter and gathered my quarters into a paper cup without once removing my eyes from her wondrous chassis, then still ogling it, I followed her to the one-arm thiefs and began feeding one just two machines away from her.

Surreptitiously I watched her, watched the movement of her fulsome breasts beneath the thin cotton blouse as she reached high for the handle and yanked it down ... watched her expression of delight as a small shower of coins dropped into the tray. Again she fed the machine and again a small win. It was my cue.

'You're having some luck there.'

She shot me a quick glance, smiled, and said, 'A little ... but I'm after the big one.'

Are you, I thought ... then you've come to the right place, love.

'Have you ever won a jackpot in here?' I asked casually.

'No - not in here. I haven't played in here before.'

'Well, they're certainly winnable. A woman won two fifties in about two minutes the other night - right over there.'

'Two! How fabulous.'

'Shows it can be done.' _

'But not on this thing - it's cold, I can feel it.'

She moved away down the line, taking my heart with her. After a while, trying not to make it *too* obvious, I followed.

'That was very interesting ... what you said about that machine over there. Can you really feel if it's cold?'

She gave a laugh. 'Sure! The fruits are all over the place - no sense of promise.'

'I see. Well, if I come across a hot one I'll let you know.'

She smiled but didn't reply and a moment later moved on again, this time rounding the bank of machines to the ones on the far side which backed the one I was playing, so that now she was facing me.

'Any warmer round there?' I grinned.

She looked up and shrugged. 'Nothing ye ... whoops! ... hey ... ten! First ten tonight! '

'Well done. You know, with your luck you ought to try roulette or blackjack.'

She shook her golden head. 'No, I'm not interested in those - only in the bandits. I adore them.'

'Do you play them ... at home?'

'Oh, sure. There are three at daddy's golf club and I knock hell out of 'em.'

'Won any jackpots there?'

'Eleven times ... but they're only ten bucks a time.'

'Well - it's better than playing golf.'

'Sure,' she laughed.

"Where *is* home?' I asked, pushing my luck.

She glanced up, really looking at me for the first time, her expression guarded, telling me I was asking too many questions. 'Vermont,' she answered, in a tone that added 'and that's your lot'.

'Oh, really? I'm from London.'

'Is that right?'

End of conversation.

A couple of pulls later she moved away - right away, over to the next bank of machines; rather pointedly, I felt. I was losing ground, losing her ... and I couldn't follow without arousing suspicion, not all the way over there. She might call the management, make a scene. I had to think of something to re-make the contact in a way she wouldn't mind. But what?

A jackpot! If I won a jackpot, that would ... don't be bloody ridiculous. It might take a month! Well, how about half a jackpot ...? Ten quarters ...? Five ...?'

I had it! A scheme so diabolical it left me quite breathless. Casually I strolled round the bank of machines to the one she'd just been playing ... popped in a quarter — pulled down the handle ... and *then* started throwing quarters into the tray!

'Hey ...! ' I laughed jubilantly. 'You won ten! '

She looked round, frowning at me. '*I* won ten? How come?'

'You left a quarter in the tray and I played it for you! '

She came over, hesitantly. 'Really?'

'No kidding - it was in the tray when I got here. Here ... give me your hand.'

'Oh, no ... I couldn't! It's not fair.'

'Certainly it's fair ... if you'd seen the quarter you'd have played it and won. Here ...' I opened her hand and dropped the quarters in.

'Well., that's very nice of you.'

'No, it isn't - it's a matter of principle. A fella doesn't go around pinching a lady's quarters ... Well, not *those* quarters.'

She laughed. 'Well, thank you ...'

'You know ... this could well be an omen - maybe we were destined to break the bank in partnership! You pop in the quarters and I yank the handle. Tobin and ... what's your name?'

'Telford.'

'I *like* it - Tobin and Telford - professional bank-busters. *Or* Telford and Tobin, I don't really mind. Come on, let's give it a whirl. Here ...' I handed her a quarter. 'Load one.'

With a shrug and a laugh she dropped the coin in the slot.

'Right ...' I said, flexing my fingers like a safe-cracker. 'Here comes the first jackpot!'

I took a grip on the handle, eased it half-way down, relaxed ... then gave a good yank.

'Note the technique, madam ...' I murmured as the fruits whirled round. 'It's known in the profession as the Tobin Faul- ter. I learned it from a barmaid in Piccadilly who could pull a head on a pint of bitter like soap suds.'

Crash!

Cherry ... cherry ... plum. Down shot five quarters!

'Success!' I laughed. 'Five hundred per cent profit first go! The world is ours, Telford - *ours,* I tell you!'

She was laughing like it was her birthday. In went the next quarter, down came the handle - and down into the tray rattled twenty-five quarters ! Unbelievable! She was ecstatic.

I glanced across at Stud and found him watching us with a beaming grin, patently happy to be back in the hunt.

'You want to go on?' I asked her.

'Well, sure ...' she frowned. 'Don't you?'

'Well ... I've got a feeling our luck may not hold on *every* quarter.'

'I've got a rule - never to take home any loose change. It's either jackpot or nothing!'

'And I'm sure the management wholly approve,' I grinned. 'O.K., partner - jackpot or nothing.'

It took us about half an hour to lose the lot but what a delightful half hour it was.

'Well, that's it,' I sighed, turning over the empty cup.

'Well, I think we did very well. Ten dollars usually lasts me about four minutes.'

'Hey, that's worth celebrating. Come on - I'll buy you a drink.'

'Oh,' she frowned, glancing at her watch. 'I'd love to ... but I'm expecting to meet someone at eleven.'

I died. 'Oh. Well ... couldn't you manage a quick one - it's only ten to?'

She gave it consideration, glancing over at the Gallery Bar. 'Mmm ... I'll be able to see them arrive from over there, won't I? Yes, all right - a quick one.'

In low spirits I walked with her to the bar. What a death blow. But then it had to be expected with a girl like her, there *had* to be a fella around somewhere.

She ordered Bacardi and coke and I gave her a cigarette.

'You know,' I said, lighting it for her and trying not to think about losing her in ten minutes, 'we've been business partners for over half an hour and I don't even know your first name. I'll have to have it for the letterheads, you know ...'

She laughed, 'It's Frenzy.'

'Frenzy?'

'A corruption of Francie - which is short for Francine. The kids at school started and it stuck - it's supposed to describe the way I dance.'

'And does it?'

'Well,' she laughed, 'I guess I do go kinda berserk at times.
I love dancing.'

'Now, that I'd like to see. I get a vision of riotous red hair and abandoned limbs.'

'You've been peeking,' she grinned.

'That I've gotta see.'

'And while we're on it - what's *your* first name, partner?'

'Russ ... short for Russell - and a corruption of Rust. And

that's how *I* dance - like I was rusted up.'

'Y'know, somehow I don't believe that.'

'Well, maybe I'm not *quite* so bad as that. I manage to get around.'

'I'm sure,' she smiled, raising a brow. 'That was a *very* cute trick you pulled back there, Tobin. Ten out of ten for quick thinking.'

'Mm?'

'Oho - and *can't* he play the innocent. O.K. - another ten out of ten for acting. No criticism, mind you - I rather liked it. It had ... *style* - very original - pretending I'd left a quarter in the tray.' She leaned towards me, fixing me with an accusing eye. 'Tobin ... I have never left a quarter in a bandit tray in my life! No way ... not ever ... *never!* '

I burst out laughing.

'Besides,' she went on, 'I counted the coins you gave me ... and there were twelve! You're a lousy con-man you know - you're not thorough.' She leaned back, smiling warmly. 'But I must admit I *did* like the style.'

The drinks arrived almost un-noticed.

'O.K.,' I said, holding up my hands, 'I admit everything. So - you knew all along! '

'Sure, I knew - we're not hicks in Vermont, you know.'

'I'm sure,' I laughed. 'Well, anyway, thank you ...'

'What for?'

'For going along with the gag.'

She smiled nicely. 'It was fun.'

'And now,' I said, 'I'm going to admit something else to you...'

'Oh...?'

'I stalked you shamelessly right across the room. I was sitting up here with a pal when I spotted you at the machines and just *had* to get close to you ... to smell your perfume ...' 'And ...?' she grinned.

'It made me go funny in the head.'

She laughed, delighted, then gave a start as something over by the door took her attention. 'Hey — there's the gang now! '

Frowning, I looked across. A dozen youngsters had come

in, all around Frenzy's age, late teens and early twenties. I turned back to her, puzzled. 'Is that ... are they who you're waiting for?'

'Sure - they're some of the gang off the boat.' Her eyes crinkled. 'You thought I was waiting for a fella, huh?'

'Well, of course.'

'I could tell - your chin hit the floor.'

'And you let it stay there.'

'Of course,' she said archly. 'It was my revenge for the trick you pulled. Come on - meet the gang ...'

'Me?'

'Sure, why not? Wouldn't you like to?'

'I'd love to, but...'

'What but?'

'Well, won't you be going off somewhere with them?'

'Yes. Come on!'

As we hurried across the casino I said, 'What's all this about a boat? Are *you* off one?'

'Yes - a student cruise boat. We've been to Europe for a month - educational sabbatical. We're on our way home now - get to Miami tomorrow.'

'Really? How many are there of you?'

'Three hundred and fifteen.'

'Good God. Have you had a good time?'

She only had time to grin before we reached the gang.

'Hi, everybody!' she called. 'Meet Russ Tobin - he's a pro one-arm bandit player.'

Everybody said 'Hi!' and continued talking among themselves.

They were a nice-looking bunch of kids with one or two fair pieces of crumpet among them including a rather well-endowed blonde in a yellow sweater who was now talking to Frenzy, making a report in excited tones.

'Listen - we found a place on Bay Street - real gropey dive but they sure groove. It's the Boogaloo.'

'Great - let's go, then.'

The blonde flashed a look at me. 'Is Russ coming?'

Frenzy turned to me. 'Sure he's coming, he *loves* dancing, don't you, partner?'

'Mm? What's all this?'

'We're going dancing - to the Boogaloo. You want to come?'

'Well, certainly ...'

'Right - let's go!'

'Oh ... well, listen ... I'd better nip over and tell my pal. He's a croupier over there. He's off duty at midnight and I'm sure he'd give his arm to join us. Would you mind?'

'Heck no ...' said Frenzy, turning to look across the room. 'Which one is he?'

I pointed. 'The ugly fella on the first roulette table.'

She peered across, a little too intently for my liking. 'Say, ... he's cute.'

'Well... not really.'

'Sure - let's go over and tell him ..

'Er ... well, I think you'd better stay here. *I'll* just nip over ... they don't like being interrupted while they're dealing.'

She shrugged. 'O.K. I'll be seeing him later.'

Mm, will you, I thought. I didn't like the sound of this. I was beginning to regret my generosity. I hurried across the floor and stood close until the play had ended, then Stud took a step away while the next bets were being placed.

'Any luck?' he grinned.

'Buckets of it! She's off a student cruise boat that's in dock for tonight. They're sailing to Miami tomorrow. Those are some of her mates over there ... not bad, huh?'

'Not bad at *all*,' he murmured, looking across the room, breaking into a lecherous grin. I turned to find Frenzy waving and smiling at him.

'And you can cut *that* out for a start, Ryder ...'

'She is *gorgeous*,' he breathed.

'And she's also mine - you do your own grafting. Listen, we're all off to the Boogaloo to do a spot of dancing. How about joining us when you're finished?'

'Try and stop me,' he grinned, eyes riveted on the far side of the room.

'Ryder...'

'Hm mm?'

'Your chips are getting cold. I'll see you later.'

'Count on it,' he said, wiggling his fingers at Frenzy.

I headed back to her.

'Hey, he's kinda sexy,' she smiled.

'Stud ...?'

She giggled. 'Is that his name? Kind of appropriate by the look of him.'

'He doesn't like girls,' I said, getting narked. 'He only waved because I asked him to ..

She gave me an old-fashioned glower. *He doesn't like girls?* What is he - queer or something?'

'Well ... no ... no, he's straight enough but he just doesn't bother with them. Too keen on his hobby.'

'Oh? What's that?'

'He's a taxidermist ... stuffs things. Spends all his spare time doing it.'

'I'll just bet,' she grinned, taking my arm as we all moved off.

The Boogaloo is an 'atmosphere' joint - which means you can't see your hand in front of your face even in the well-lit parts. They must have saved a fortune on decoration.

There is an atmosphere bar of scrubbed wood, an atmosphere dance floor, two snogs wide and one grope long, and several atmosphere alcoves, blacker than a coal-hole, with couches on which all the serious fornication takes place.

The gang hit the place like a tornado and headed straight for the dance floor to get the blood moving. Soon everyone was grooving, especially Frenzy, who was doing four times more work than the rhythm demanded and was really something to see. Everything was flying and bouncing and shaking in quadruple time, her hair swirling like a bull-fighter's cape, and I was enjoying the sexy spectacle so much I forgot my own dancing and concentrated on her.

When the record finished she threw back her head, gasping, *'Oh,* that was great ... come on, let's get a drink.'

Most of the gang had by this time taken over one of the

alcoves and we joined them - or rather attempted to. And after crashing into a table, treading on somebody's toe, thumping somebody else in the ear with an elbow, I found myself hurtling backwards into a black abyss and sank deep into marshmallow cushions three feet below.

A nice-smelling body dropped down beside me.

'Is that you?' I enquired.

'Sure, it's me - but who's that?'

'Me.'

'Incredible. Don't go to the can without me, we may never meet again. Hey, out there, who's got the drinks?'

A glass of something was pushed into my hand. 'Thanks,' I said.

'You're welcome.'

'Who said that?'

'Liz.'

'Thanks, Liz.'

I sniffed at the glass and took a sip. It tasted like battery acid.

A hand crept on to my knee. 'Cheers,' said Frenzy.

'I wish I could see your face.'

'Why?'

'I want to kiss it.'

There was a pause. 'Do you, now?'

'Very much.'

Another pause, then her hand took mine and lifted it to her cheek. 'It's here.'

I leaned towards her, meeting her warm, soft mouth. She let me play for a moment then broke away. 'That's enough, I don't know you.'

'The name's Tobin.'

'Tobin who?'

She was irresistible ... her perfume, warmth, just too much.

I slipped my arm around her, brought her close, expecting her to resist but she didn't.

'You smell wonderful,' I murmured, nuzzling her ear. 'What's it called?'

'It's called "Down Boy!"'

'A howling contradiction.'

'I ... don't know what you mean,' she said innocently, putting her hand on my thigh.

'Be careful,' I warned her.

'Why?'

'A millimetre higher and I cannot be held responsible for my actions.'

Up went her hand. I plunged, bit her neck, her ear.

'Hey ...' she chuckled.

'Mm?'

I pulled her down and across me, holding her tight, and she came willingly, finding my mouth. After an hour or so she eased me away, panting breathlessly, 'I . .. think we'd ... better dance! '

'You do?'

'I *know* we'd better! '

With enormous difficulty we got up off the couch and squeezed through the gang out on to the floor where we immediately resumed total confrontation. She was a glutton - one of nature's real kissers, and things were fast reaching flashpoint when a thump on the back shocked me out of Happyland and had me whirling to face the aggressor, ready to kill.

There was no one there.

Suddenly Frenzy was gone from my arm. I whirled again, coming face to face with Ryder, grinning his lips off.

'Gentlemen's Excuse Me,' he explained, turning to Frenzy.

'Hi... nice to see you again.'

'Ry ... der! ' I howled.

'Stud Ryder's the name,' he oozed at her. 'What's yours?'

'Frenzy Telford,' she grinned, highly amused by his puerile humour. 'Where did you appear from?'

'The casino. I ran out, quit my job - just to be with you. Couldn't wait another moment. You captured my heart from across the room - so I gave all my chips away and ran all the way here.'

'How very sweet,' she smiled, cocking an eye in my

direction. 'But ... I thought you didn't like girls.'

'Huh! Who said that ... who *said* that?' He turned and glared at me. 'Tobin!'

'So ...' I shrugged, 'this *isn't* one of your queer nights.'

'Rat!'

'Fink!'

Frenzy laughed and held out her arm to me. 'Come and join us!'

I joined them.

'Listen ...' she said, 'I've just had a great idea. How'd you fellas like to come to a fancy-dress party?'

'Mm?' Stud's brows shot up. 'Party?'

'Where? When? Whose?' I asked.

'On the boat and right now. It's our last night of the cruise and tonight everything goes. We sail at three tomorrow and nobody plans going to bed until we hit Miami - well... not alone, anyway.'

'Fantastic!' gasped Stud.

'Terrific!' said I.

'There's ... only one thing .. .'

'Oh,' we chorused.

'One teensy weensy drawback ..

'And what's that?' I asked glumly.

'You're not allowed on board.'

'Oh ...' Stud and I looked at each other, just a teensy weensy bit puzzled.

'But ...' she went on cannily, 'there are ways. Come - let us confer with the others.'

Stud and I remained at the entrance to the alcove while she disappeared from view to chat with the gang.

'Well, well,' he chuckled at me. 'And what do we have here, Russell?'

'I know what *I* had before you broke it up, you bum.'

'I felt it my duty,' he said gravely. 'Such goings on in a pubic ... er, public place constitute a serious hazard to youth. But, listen - what d'you reckon to this party?'

'*I'm* all for it, Ryder - I've got some unfinished business to attend to.'

'Yeah, well, you're all fixed up. You reckon there'll be

plenty of spare there?'

'Huh! Since when did that trouble the Pied Piper of Paradise? If there isn't, you'll just barge in and filch some other poor sod's, I'm sure - I've seen it happen.'

'True, true.'

'Here she comes ! '

Frenzy emerged from the Black Hole of Bay Street, wincing at the blinding gloom. 'O.K. - it's all fixed! We're leaving right now to go back on board. You two come with us and wait on the dock. We've got an *ingenious* plan!'

Ten minutes later Stud and I were standing alone in the deep shadow of a warehouse, not fifty yards from the gangway leading up into the side of the huge white boat. The kids had just run up it in high spirits (all part of the plan!) and promised to be back for us within fifteen minutes with fancy-dress costumes in which we were to be smuggled on board, the excitement of the plot appealing to our over-rested libidos enormously and to mine in particular - after the session with Frenzy in the Boogaloo. That was business just *begging* to be finished and I could concentrate on nothing else.

The boat at this close range was a stirring sight - a towering, glittering city of light, throbbing with life and music, coming from a stem sun-deck. Fairy-lights had been strung out along this deck and we could see several people in fancy-dress leaning against the rail, drinking and chattering. To us, as onlookers, it was an exciting, inviting spectacle and we couldn't wait to get up there.

'How many students *are* there on the cruise?' asked Stud, craning his neck to watch the activity on the sun-deck.

'Frenzy said three hundred and fifteen.'

'Good God ... and half of them women? Boy, I'll bet there's been some goings on going on at night ... musical bunks and "Guess who's sleeping in *my* cabin! " I can't altogether see our Frenzy going to bed with The Rise and Fall of the Roman Empire. The Rise and Fall bit yes,...'

"Will you cut out this *"our* Frenzy" terminology, Ryder? I do not recall ever inviting you to share any part of my bird.

But I'd lay money you're right about the musical bunks. Three hundred and fifteen lusty kids close-closeted in there for a month! The mind throbs .. .'

'Hey!' He gave a start, peering at the top of the gangway. 'Here comes something ... it is them isn't it?'

I couldn't be sure. The first three figures on the gangway were dressed as a cavalier, a Zulu and a cowboy. Down they ran, hesitantly, throwing glances behind them as though being chased. Suddenly a horse's head appeared through the exit hatch! It was a pantomime horse, white with spots, the sort that holds two people. It paused in the doorway, peering down quizzically at the three fleeing figures, then began to give chase.

Behind it, now, the rest of the gang quickly appeared, ran down after it, smacking it on the rump with a whip, whooping and yelling, making a heck of a noise.

The first three characters reached the quay and ran on, heading straight for us, then came the horse, closely followed by the others, all in costume. I spotted Frenzy, looking wildly sexy in a see-through Eastern costume with bare mid-riff and damn-near everything else.

'Quickly - out!' she commanded, reaching us the same time as the horse.

Zzzzziiiippppp! ! The horse fell apart at the Velcro seam, revealing two lads dressed in gypsy costume.

'Quickly in! ' she commanded Stud and me.

Eh!

I gaped at Stud and he started grinning. 'Yeah - crazy!'

'Hurry up!' urged Frenzy. 'We've got to make it seem like a chase round the warehouse! '

'Right - heads or tails?' Stud asked me.

I shrugged - fool that I am.

'O.K. - I'll take the head,' he said, holding his hand out for the forelegs.

'Any knack to this?' I asked the gypsy who was handing the rear legs to me.

'Yeah,' he gasped, 'learn to suffocate - the rest is up to the guy in front.'

Quickly we climbed into the daft costume. I caught Stud

round the waist, bent down, the top of my head against his backside, the "skin" was pulled over my head and the Velcro was fastened.

'Hey, it's dark in here ! ' Stud protested, pulling on the head.

'It's not so flaming light in here, either!' I said. 'Now, you just watch where you're going, Ryder - because wherever it is, I go with you! Stay out of that bleeding harbour! '

'Roger, Hindlegs! '

'Giddup! ' Crack! Someone gave me a whack on the arse with the whip and we were off at a flat-out gallop, Stud shouting out the leg sequence. 'Left... right .. left. .. right - hey, terrific! '

'Might ... be ... for you ... Ryder ... but it's hell ... back here!'

'Stay with it, Hindlegs - only another seven furlongs to go - and don't forget - your *oats* are waiting for you at the end! '

'Ugh! Ryder ... can you see where you're going?'

'Not a damn thing - someone's towing me by the nose!'

Crack!

'Ouch! Who's the nutter with the bleeding whip - I'll kill him!'

'It's me! ' said Frenzy.

CRACK!!

'*Who's* a nutter! ?'

'Not you ... not you ... ooh ... ow! ' I mis-stepped with Stud and he caught me a kick on the shin. 'Ow, Jesus Christ, that hurt ...! '

'Stop hopping, man, you're pulling my trousers down!'

'It's all right for you, Foreskin ... ! '

'Hang on! ' called a voice, 'here we go up the gangway! '

Clatter ... clump ... thud ... up the steeply-rising boards. Then I tripped over one of the cross-treads. Down I went! Stud came with me, cracking his knee. 'OW! '

'Get up ... get up! ' Frenzy whispered. 'They're watching us in the hatch!'

'The head's falling off!' gasped Stud. 'I can't see!'

'You don't have to! I'll lead you! Come on - get up!'

We staggered to our feet and started up the ramp again at a fast limp.

'Have we got to stay in this flaming thing all *night?*' I hissed at Frenzy.

'No! Only till you get to my cabin - we've got some more costumes for you there!'

'Thank God for that - me back's killing me!'

'Ssssh! We're nearly at the top!'

The steep gradient suddenly flattened and we were inside the boat.

'Now ... GO!' whispered Frenzy.

Stud plunged away, dragging me with him. A cheer went up, then ... whoomf! Some blithering idiot landed on my back.

'Yyyiiiipppeee! Ride em, cowboy!'

'Gerrof, yuh daft sod!'

My knees buckled ... down came Stud's trousers - round his knees. He staggered ... pitched forward ... and with a howl of dismay down he went, me on top of him and the bloke on my back on top of me.

Another loud cheer went up. Hands tugging at us urgently. Frenzy whispered frantically, 'Get up, get up ... there are teachers all around you!'

I was hauled to my feet. Stud got to his and we were off again, completely out of kilter, me tripping over Stud's feet every few steps.

'Stairs!' Frenzy shouted.

Clatter ... thud ... clump. Like a couple of blind drunks we fell down them, then Stud broke into a trot down a straight, me going like hell to keep up with him. Suddenly he turned a corner so sharply I kept going and slammed into a wall.

'STUD!' I gasped. *Tell* me when you're turning!'

'How the hell did *I* know - the eyeholes are under my chin!'

Then he stopped so abruptly I butted him hard in the ass. 'Whoops! Watch it, Russell!'

'Quick - in here!' ordered Frenzy.

We clattered over a threshold and the door was shut. Zzzziiippp! Light blinded me. I creaked upright, easing my screaming back. 'Do we have to go through all *that* again to get *off* the boat? I think I'll jump!'

We were in a large cabin bulging with kids putting the final touches to their costumes. A Roman gladiator was tying his toga together with string and a skinny Tarzan was sticking false hair on his chest with nail varnish. In a corner the busty blonde I'd seen in the casino was trying to squeeze her billowing boobs into a sarong four sizes too small and giving us a right old eyeful in the process, though no one else seemed to notice.

'Now ...' said Frenzy, eyeing Stud and me for size. 'Let's see what we can find you two. We need something that will hide you, of course ...' She crossed to a huge wicker basket and began pulling out costumes. 'Ah! Here - that'll do for you, Stud ...' she threw him a pair of breeches ... frilly shirt ... cocked hat ... a mask. 'Dick Turpin - the mask will hide you O.K.?'

'Great,' said Stud, climbing out of the forelegs.

'Super,' I lisped at him. 'You'll look a right Dick ... Turpin in that lot.'

'Jealousy, sweetie ... will get you a thick ear.'

'Bitch!'

'Madam!'

'Right - just *try* and get a dance with me!'

'Now ...' Frenzy was saying contemplatively, looking me up and down, '... what can we find for Russ.' She turned to the others, 'Hey, you guys ... got anything to hide Russ in?'

'Yeah,' said a small red-headed bloke, 'the armour - under the bunk.'

'Yeah!' exclaimed Frenzy. 'Just the thing.'

The red-headed guy dived under the bunk and pulled out a full suit of plastic armour.

'There y'go,' said Frenzy. 'Get into that.'

I must say the idea rather appealed to me - for about three minutes. It was as she snapped the last piece of breast-plate into place that I began to have serious doubts. I felt like a bad accident case sealed in plaster.

'Now the helmet ...' she said, delighted with the result.

On it went, almost severing my ears as she thumped it into place.

'There - how's it feel?' she laughed, lifting the visor and peering in.'

'Terrific,' I said between clenched teeth. 'Like I've been starched.'

'You'll probably win. And how's Dick Turpin doing?'

'I'm doing great,' grinned Stud, slipping his mask into place and putting his tricorn on.

'You look beautiful - very dashing,' she smiled, far too warmly for my liking. 'O.K. - let's go. Russ ... pull down your visor.'

I tried . .. but the plastic was too stiff. I couldn't bend my arm to reach my face. 'I can't... get at it.'

'I'll do it.'

Clang!

'But ... how do I get it open again?' I asked, my voice booming around the helmet.

'I'll be around,' she promised. 'Right - let's go!'

She pulled open the door and out I marched - stiff-legged, stiff armed and stiff everything else. I was rigid!

'This is bloody ridiculous,' I muttered to Stud who was swaggering along in style, quite fancying himself as a highwayman, pistols in his belt and hat at a jaunty angle. 'Hey ...! What happens when I want a pee?!'

'Ask the galley for a can-opener!' he chortled.

'Very funny ... and how the hell do I *dance* in this thing?'

'With great difficulty, I'd have thought,' he cackled. 'Jeez, you look a dilly.'

'I feel a right bloody narna, mate.'

We reached the stairs and that was it. I couldn't bend my knees to get a foot up. Stud was half-way up with Frenzy and I was still at the bottom.

'Hey, you' two ...!'

They turned - and burst out laughing.

Then a bunch of kids was coming up behind me. They saw my predicament, lifted me bodily and plonked me down at the top.

'There y'go, Sir Lancelot - next time stay outta the rain!'

Frenzy and Stud took my arms and helped me along, killing themselves laughing.

'Aw, this is ridiculous,' I groaned. 'There's something wrong with the joints - I can't bend my knees!'

'But you look fantastic!' enthused Frenzy. 'You'll probably win first prize.'

'But I'll have to stand up all night!'

'Don't worry — a couple of belts of our fruit punch and your troubles will disappear.'

Fruit punch!' I winced, suddenly realizing that, of course, no booze would be allowed on board!

'Like you never tasted,' she grinned.

Stud went ahead to open a door then, with Frenzy, helped me over the raised threshold. 'Easy does it, old timer ...'

'Ryder ..

We emerged on to the sun-deck that was crowded with kids all knocking themselves out to some wild music coming from the tannoy system. It was real bedlam.

To our left, white-uniformed crew members were dispensing the fruit punch from six huge bowls arranged down a long, cloth-covered table. Beyond this was another table with a mountain of cold snacks on it. Expense had obviously not been spared.

'Quite a party,' I said to Frenzy, shouting over the racket and deafening myself in the helmet.

'Yeah, this is the big night!' she agreed. 'Tonight they convince us it's all been worth three thousand bucks so we can go home and tell mummy and daddy! Come on - let's get a glass of that junk!'

We crossed to the drinks table and picked up big glass cups of the punch. Stud sipped his and made a face. 'Oh, boy ... takes you right back to childhood.'

'Hold it,' said Frenzy, looking round the deck. 'O.K. - come this way.'

She led us across the deck to where a cluster of kids were drinking and laughing. As she got close she said something to them and they parted, revealing in their midst a bloke dressed in full Scottish Highlander regalia - bagpipes under his arm. Stud and I followed her into the group and were suddenly surrounded by them again. Frenzy turned to us, grinning mysteriously. 'Vodka O.K. for you two?'

'Vodka!' we chorused. 'Yes, terrific!'

She turned to Angus and nodded. 'O.K. - shoot!'

Down came his blow-pipe. A squeeze on the bag and a sweet stream of Russian ruin shot into her fruit punch.

She backed away, taking a sip and gasping. 'Next...!'

'In ... genious,' grinned Stud, stepping forward. 'And they say higher education doesn't pay.'

'Serves 'em right for teaching us to use our initiative,' she said, taking another gulp. 'Oh, *boy,* that is fruity!'

When Stud and I had received our shots we joined Frenzy in a stroll round the deck, surveying the scene.

'How many outlets are there?' Stud asked her. 'Just the one?'

'Heck, no ... three.' She nodded. 'See the Greek goat-herd with the goatskin bag over his shoulder ... he's carrying about a gallon . ..' She looked around the deck. 'And the guy dressed as the gasoline pump? He's got another load.'

'All vodka?' I asked.

'Sure - no smell, no hangovers. We've fooled 'em for a month.'

'Er ... if it's not too much trouble - would one of you *please* open my visor - I'm gasping for a drink.'

'We'll find you a straw,' laughed Frenzy, yanking the thing up. 'You can stick it through the slit.'

I took a good long gulp, nodded my head and the thing clanged shut. It was like being slammed in solitary.

'Er, as it's impossible to smoke,' I said to Frenzy with barely concealed cynicism, 'would you care to dance?'

'I'll try anything once,' she laughed, lumbering Stud with our drinks.

It was ridiculous. Stiff-legged and stiffer-armed I clumped around the deck like Frankenstein's monster, treading on her toes eight times a minute.

'Ow!'

'Oh, I'm sorry, Frenzy ..

'So am I - about the costume. It was a lousy idea, wasn't

it?'

'It was a very good idea, it's not your fault. Look - you have a dance with Stud. I'll find a quiet corner and get some air.'

Stud, the skunk, was delighted. 'We'll drop by from time to time and drip-feed you! ' he hooted as he took the floor with her.

I watched them disappear, already engrossed in each other, and I headed for the drinks table to find a straw.

'Hey, mac ... will yuh pass me anudder one a dem tings?'

I turned - and came face-to-face with a full-grown gorilla, its face so grotesque, mouth half-open in a terrifying snarl, fangs savagely bared, that I backed into the table and slopped punch ail over the place.

'Wha's the matter?' chuckled the guy inside. 'Ain't you ever seen a gorilla at a party before?'

'N ... Not usually this early.'

He gave a chesty chortle, raised his hand and stuffed a corned beef sandwich down the gaping red hole.

'Pass me one of dem glasses, will yuh?'

I did so and from nowhere he produced a straw, stuck one end in the cup, the other down the hole, and sucked hard and long, emptying the glass. 'Man, oh man, that's lousy.'

Funny, I thought - doesn't he know about the vodka?
, 'Er, where did you get the straw - I could use one myself?' 'End of the table - back of the punch bowl.' 'Thanks.'

I moved off, collected a straw, stuck it through a slit in the visor, took a monstrous slug and began to feel much better.

'Take it easy ... all that lousy fruit'll kill yuh.'

I turned. It was the gorilla. It looked like I'd collected a pet.

'Are you ... a student?' I asked it.

'The hell,' he cackled. 'I'm a stoker. How 'bout you?'

I felt I could trust him. 'No, I'm, er, sort of a stowaway. Some of the kids smuggled me on board. That's why I'm wearing this outfit - what's your excuse?'

He chuckled again. 'Me ...? I reckon I can get me a piece of sweet ass wearin' this thing. Some a these little pigeons really fly - y'know?'

'Is that right?'

'Listen ...' he reached for a sausage and stuffed it down the hole, 'I bin wid dese wing-dings a goddam month an' I should know! There's bin more shaftin' on dis tub than in Hamboig on navy pay-night. De monkeys is doin' it all over the place - in the paint-locker ... the engine room. I even caught two a dem takin' a knee-trembler in a vent-shaft.'

'No kidding,' I laughed. 'But do you need the costume to get it?'

He cackled again. 'Sure I need it - I'm uglier than the gorilla! ' He swung round and faced the crowd of dancing kids. 'One of them cuckoos is bound ta fancy screwing a gorilla ... an' I reckon it's de red broad in the Minnie Ha Ha get-up. She ain't bin ta bed solo since she came on board. Well, I'll be seein' yuh.'

'Best of luck.'

'Sure thing.'

He waddled off, stuffing a pork pie down his throat and scratching his armpit with unconscious realism.

I turned back to the table for my drink and almost collided with Scarlett O'Hara in pink-and-white pinafore dress, long lace pantaloons, pink ribbons in her long plaits. She was a nice little thing with big, vacuous blue eyes which were pelmeted by eighteen pairs of false-eyelashes which she now batted at me so hard I could feel the draught. Her first slurred words confirmed what her eyes had already told me - she was shickered.

"Hi, in there - and who are you? Is that you, Billy John?'

I put on my Clark Gable voice. 'No, Scarlett, it's me - Rhet Butler. Don't you recognize me?'

She giggled and hiccoughed. 'Well, sho' 'nough, Rhet, baby - but why you hidin' in there?'

'I can't get the damned thing off, Scarlett - mah ears is too big.'

She giggled again, wrinkling her nose. 'Open up an' let

me have a look at you, who-ever-you-are.'

'I can't do that, either,' I said seriously. 'My arms won't reach - look.'

'Here, let me ...' She yanked up the visor and she peered at me, mystified, fluttering her rug-fringe lashes. 'Do I know you?'

'Nope,' I said, feeling suddenly quite rosy from the voddie and happy to have found a playmate.

'Hey ...' she said suspiciously, 'you're not one of us!'

'Nope - I'm a stowaway. Sir Russell Tobin - at your service ... dragons slain, damsels rescued, round tables sat at. Knight work a speciality ... sorry about that.'

'You're English! Well, how beautiful!'

'Hm?'

'How *gorgeous* ... I just love Englishmen ... *adore* Tom Jones. Russ ... Corbin, was it?'

'Nearly right. Tobin. T for Tobin, O for Obin, B for Bin, I for In and N as in Nutter. And what's your lovely name?'

'Eloise Byrd - with a Y.'

'Enchanting. Eloise, love - have you got a few minutes to spare?'

She fluttered those things again. 'I've got all night.'

'Better still. I need help, Eloise ... I can't smoke, I can't eat...
I'm as helpless as a turtle on its back.'

'Mah pleasure ...' she smiled, focusing on a big sausage and reaching for it. 'Here, honey ... take a bite.'

I took one, noticing with what relish she watched the action, then she transferred the banger to her own mouth and slowly, deliberately, sank her little white teeth into it, wrinkling her nose sexily at me as she devoured the succulent mouthful.

'Mmmm ... scrumptious,' she breathed. 'There is simply *nothing* like a big ... meaty ... sausage.'

'Nothing,' I gulped.

'Would you like a drink, honey?'

'Please.'

She lifted the straw to my lips and watched me drink with droop-lidded concentration, weaving nicely from side to side. Then, when I'd finished, she drained the glass, plonked it down on the table, picked up a full one and peered across the deck, finding the guy dressed like a petrol pump.

'Sssh, stay here,' she said, finger at her lips. 'I shall return.'

She was back in under the minute, sucking the top off the overflowing glass as she arrived.

'Here, have a drink ...'

While I was taking it she beamed a joyful, alcoholic smile and said, 'I... am having a *lovely* time - *now,* thanks to you.'

'Why me?'

' 'Cos you're nice. *But* ... are *you* having a lovely time?'

'I'm having a smashing time ... *now,* thanks to you.'

'That's nice - have a drink.'

'I'm getting loaded.'

'Good! We'll get loaded together - partners, right down the line. You know ... you look *awfully* uncomfortable in that thing ..

'Funny you should say that..

'Wouldn't you like to take it off?'

'My most fervent wish, Eloise, is to take this off.'

She shrugged. 'O.K. - so take it off! '

'How can I? They'd clap me in irons ... kick me off the boat...'

'Mmm,' she went, then she brightened. 'Aha ... I have an idea ...'

'You do?'

'Huh - listen, I know a place - a nice, little hidie-hole. We could have a party all by ourselves, what d'you say? Would you like to see my liddle hidie-hole?'

'Eloise ... nothing would give me greater pleasure.'

'O.K. - come on.'

She dropped my visor, took my hand and away we trudged. Down ... down ... down we went, staircase after staircase, deep into the bowels of the ship, leaving the passenger accommodation far behind, creeping along the unglamorous passageways of the cargo sections, finally halting at a heavy steel door marked 'Bedding

Stores'.

Shushing me to be quiet and grinning mischievously, she pushed up the securing bar, pulled open the door and waved me in. She followed and closed the door, putting us in darkness so black that my head swam. I went dizzy, staggered, fell against a soft yielding wall and then the light came on. I was leaning against a stack of mattresses.

'Hey ... you all right, honey?' she said anxiously, coming to me.

I nodded. 'Yes ... it's this damned helmet ... gives me claustrophobia. That and the vodka.'

'Sure - come on, let's get you outta this contraption.'

She led me round the stack of mattresses to a cleared space between several stacks and eased off my helmet. I came out of it with enormous relief and a face streaming with sweat.

'For gosh ... *sakes* - just look at you! It must've bin *murder* in there. You feel better now?'

'A bit dizzy,' I laughed; shaking my head. 'Phew! '

'Come on - get the rest of it off and have a lie down. We can lay a couple of these mattresses down.'

I ripped off the armour then my jacket and tie, discovering my shirt was wet through, so I took that off and hung it on one of the stacks. 'By golly, that feels better.'

'Here - give me a hand with one of these, honey ...'

We pulled two mattresses down and laid them side by side, making a cozy bed.

'There - how's that?' she grinned.

'That - is beautiful.'

'Sit down ... take your shoes off ... make yourself comfortable, I'll be back in a minute.'

Puzzled, I did as I was told, sank gratefully to the mattresses and was sitting there with my eyes closed, my back against the stack, when she returned carrying a bottle of booze and two beakers.

'Ready-mixed,' she grinned excitedly. 'I keep it hidden in the corner.'

'Good God, you're really organized. How did you stumble on this place.'

'I looked for it,' she said, with surprising forthrightness. 'I can't stand crowds.'

'Me, neither.'

'Rubbing shoulders with three hundred and fourteen kooks for a month could drive a woman to drink,' she laughed, then knelt down, poured a couple, corked the bottle and sat cross-legged at the side of me, releasing a sigh of enormous contentment.

'Oh ... *boy,* this is nice ... cheers.'

'Cheers,' I grinned. 'Won't we be disturbed?'

She shook her head. 'Not a chance. Have you got a cigarette, honey?'

'Sure.'

I gave her one, lit one for myself.

'Great shame you weren't with us from the start,' she said regretfully. 'That woulda been nice.'

'You think so?' I grinned.

'Sure ...' she looked at me, kicking me under the heart with the gleam in her eye. 'Don't you think so?'

'Yes,' I croaked. 'I think maybe it would.'

We came together, gazing at each other. Her mouth was warm and yielding, languid with need. Her hand came up to touch my shoulder then stayed to probe and knead. She was coming to the boil fast. She broke away, murmuring in my ear, 'I want to hold all of you ...' and was suddenly on her feet, ripping away the costume.

Trousers abandoned, I reached for her. She lay over me, velvet soft and cuddly, smiling down at me. 'I ... don't want to do it yet ... I want to play ... get really high ... O.K.?'

'Sure,' I laughed.

'Oh ... why does it always happen like this - on the last night? We could have had the whole damn month.'

'Well, never mind. We'll just have to make up for it.'

'Yes,' she said earnestly. 'We will.'

She leaned across and picked up her drink, offered me a sip, took a good one herself and set the glass down again.

The party had begun.

CHAPTER FOURTEEN

'Russ...?'

Her voice was a strange ethereal thing, too distant, too nebulous to fully pluck me from sleep. It had been a heck of a party ... a rapturous cavort with a lovely lass, in itself not capable of bashing me flat but as an adjunct to all the other high old times I'd endured in the past few days quite sufficient to do just that.

I was out, gone, smashed, blitzed, pooped, destroyed, and couldn't have managed a moment's concern if the boat had been sinking.

I answered with a groan but was already on my way back down to blissful limbo before her next word.

'I've gotta go, honey ..

'Mmm ...?'

'They do a night check on the cabins.'

'Mmm.'

'You going to stay here a while?'

'Mmm.'

'Don't over-sleep now ...

'Uh uh.'

'You O.K. to get off the boat?'

'Mmm.'

'It was a great party, honey ... thank you.'

'Than' you, ba ... by ...'

'You sure, you're all right?'

'Fine ... fine.'

'O.K. ...'

And that was all. Sometime later I moved in sleep and opened an eye, saw before me a beckoning sea of cozy mattresses and lowered myself into it - totally. I was gone.

I awoke with a start, sober and alert. Something was wrong ... something was different. The lighting was different! Time, I knew, had passed - a great deal of it! With pounding heart I got to my feet, staggered dizzily, fell against the stack of mattresses then stepped round it and saw the porthole. Sunlight was streaming in!

Daylight! Panic battered me. I had to get off the boat!

I dived for my clothes, felt for my watch in the pocket. Eleven o'clock! Ridiculous ... I couldn't have slept that long. The watch had stopped! I stuck it in my ear, quailing at its tick. It flaming well *was* eleven o'clock!

Oh, my *God* ... I rammed the shirt over my head, pulled on my trousers, jacket, jammed the tie in the pocket, pulled on my socks inside out, trod into my shoes and staggered across the mattresses to the door.

I listened at it ... eased up the securing bar and opened it a crack. Now I could hear sounds but very distant. I peered out of the door. The corridor was empty. I slipped out, closing the door and feeling a touch easier. Now all I had to do was get off the bleeding boat!

I started off to the right, trembling with apprehension, and within a few yards stopped dead at the sound of whistling coming from an open doorway. Whipping out my handkerchief, I buried my face in it and started off at a fast clip, intending to flash past the door, but as I reached it a steward carrying a tray came hurtling out and we almost collided.

'Whoops! sorry, sir ...' he said, very astonished.

'Sor ride,' I muttered, face down, hidden by the hanky.

His eyes narrowed suspiciously. I must have looked a right crumpled sight. 'Er ... you all right, sir ...?'

'Yes, fide, thang you.'

'Boy, oh, boy - that's a beaut of a cold you've got there. Heck of a way to finish a trip, hm? Er ... were you lookin' for someone, sir ...?'

He was *very* suspicious.

'No - just walking. Er ... whad deck is dis, steward?'

'Deck? It's "E" Deck, sir ...'
'Danks berry butch.'
'You're welcome .. .'

I hurried on, knowing he was watching me, and thankfully turned the corner out of his sight. 'E' Deck ... mmm, but which deck was the exit hatch on? I came to another corner and turned right, went along again and had to turn right again, went along that and ran smack into the same bloody steward.

'Well, well ... hello *again,* sir,' he cracked. 'Get lost?'

'Er ... yes,' I laughed. I couldn't keep this handkerchief act up much longer, he really *would* get suspicious. I'b looking for the deck where the gangway is - where we come on board.'

'The entrance hatch ! ' he laughed. 'Heck, that's on "C" Deck, sir - two decks up.'

'Oh. Well, danks berry butch again.'

'Boy, you got a real streamer, ain't you - your eyes look terrible.'

'Yeah, I feel lousy. I think I'll go to bed.'

He gave me a strangely quizzical look, 'Bed, sir .. .'

'Well, danks a lot...'

I gave a damn good sneeze that made him back away and then I was off, reached the end of the corridor and turned left, broke into a half-run down a long corridor and slowed as I came into a crowded vestibule, feeling, incredibly, safer among all, these people.

Locating the stairs, I pushed through the crowd, still covering my face with the hanky, ran up the first flight, then the second and emerged at the 'D' Deck foyer which was also crowded. An older man, presumably a teacher, was addressing about fifty kids who were all talking together and taking no notice of him.

'Now, I must impress upon you that *all* your luggage must be labelled correctly. It'll be no use complaining that things have gone astray ..

I squeezed around the edge of the crowd, meeting nobody's eye, and beat it up the next flight of stairs, emerging once again into mayhem. The 'C' vestibule was choked with kids, teachers, luggage, ship's officers, stewards. I slipped around them ... 'Aaaa .. . tshoo! ' and reached a side-wall close to the gaping hatch from which the blessed gangway plunged to freedom.

Oh, how good it felt to smell fresh air ... see the sunlight. But how was I going to get down it without attracting attention !

Handkerchief over my face, I did a surreptitious recce of the situation. There was, thank God, no one guarding the gangway, but even so - with sailing time drawing close anyone going down it would be spotted immediately. How was I going to *do* it?

The idea came when I spotted the abandoned newspaper on a ledge. Brashness! I'd take the bull by the proverbials and simply stroll down the gangway, nonchalantly reading the newspaper. If anyone challenged me I'd ignore them, carry on reading and walking as though I hadn't heard them, then, when I hit the quay, I'd take off ... run like hell! It was no distance at all across the quay and into Rawson Square - a couple of hundred yards at the most. And once I reached the square I'd be swallowed up instantly by the crowds in the Straw Market.

The plan was set. With parched throat and trembling legs I strolled across to the newspaper, picked it up and quickly opened it to hide my face, then strolled nonchalantly back, changing course for the escape hatch as though needing better light to read by.

I reached it ... my foot was actually touching the gangway. I searched the crowd ... no one was taking a blind bit of notice of me. It was all clear ... all systems go! All I had to do was step on to the gangway and take off. Well ... here goes - on the count of three! One ... two ... THREE! GO !

I couldn't move; I was stuck, paralyzed, sick with fright! Go on, you berk - move! Just step up and keep moving! No one gives a damn about you. Go on ... take that first step ... NOW!

I took it. I was actually on the gangway ... second step ... third step ... fourth ... I was through the hole! Sunlight hit me, warm and comforting. Clomp ... clomp ... clomp ... eyes glued to the paper I thumped down, positive that four hundred pairs of eyes were on me. But nothing happened. I was well clear of the ship ...! I was going to make it! Tenth step ... eleventh ... twelfth ... I was more than a third of the way down ... fifteenth ... sixteenth ... seventeenth ... more than halfway ! Whatever happened now I was going to make it! I could run for it ... run like hell for the market. Never again! No more mad ideas for me! I was going to play it safe, keep it cozy, stay on my own comforting doorstep ...

'Hey, you down there ...! '

Oh, Jesus! The voice bellowed out of the hatch, clutching my vitals, freezing my blood.

'Hey, you on the gangway ... STOP! '

Clomp ... clomp ... clomp ... I moved faster, driven by shrivelling fear.

'HEY ...! YOU READING THE PAPER! STOP ...! WHERE D'YOU THINK YOU'RE GOING!'

Home, mate - as fast as these rubbery legs will carry me! Clompity ... clompity ... clomp! I hurled the paper aside, all pretence abandoned, and fled down the last few feet of gangway. The quay rushed up to meet me and I hit it on the flat-out run.

Now a barrage of irate voices beat down on me. 'STOP THAT MAN! STOP HIM! ! '

In a blind, panic-stricken gallop I hared across the wharf, heart bursting, sight blurred but not too blurred to see a uniformed figure come charging out of a wooden hut and head towards me at a hell of a lick. A cop! He was a huge Bahamian cop ... coming at me heaven's hard and ... my God! ... reaching for his holster on the run! He was pulling out his gun ...! Pointing it at me ... taking aim! '

'STOP RIGHT THERE - Y'HEAR!'

By *God* I stopped ... almost fell down, shaking, trembling ... no strength at all. I'd confess! What could they get me for? ! Illegal boarding of a cruise boat for a party, that was all! Nothing! I'd get a ticking off. I'd plead ignorance ... drunkenness ... an irresistible compulsion for boats. O.K.,

Tobin, it was naughty, but not serious. Don't do it again. You're damn *right,* I won't your Honour ...

'GET YUH HANDS HIGH, MISTER ...' the cop was bellowing. 'UP IN THE AIR!'

I was scraping cloud. He came up to me, slowly, at a half crouch, eyes wild, that damn gun pointing at my belly, its hole an inch across, straining to blast me.

'Don't ... sh ... sh ... shoot! ' I croaked, lowering a hand to wipe away streaming sweat from my face.

'DON'T MOVE!'

'I won't... I won't! '

'DON'T MAKE ME SHOOT YOU, FELLA!'

'I won't... p ... please believe me! '

He crept closer, came right up to me, sweating buckets, breathing hard through flared nostrils - enormous! Built like Garth ... muscles bulging through his shirt. And this guy needed a *pistol!*

'O.K. ...' he panted, his wild, white eyes flicking over me, ready for the slightest move. 'Now ... nice and easy, huh ...? Turn around ...'

I turned and he moved in close behind me, began thumping me up and down. 'O.K., you're clean ... that's real nice ...' He sounded a touch more relaxed - but only a touch - and he didn't put that gun away.

'O.K. ... turn round ... let's have a good look at yuh ...'

I faced him, my eye-line level with his third shirt button, and he covered me methodically with a hard, narrow-eyed gaze. 'What's your name, man?' he panted.

'T ... T ...'

'O.K., take it easy. I ain't gonna shoot you - not just yet anyway. Let's have it again ... nice 'n' slow.'

'Tobin ...' I squeaked. 'Russell Tobin.'

'Huh huh. You English?'

'Yes. I'm ... on holiday here.'

His eyes narrowed even narrower. 'Say 'gain.'

'I'm on holiday ... vacation ... here.'

'Here?'

'Yes ..I pointed a trembling finger vaguely in the direction of the Holiday Inn, 'on Paradise Island ... I'm staying at the Holiday Inn ..

He gave a curious, puzzled frown and stepped back a pace, relaxed on one hip and thrust his hands on them, looking at me very strangely from under the peak of his cap. 'Holiday ... Inn ..he repeated slowly. 'An' ... where did yuh say that was 'xactly?'

I gave a nervous, bemused laugh. He was playing flaming games with me! 'Well - on Paradise Beach ... just across the bridge! '

For an aeon he continued to peer at me, wearing a frown of bewilderment that astounded me, then, with a shake of the head, said, 'Mister ... would you mind tellin' me just where this ... Paradise Island ... is supposed to be here 'bouts?'

My mouth dropped open. This was ridiculous ... crazy! Was it possible he didn't *know?* 'Well ... it's ... it's along *Bay* Street... and over the bridge! '

'Ah,' he said, nodding at last to my immense relief. 'Bay Street...'

"Yes! ' I laughed. 'Then over the ...'

Anger clouded his brow, his eyes snapped. 'And just where the hell is *Bay* Street! ' he bellowed.

I shot back, stared at him.

'Look, mister ... are you on drugs ... are you some kinda *nut* or somethin'! ? Just where the hell d'you think you're standin' right now - huh?'

'S ... Standing?' I stared at my feet. 'Well, I'm standing on ... P ... P ... Prince George's Wharf ..

'Prince ... George's ... Wharf?' he gaped incredulously. 'Prince George's Wharf *where,* man! ?'

'Prince George's Wharf - *Nassau'.'* I shouted, getting me paddy up now, aching to add 'you daft bastard! '

Now he *really* stared at me, mouth open, for about a minute, then suddenly he relaxed and nodded. 'O.K. ... now ... just you do somethin' for me, huh? Can you *read,* mister ...?'

Insulting bugger. 'Of course I can read,' I said, stung by his condescending tone.

'O.K. ... well, you jerst turn round an' tell me what you

see painted in letters twenty feet *high* on that buildin' back there - go on, you jerst *do* that.'

I knew by his tone before I turned that whatever was behind me was going to shock me to the roots ... and it did. It was a dream ... a terrible ... shattering ... bewildering ... living nightmare ...

'Go on,' he insisted. 'Read it to me - out loud.'

'It says "Welcome ... to ... Miami... Florida," ' I croaked.

'Good boy - right first time. "Welcome to Miami, Florida". An' would you know off-hand which *country* li'l ole Florida is in, *Mister* Tobin?'

'It's in ... the U.S.A.,' I whispered, numb, destroyed.

'By ... *golly,* that's right - it's in the United States of Amurica. Now, tell you what we're gonna do ... we're gonna take a walk to that li'l ole hut over there and you're gonna tell me what *else* you know - like for instance ... why you wus tryin' to slip into the United States of Amurica without waitin' for an invitation ... an' how come you've got no passport ... an' no luggage ... an' why you wus sneakin' off that boat like that... an'...'

Oh, Gawd ...

Well, there it is ... if I get a chance before they drop the cyanide capsule under the chair, I'll let you know what happened. If not, think kindly of me and switch to Enid Blyton.

One thing's for certain, though - if I ever get out of this alive I shall never, *never* ... aw, what's the use?

Tarra.

' 'Kay, Tobin ... let's try it all again - from the top, nice an' slow ... an' do try and stop shakin', man ...'

ABOUT THE AUTHOR

Stanley Morgan is a best-selling British author whose 32 books have been enjoyed by countless millions around the world.

An inveterate world-traveller, he left Liverpool in the 1950s to study radio drama in Canada, and then moved to Southern Rhodesia to work on a tobacco farm, whilst performing part time in local theatre productions. He returned to London in the 1960s and became a successful actor and a leading voice-over in TV commercials. He appeared in the first James Bond film, Doctor No amongst many other British films of the era. In-between acting jobs he began to write. and his first novel 'The Sewing Machine Man' was published in 1968.

Featuring his popular 'Russ Tobin' character, he then went on to write 17 more books in the series during the 1970s, selling over ten million copies in the process. He later moved to the US and continued to write more serious thrillers, before returning for a final Russ Tobin book in 2005.

http://www.stanleymorgan.co.uk

Made in the USA
Las Vegas, NV
29 January 2025